NATIVE AMERICAN MYTHS AND LEGENDS

NATIVE AMERICAN MYTHS AND LEGENDS

This edition published in 2025 by Sirius Publishing, a division of
Arcturus Publishing Limited,
26/27 Bickels Yard, 151–153 Bermondsey Street,
London SE1 3HA

Copyright © Arcturus Holdings Limited

All rights reserved. No part of this publication may be reproduced, stored in a retrieval system, or transmitted, in any form or by any means, electronic, mechanical, photocopying, recording or otherwise, without prior written permission in accordance with the provisions of the Copyright Act 1956 (as amended). Any person or persons who do any unauthorised act in relation to this publication may be liable to criminal prosecution and civil claims for damages.

ISBN: 978-1-3988-5176-4
AD011968US

Printed in China

Contents

Introduction 9

PART 1: CREATION MYTHS 11

1. Genesis (Zuni) 13
2. The Creation or Age of Beginning (Navajo) 19
3. How Kemush Created the World (Klamath) 30
4. How the World Was Made (Cherokee) 32
5. The Making of Lakes and Mountains (Haida) 35
6. Pokoh, the Old Man (Pai Ute) 37
7. Old Man Above and the Grizzlies (Shasta) 38
8. The Naming of Creation (Nez Percé) 40
9. The Gifts of the Sky God (Chitimacha) 41
10. The Flood (Miwok) 43

PART 2: NATURE ORIGIN MYTHS 45

11. Kana'tĭ and Selu: The Origin of Game and Corn (Cherokee) .. 47
12. Origin of the Buffalo (Teton) 55
13. The Coming of the Salmon (Bella Coola) 56
14. Origin of the Saguaro and Palo Verde Cacti (Pima) 59
15. Discovery of the Wild Rice (Ojibwa) 60
16. Origin of Tobacco (Menomini) 62
17. Origin of Maple Sugar (Menomini) 63
18. Origin of the Bear (Cherokee) 64
19. Origin of the Black Snakes (Passamaquoddy) 66
20. Origin of Strawberries (Cherokee) 68
21. Creation of the Killer Whale (Tlingit) 69
22. The Maiden with Golden Hair (Chippewa) 70
23. Origin of the Violet (Iroquois) 72
24. The Corn Maidens (Zuni) 75
25. The Course of the Sun (Sia) 83
26. The Quarrel of Sun and Moon (Sioux) 85
27. The White Hawk (Shawnee) 86

CONTENTS

PART 3: MYTHS ABOUT DEATH, SPIRITS AND GHOSTS 91

- 28. Old Woman Who Never Dies (Mandan) 93
- 29. Duration of Human Life (Haida) 95
- 30. How Death Came (Lillooet) 96
- 31. The Daughter of the Sun (Cherokee) 97
- 32. A Visiting Ghost (Teton) 100
- 33. The Forked Roads (Omaha) 101
- 34. The Death Trail (Choctaw) 102
- 35. The Spirit Land (Arapahoe) 103
- 36. The Ghost Land (Tlingit) 104
- 37. The Memaloose Islands (Klickitat) 106
- 38. The Ghost's Resentment (Dakota) 108
- 39. The Ghost Bride (Pawnee) 111
- 40. Journey to the World of Souls (Wyandot) 113
- 41. Chinook Ghosts (Chinook) 116

PART 4: MYTHS ABOUT THE WEATHER 119

- 42. How the Seasons Came to Be (Ojibwa) 121
- 43. As-ai-yahal (Tillamook) 124
- 44. Chinook Wind (Yakama) 126
- 45. The Hill Giant (Inuit) 128
- 46. Mink's War with the Southeast Wind (Kwakiutl) 132
- 47. Origin of the Winds (Inuit) 134
- 48. Capture of the Wind (Chilcotin) 136
- 49. Keeper of the Winds (Algonquin) 137
- 50. The Children of Cloud (Pima) 140
- 51. The Thunder People (Passamaquoddy) 142
- 52. Bear and the Fawns (Miwok) 145
- 53. How the Hunter Destroyed Snow (Menomini) 151

PART 5: "WHY?" MYTHS 153

- 54. Why the Sun is Bright (Lillooet) 155
- 55. Why the Moon is Pale (Wyandot) 156

CONTENTS

56. Why James Bay is Salt (Cree) 157
57. Why Lightning Strikes the Trees (Thompson River) 158
58. Why the Aspen Leaves are Never Still (Blackfoot) 159
59. Why There are No Snakes on Takhoma (Cowlitz) 161
60. Why the Mole Lives Underground (Cherokee) 162
61. Why the Blackbird has Red Wings (Chitimacha) 163
62. Why the Birds have Sharp Tails (Biloxi) 164
63. Why the Squirrel Coughs (Algonquin) 165
64. Why the Frogs Croak (Algonquin) 166
65. Why the Oaks and Sumachs Redden (Fox) 168
66. Why the Possum's Tail is Bare (Cherokee) 170
67. Why the Deer's Teeth are Blunt (Cherokee) 172
68. Why Brother Bear Wears a Stumpy Tail (Ojibwa) 174
69. Why the Baby Says "Goo" (Algonquin) 176
70. Why the Turkey Gobbles (Cherokee) 178
71. Why the Wolves Help in War (Dakota) 179

PART 6: MYTHS ABOUT HEROES AND TRICKSTERS 181

72. How the Rabbit Stole the Otter's Coat (Cherokee) 183
73. Rabbit and the Turkeys (Omaha) 185
74. How Rabbit Caught the Sun in a Trap (Omaha) 186
75. How Rabbit Killed the Giant (Omaha) 188
76. White Plume (Sioux) 191
77. Coyote and Gray Fox (Ponca) 199
78. Coyote and the Dragon (Nez Percé) 200
79. How the Rabbit Lost His Tail (Sioux) 201
80. Unktomi and the Arrowheads (Sioux) 206
81. How Master Lox Played a Trick on Mrs. Bear (Micmac) 208
82. How the Ermine Got its Necklace (Athabascan) 211
83. The Legend of O-na-wut-a-qut-o (Ojibwa) 214
84. The Adventures of the Great Hero Pulowech, or the Partridge (Micmac) 218
85. The Peace with the Snakes (Blackfoot) 223
86. The Adventures of Kivioq (Inuit) 231
87. Nanebojo and the Geese (Ojibwa) 235

CONTENTS

88. Ûñtsaiyǐ, the Gambler (Cherokee) 237
89. The Fallen Star (Dakota) 242
90. The Destruction of Monsters (Shuswap) 248
91. The Boy Who Became a God (Navajo) 250
92. The Adventures of Tcikápis (Cree) 254
93. The Story of Ashish (Klamath) 257

PART 7: MYTHS ABOUT BIRDS 259

94. Origin of Birds (Ojibwa) 261
95. The Origin of the Raven and the Macaw, Totems of Winter and Summer (Zuni) 262
96. The Thunder Bird (Comanche) 265
97. When Chickadee Climbed a Tree (Shuswap) 266
98. Story of the Hummingbird (Shoshone) 267
99. Owl and Raven (Inuit) 270
100. Ball Game of the Birds and Animals (Cherokee) 271
101. The Race Between Humming Bird and Crane (Cherokee) 273
102. Prairie Falcon's Marriage (Miwok) 274
103. Redbird and Blackbird (Ojibwa) 279
104. War with the Sky People (Thompson River) 280
105. The Eagle and the Hunter (Wyandot) 281
106. Sedna, Goddess of the Sea (Inuit) 283

PART 8: MYTHS ABOUT FIRE AND LIGHT 287

107. The Origin of Daylight (Nanaimo/Tlingit) 289
108. Old Man Steals the Sun's Leggings (Blackfoot) 290
109. The Northern Lights (Wabanski) 295
110. The Theft of Fire (Miwok) 297
111. How Beaver Stole Fire from the Pines (Nez Percé) 299
112. The Flying Heads (Wyandot) 301

Introduction

Curiosity is a quality that transcends all cultures. To be human is to question the things around us and to wonder not only how, but *why* things work the way they do. Before scientific theory governed our quest for knowledge, early humanity used the arts of storytelling and mythology to seek answers and convey ideas about the world. The indigenous culture of North America is rooted in the tradition of oral and written mythology. These tales create a rich tapestry, woven together by the stories and traditions of various Native American tribes and peoples. Mythology lays the groundwork for every area of life; it tells us how to raise our children, why the sun is powerful enough to cut through the darkness of night, and inspires us to hold tightly to our shared history.

Perhaps you are a parent looking for a way to teach your children about the importance of patience. You could turn to the tale of the Origin of the Raven and the Macaw from the Zuni tribe, indigenous to what would be known as modern day New Mexico. Readers of this myth quickly learn that speed is not always more valuable than restraint, and that the reward one waits for is often more abundant than a prize easily won. Or maybe you live near a body of water and wonder why the frogs are so loud. The Algonquin tribe would tell you that it is because the voices of an ancient tribe still argue about how much water their people need.

If one were to look closer and pull at the threads of these stories, they would quickly discover common tropes, such as an emphasis on morality or warnings of a character type known as the "trickster." The Sioux tribe recounts a story in which a young warrior, White Plume, is deceived by the Spider Unktomi. White Plume remains steadfast in his quest to save a neighboring tribe from a curse and, with the help of his future bride, saves the girl's village and banishes Unktomi into the shadows. A similar tale has been passed down through the Cherokee tribe, which chronicles the trials of a young boy as he battles to

INTRODUCTION

outsmart the gambler Ûñtsaiyǐ'. Honor triumphs over deceit and wrongdoers are punished for eternity while the other characters are remembered as heroes.

Although each tribe has their own individual stories, many groups overlap in terms of the central themes of their myths. These stories have survived for centuries because at their core, they represent the most important values of their respective groups. This diverse, although not comprehensive, collection of myths will not only shed light on a persevering and resilient culture, but will entertain and inspire those who immerse themselves in the following pages.

Part 1:
Creation Myths

Genesis
(Zuni)

Retold by Frank Hamilton Cushing

THE GENESIS OF THE WORLDS, OR THE BEGINNING OF NEWNESS

Before the beginning of the new-making, Áwonawílona (the Maker and Container of All, the All-father Father), solely had being. There was nothing else whatsoever throughout the great space of the ages save everywhere black darkness in it, and everywhere void desolation.

In the beginning of the new-made, Áwonawílona conceived within himself and thought outward in space, whereby mists of increase, steams potent of growth, were evolved and uplifted. Thus, by means of his innate knowledge, the All-container made himself in person and form of the Sun whom we hold to be our father and who thus came to exist and appear. With his appearance came the brightening of the spaces with light, and with the brightening of the spaces the great mist-clouds were thickened together and fell, whereby was evolved water in water; yea, and the world-holding sea.

With his substance of flesh (*yépnane*) outdrawn from the surface of his person, the Sun-father formed the seed-stuff of twain worlds, impregnating therewith the great waters, and lo! in the heat of his light these waters of the sea grew green and scums (*k'yanashótsi-yallawe*) rose upon them, waxing wide and weighty until, behold! they became Áwitelin Tsíta, the "Four-fold Containing Mother-earth," and Ápoyan Tä´chu, the "All-covering Father-sky."

PART 1: CREATION MYTHS

THE GENESIS OF MEN AND THE CREATURES

From the lying together of these twain upon the great world-waters, so vitalizing, terrestrial life was conceived; whence began all beings of earth, men and the creatures, in the Four-fold womb of the World (Áwiten Téhu'hlnakwi).

Thereupon the Earth-mother repulsed the Sky-father, growing big and sinking deep into the embrace of the waters below, thus separating from the Sky-father in the embrace of the waters above. As a woman forebodes evil for her first-born ere born, even so did the Earth-mother forebode, long withholding from birth her myriad progeny and meantime seeking counsel with the Sky-father. "How," said they to one another, "shall our children, when brought forth, know one place from another, even by the white light of the Sun-father?"

Now like all the surpassing beings (*píkwaiyin áhâi*) the Earth-mother and the Sky-father were *'hlímna* (changeable), even as smoke in the wind; transmutable at thought, manifesting themselves in any form at will, like as dancers may by mask-making.

Thus, as a man and woman, spake they, one to the other. "Behold!" said the Earth-mother as a great terraced bowl appeared at hand and within it water, "this is as upon me the homes of my tiny children shall be. On the rim of each world-country they wander in, terraced mountains shall stand, making in one region many, whereby country shall be known from country, and within each, place from place. Behold, again!" said she as she spat on the water and rapidly smote and stirred it with her fingers. Foam formed, gathering about the terraced rim, mounting higher and higher. "Yea," said she, "and from my bosom they shall draw nourishment, for in such as this shall they find the substance of life whence we were ourselves sustained, for see!" Then with her warm breath she blew across the terraces; white flecks of the foam broke away, and, floating over above the water, were shattered by the cold breath of the Sky-father attending, and forthwith shed downward abundantly fine mist and spray! "Even so, shall white clouds float up from the great waters at the borders of the world, and clustering about the mountain terraces of the horizons be borne aloft and abroad by the breaths of the surpassing of soul-beings, and of the children, and shall hardened and broken be by thy cold, shedding downward, in rain-spray, the water of life, even into the hollow places of my lap! For therein chiefly shall nestle our children mankind and creature-kind, for warmth in thy coldness."

Lo! even the trees on high mountains near the clouds and the Sky-father crouch low toward the Earth-mother for warmth and protection! Warm is the Earth-mother, cold the Sky-father, even as woman is the warm, man the cold being!

"Even so!" said the Sky-father; "Yet not alone shalt *thou* helpful be unto our children, for behold!" and he spread his hand abroad with the palm downward and into all the wrinkles and crevices thereof he set the semblance of shining yellow corn-grains; in the dark of the early world-dawn they gleamed like sparks of fire, and moved as his hand was moved over the bowl, shining up from and also moving in the depths of the water therein. "See!" said he, pointing to the seven grains clasped by his thumb and four fingers, "by such shall our children be guided; for behold, when the Sun-father is not nigh, and thy terraces are as the dark itself (being all hidden therein), then shall our children be guided by lights—like to these lights of all the six regions turning round the midmost one—as in and around the midmost place, where these our children shall abide, lie all the other regions of space! Yea! and even as these grains gleam up from the water, so shall seed-grains like to them, yet numberless, spring up from thy bosom when touched by my waters, to nourish our children." Thus and in other ways many devised they for their offspring.

THE GESTATION OF MEN AND THE CREATURES

Anon in the nethermost of the four cave-wombs of the world, the seed of men and the creatures took form and increased; even as within eggs in warm places worms speedily appear, which growing, presently burst their shells and become as may happen, birds, tadpoles or serpents, so did men and all creatures grow manifoldly and multiply in many kinds. Thus the lowermost womb or cave-world, which was Ánosin téhuli (the womb of sooty depth or of growth-generation, because it was the place of first formation and black as a chimney at night time, foul too, as the internals of the belly), thus did it become over-filled with being. Everywhere were unfinished creatures, crawling like reptiles one over another in filth and black darkness, crowding thickly together and treading each other, one spitting on another or doing other indecency, insomuch that loud became their murmurings and lamentations, until many among them sought to escape, growing wiser and more manlike.

PART 1: CREATION MYTHS

THE FORTHCOMING FROM EARTH OF THE FOREMOST OF MEN

Then came among men and the beings, it is said, the wisest of wise men and the foremost, the all-sacred master, Póshaiyaŋk'ya, he who appeared in the waters below, even as did the Sun-father in the wastes above, and who arose from the nethermost sea, and pitying men still, won upward, gaining by virtue of his (innate) wisdom-knowledge issuance from that first world-womb through ways so dark and narrow that those who, seeing somewhat, crowded after, could not follow, so eager were they and so mightily did they strive with one another! Alone, then, he fared upward from one womb (cave) to another out into the great breadth of daylight. There, the earth lay, like a vast island in the midst of the great waters, wet and unstable. And alone fared he forth dayward, seeking the Sun-father and supplicating him to deliver mankind and the creatures there below.

THE BIRTH FROM THE SEA OF THE TWAIN DELIVERERS OF MEN

Then did the Sun-father take counsel within himself, and casting his glance downward espied, on the great waters, a Foam-cap near to the Earth-mother. With his beam he impregnated and with his heat incubated the Foam-cap, whereupon she gave birth to Úanam Achi Píahkoa, the Beloved Twain who descended; first, Úanam Éhkona, the Beloved Preceder, then Úanam Yáluna, the Beloved Follower, Twin brothers of Light, yet Elder and Younger, the Right and the Left, like to question and answer in deciding and doing. To them the Sun-father imparted, still retaining, control-thought and his own knowledge-wisdom, even as to the offspring of wise parents their knowingness is imparted and as to his right hand and his left hand a skillful man gives craft freely surrendering not his knowledge. He gave them, of himself and their mother the Foam-cap, the great cloud-bow, and for arrows the thunderbolts of the four quarters (twain to either), and for buckler the fog-making shield, which (spun of the floating clouds and spray and woven, as of cotton we spin and weave) supports as on wind, yet hides (as a shadow hides) its bearer, defending also. And of men and all creatures he gave them the fathership and dominion, also as a man gives over the control of his work to the management of his hands. Well instructed of the Sun-father, they lifted the Sky-father with their great cloud-bow into the vault of the high zenith, that the earth might become warm and thus fitter for their children, men and the creatures. Then along the trail of the sun-seeking Póshaiyaŋk'ya, they sped backward swiftly on their floating fog-shield, westward to the Mountain of Generation. With their magic knives of the thunderbolt they spread open the uncleft depths of the mountain, and still on their cloud-shield—even as a spider in her web descendeth—so descended they unerringly, into the dark of the under-world. There they abode with men and the creatures, attending them, coming to know them, and becoming known of them as masters and fathers, thus seeking the ways for leading them forth.

THE BIRTH AND DELIVERY OF MEN AND THE CREATURES

Now there were growing things in the depths, like grasses and crawling vines. So now the Beloved Twain breathed on the stems of these grasses (growing tall, as grass is wont to do toward the light, under the opening they had cleft and whereby they had descended), causing them to increase vastly and rapidly by grasping and walking round and round them, twisting them upward until lo! they reach forth even into the light. And where successively they grasped the stems ridges were formed and thumb-marks whence sprang branching leaf-stems. Therewith the two formed a great ladder whereon men and the creatures might ascend to the second cave-floor, and thus not be violently ejected in after-time by the throes of the Earth-mother, and thereby be made demoniac and deformed.

Up this ladder, into the second cave-world, men and the beings crowded, following closely the Two Little but Mighty Ones. Yet many fell back and, lost in the darkness, peopled the under-world, whence they were delivered in after-time amid terrible earth shakings, becoming the monsters and fearfully strange beings of olden time. Lo! in this second womb it was dark as is the night of a stormy season, but larger of space and higher than had been the first, because it was nearer the navel of the Earth-mother, hence named K'ólin tehuli (the Umbilical-womb, or the Place of Gestation). Here again men and the beings increased and the clamor of their complainings grew loud and beseeching. Again the Two, augmenting the growth of the great ladder, guided them upward, this time not all at once, but in successive bands to become in time the fathers of the six kinds of men (the yellow, the tawny gray, the red, the white, the mingled, and the black races), and with them the gods and creatures of them all. Yet this time also, as before, multitudes were lost or left behind. The third great cave-world, whereunto men and the creatures had now ascended, being larger than the second and higher, was lighter, like a valley in starlight, and named

PART 1: CREATION MYTHS

Áwisho tehuli—the Vaginal-womb, or the Place of Sex-generation or Gestation. For here the various peoples and beings began to multiply apart in kind one from another; and as the nations and tribes of men and the creatures thus waxed numerous as before, here, too, it became overfilled. As before, generations of nations now were led out successively (yet many lost, also as hitherto) into the next and last world-cave, Tépahaian tehuli, the Ultimate-uncoverable, or the Womb of Parturition.

Here it was light like the dawning, and men began to perceive and to learn variously according to their natures, wherefore the Twain taught them to seek first of all our Sun-father, who would, they said, reveal to them wisdom and knowledge of the ways of life—wherein also they were instructing them as we do little children. Yet like the other cave-worlds, this too became, after long time, filled with progeny; and finally, at periods, the Two led forth the nations of men and the kinds of being, into this great upper world, which is called Ték'ohaian úlahnane, or the World of Disseminated Light and Knowledge or Seeing.

The Creation or Age of Beginning
(Navajo)
As told by Aileen O'Bryan

THE FIRST WORLD

These stories were told to Sandoval, Hastin Tlo'tsi hee, by his grandmother, Esdzan Hosh kige. Her ancestor was Esdzan at a', the medicine woman who had the Calendar Stone in her keeping. Here are the stories of the Four Worlds that had no sun, and of the Fifth, the world we live in, which some call the Changeable World.

The First World, Ni'hodilqil, was black as black wool. It had four corners, and over these appeared four clouds. These four clouds contained within themselves the elements of the First World. They were in color, black, white, blue, and yellow.

The Black Cloud represented the Female Being or Substance. For as a child sleeps when being nursed, so life slept in the darkness of the Female Being. The White Cloud represented the Male Being or Substance. He was the Dawn, the Light-Which-Awakens, of the First World.

In the East, at the place where the Black Cloud and the White Cloud met, First Man, Atse'hastqin was formed; and with him was formed the white corn, perfect in shape, with kernels covering the whole ear. Dolionot i'ni is the name of this first seed corn, and it is also the name of the place where the Black Cloud and the White Cloud met.

The First World was small in size, a floating island in mist or water. On it there grew one tree, a pine tree, which was later brought to the present world for firewood.

Man was not, however, in his present form. The conception was of a male and a female being who were to become man and woman. The creatures of the First World are thought

PART 1: CREATION MYTHS

of as the Mist People; they had no definite form, but were to change to men, beasts, birds, and reptiles of this world.

Now on the western side of the First World, in a place that later was to become the Land of Sunset, there appeared the Blue Cloud, and opposite it there appeared the Yellow Cloud. Where they came together First Woman was formed, and with her the yellow corn. This ear of corn was also perfect. With First Woman there came the white shell and the turquoise and the yucca.

First Man stood on the eastern side of the First World. He represented the Dawn and was the Life Giver. First Woman stood opposite in the West. She represented Darkness and Death.

First Man burned a crystal for a fire. The crystal belonged to the male and was the symbol of the mind and of clear seeing. When First Man burned it, it was the mind's awakening. First Woman burned her turquoise for a fire. They saw each other's lights in the distance. When the Black Cloud and the White Cloud rose higher in the sky First Man set out to find the turquoise light. He went twice without success, and again a third time; then he broke a forked branch from his tree, and, looking through the fork, he marked the place where the light burned. And the fourth time he walked to it and found smoke coming from a home.

"Here is the home I could not find," First Man said.

First Woman answered: "Oh, it is you. I saw you walking around and I wondered why you did not come."

Again the same thing happened when the Blue Cloud and the Yellow Cloud rose higher in the sky. First Woman saw a light and she went out to find it. Three times she was unsuccessful, but the fourth time she saw the smoke and she found the home of First Man.

"I wondered what this thing could be," she said.

"I saw you walking and I wondered why you did not come to me," First Man answered.

First Woman saw that First Man had a crystal for a fire, and she saw that it was stronger than her turquoise fire. And as she was thinking, First Man spoke to her. "Why do you not come with your fire and we will live together." The woman agreed to this. So instead of the man going to the woman, as is the custom now, the woman went to the man.

About this time there came another person, the Great-Coyote-Who-Was-Formed-in-

THE CREATION OR AGE OF BEGINNING

the-Water, and he was in the form of a male being. He told the two that he had been hatched from an egg. He knew all that was under the water and all that was in the skies. First Man placed this person ahead of himself in all things. The three began to plan what was to come to pass; and while they were thus occupied another being came to them. He also had the form of a man, but he wore a hairy coat, lined with white fur, that fell to his knees and was belted in at the waist. His name was Atse'hashke', First Angry or Coyote. He said to the three: "You believe that you were the first persons. You are mistaken. I was living when you were formed."

Then four beings came together. They were yellow in color and were called the tsts'na. or wasp people. They knew the secret of shooting evil and could harm others. They were very powerful.

This made eight people.

Four more beings came. They were small in size and wore red shirts and had little black eyes. They were the naazo'zi or spider ants. They knew how to sting, and were a great people.

After these came a whole crowd of beings. Dark colored they were, with thick lips and dark, protruding eyes. They were the wolazhi'ni, the black ants. They also knew the secret of shooting evil and were powerful; but they killed each other steadily.

By this time there were many people. Then came a multitude of little creatures. They were peaceful and harmless, but the odor from them was unpleasant. They were called the wolazhi'ni nlchu nigi, meaning that which emits an odor.

And after the wasps and the different ant people there came the beetles, dragonflies, bat people, the Spider Man and Woman, and the Salt Man and Woman, and others that rightfully had no definite form but were among those people who peopled the First World. And this world, being small in size, became crowded, and the people quarreled and fought among themselves, and in all ways made living very unhappy.

THE SECOND WORLD

Because of the strife in the First World, First Man, First Woman, the Great-Coyote-Who-Was-Formed-in-the-Water, and the Coyote called First Angry, followed by all the others, climbed up from the World of Darkness and Dampness to the Second or Blue World.

PART 1: CREATION MYTHS

They found a number of people already living there: blue birds, blue hawks, blue jays, blue herons, and all the blue-feathered beings. The powerful swallow people lived there also, and these people made the Second World unpleasant for those who had come from the First World. There was fighting and killing.

The First Four found an opening in the World of Blue Haze; and they climbed through this and led the people up into the Third or Yellow World.

THE THIRD WORLD

The bluebird was the first to reach the Third or Yellow World. After him came the First Four and all the others.

A great river crossed this land from north to south. It was the Female River. There was another river crossing it from east to West, it was the Male River. This Male River flowed through the Female River and on; and the name of this place is tqo alna'osdli, the Crossing of the waters.

There were six mountains in the Third World. In the East was Sis na' jin, the Standing Black Sash. Its ceremonial name is Yolgai'dzil, the Dawn or White Shell Mountain. In the South stood Tso'dzil, the Great Mountain, also called Mountain Tongue. Its ceremonial name is Yodolt i'zhi dzil, the Blue Bead or Turquoise Mountain. In the West stood Dook'oslid, and the meaning of this name is forgotten. Its ceremonial name is Dichi'li dzil, the Abalone Shell Mountain. In the North stood Debe'ntsa, Many Sheep Mountain. Its ceremonial name is Bash'zhini dzil, Obsidian Mountain. Then there was Dzil na'odili, the Upper Mountain. It was very sacred; and its name means also the Center Place, and the people moved around it. Its ceremonial name is Ntl'is dzil, Precious Stone or Banded Rock Mountain. There was still another mountain called Chol'i'i or Dzil na'odili choli, and it was also a sacred mountain.

There was no sun in this land, only the two rivers and the six mountains. And these rivers and mountains were not in their present form, but rather the substance of mountains and rivers as were First Man, First Woman, and the others.

Now beyond Sis na' jin, in the east, there lived the Turquoise Hermaphrodite, Ashton nutli. He was also known as the Turquoise Boy. And near this person grew the male reed. Beyond, still farther in the east, there lived a people called the Hadahuneya'nigi,

THE CREATION OR AGE OF BEGINNING

the Mirage or Agate People. Still farther in the east there lived twelve beings called the Naaskiddi. And beyond the home of these beings there lived four others—the Holy Man, the Holy Woman, the Holy Boy, and the Holy Girl.

In the West there lived the White Shell Hermaphrodite or Girl, and with her was the big female reed which grew at the water's edge. It had no tassel. Beyond her in the West there lived another stone people called the Hadahunes'tqin, the Ground Heat People. Still farther on there lived another twelve beings, but these were all females. And again, in the Far West, there lived four Holy Ones.

Within this land there lived the Kisa'ni, the ancients of the Pueblo People. On the six mountains there lived the Cave Dwellers or Great Swallow People. On the mountains lived also the light and dark squirrels, chipmunks, mice, rats, the turkey people, the deer and cat people, the spider people, and the lizards and snakes. The beaver people lived along the rivers, and the frogs and turtles and all the underwater people in the water. So far all the people were similar. They had no definite form, but they had been given different names because of different characteristics.

Now the plan was to plant.

First Man called the people together. He brought forth the white corn which had been formed with him. First Woman brought the yellow corn. They laid the perfect ears side by side; then they asked one person from among the many to come and help them. The Turkey stepped forward. They asked him where he had come from, and he said that he had come from the Gray Mountain. He danced back and forth four times, then he shook his feather coat and there dropped from his clothing four kernels of corn, one gray, one blue, one black, and one red. Another person was asked to help in the plan of the planting. The Big Snake came forward. He likewise brought forth four seeds, the pumpkin, the watermelon, the cantaloup, and the muskmelon. His plants all crawl on the ground.

They planted the seeds, and their harvest was great.

After the harvest the Turquoise Boy from the East came and visited First Woman. When First Man returned to his home he found his wife with this boy. First Woman told her husband that Ashon nutli' was of her flesh and not of his flesh. She said that she had used her own fire, the turquoise, and had ground her own yellow corn into meal. This corn she had planted and cared for herself.

PART 1: CREATION MYTHS

Now at that time there were four chiefs: Big Snake, Mountain Lion, Otter, and Bear. And it was the custom when the black cloud rose in the morning for First Man to come out of his dwelling and speak to the people. After First Man had spoken the four chiefs told them what they should do that day. They also spoke of the past and of the future. But after First Man found his wife with another he would not come out to speak to the people. The black cloud rose higher, but First Man would not leave his dwelling; neither would he eat or drink. No one spoke to the people for four days. All during this time First Man remained silent, and would not touch food or water. Four times the white cloud rose. Then the four chiefs went to First Man and demanded to know why he would not speak to the people. The chiefs asked this question three times, and a fourth, before First Man would answer them.

He told them to bring him an emetic. This he took and purified himself. First Man then asked them to send the hermaphrodite to him. When he came First Man asked him if the metate and brush were his. He said that they were. First Man asked him if he could cook and prepare food like a woman, if he could weave, and brush the hair. And when he had assured First Man that he could do all manner of woman's work, First Man said: "Go and prepare food and bring it to me." After he had eaten, First Man told the four chiefs what he had seen, and what his wife had said.

At this time the Great-Coyote-Who-Was-Formed-in-the-Water came to First Man and told him to cross the river. They made a big raft and crossed at the place where the Male River followed through the Female River. And all the male beings left the female beings on the river bank; and as they rowed across the river they looked back and saw that First Woman and the female beings were laughing. They were also behaving very wickedly.

In the beginning the women did not mind being alone. They cleared and planted a small field. On the other side of the river First Man and the chiefs hunted and planted their seeds. They had a good harvest. Nadle ground the corn and cooked the food. Four seasons passed. The men continued to have plenty and were happy; but the women became lazy, and only weeds grew on their land. The women wanted fresh meat. Some of them tried to join the men and were drowned in the river.

First Woman made a plan. As the women had no way to satisfy their passions, some fashioned long narrow rocks, some used the feathers of the turkey, and some used strange

THE CREATION OR AGE OF BEGINNING

plants (cactus). First Woman told them to use these things. One woman brought forth a big stone. This stone-child was later the Great Stone that rolled over the earth killing men. Another woman brought forth the Big Birds of Tsa bida'hi; and others gave birth to the giants and monsters who later destroyed many people.

On the opposite side of the river the same condition existed. The men, wishing to satisfy their passions, killed the females of mountain sheep, lion, and antelope. Lightning struck these men. When First Man learned of this he warned his men that they would all be killed. He told them that they were indulging in a dangerous practice. Then the second chief spoke: he said that life was hard and that it was a pity to see women drowned. He asked why they should not bring the women across the river and all live together again.

"Now we can see for ourselves what comes from our wrong doing," he said. "We will know how to act in the future." The three other chiefs of the animals agreed with him, so First Man told them to go and bring the women.

After the women had been brought over the river First Man spoke: "We must be purified," he said. "Everyone must bathe. The men must dry themselves with white corn meal, and the women, with yellow."

This they did, living apart for four days. After the fourth day First Woman came and threw her right arm around her husband. She spoke to the others and said that she could see her mistakes, but with her husband's help she would henceforth lead a good life. Then all the male and female beings came and lived with each other again.

The people moved to different parts of the land. Some time passed; then First Woman became troubled by the monotony of life. She made a plan. She went to Atse'hashke, the Coyote called First Angry, and giving him the rainbow she said: "I have suffered greatly in the past. I have suffered from want of meat and corn and clothing. Many of my maidens have died. I have suffered many things. Take the rainbow and go to the place where the rivers cross. Bring me the two pretty children of Tqo holt sodi, the Water Buffalo, a boy and a girl.

The Coyote agreed to do this. He walked over the rainbow. He entered the home of the Water Buffalo and stole the two children; and these he hid in his big skin coat with the white fur lining. And when he returned he refused to take off his coat, but pulled it around himself and looked very wise.

PART 1: CREATION MYTHS

After this happened the people saw white light in the East and in the South and West and North. One of the deer people ran to the East, and returning, said that the white light was a great sheet of water. The sparrow hawk flew to the South, the great hawk to the West, and the kingfisher to the North. They returned and said that a flood was coming. The kingfisher said that the water was greater in the North, and that it was near.

The flood was coming and the Earth was sinking. And all this happened because the Coyote had stolen the two children of the Water Buffalo, and only First Woman and the Coyote knew the truth.

When First Man learned of the coming of the water he sent word to all the people, and he told them to come to the mountain called Sis na'jin. He told them to bring with them all of the seeds of the plants used for food. All living beings were to gather on the top of Sis na'jin. First Man traveled to the six sacred mountains, and, gathering earth from them, he put it in his medicine bag.

The water rose steadily.

When all the people were halfway up Sis na' jin, First Man discovered that he had forgotten his medicine bag. Now this bag contained not only the earth from the six sacred mountains, but his magic, the medicine he used to call the rain down upon the earth and to make things grow. He could not live without his medicine bag, and he wished to jump into the rising water; but the others begged him not to do this. They went to the kingfisher and asked him to dive into the water and recover the bag. This the bird did. When First Man had his medicine bag again in his possession he breathed on it four times and thanked his people.

When they had all arrived it was found that the Turquoise Boy had brought with him the big Male Reed; and the White Shell Girl had brought with her the big Female Reed. Another person brought poison ivy; and another, cotton, which was later used for cloth. This person was the spider. First Man had with him his spruce tree which he planted on the top of Sis na'jin. He used his fox medicine to make it grow; but the spruce tree began to send out branches and to taper at the top, so First Man planted the big Male Reed. All the people blew on it, and it grew and grew until it reached the canopy of the sky. They tried to blow inside the reed, but it was solid. They asked the woodpecker to drill out the hard heart. Soon they were able to peek through the opening, but they had to blow and blow before it was large enough to climb through. They climbed up inside the big male reed, and after them the water continued to rise.

THE FOURTH WORLD

When the people reached the Fourth World they saw that it was not a very large place. Some say that it was called the White World; but not all medicine men agree that this is so.

The last person to crawl through the reed was the turkey from Gray Mountain. His feather coat was flecked with foam, for after him came the water. And with the water came the female Water Buffalo who pushed her head through the opening in the reed. She had a great quantity of curly hair which floated on the water, and she had two horns, half black and half yellow. From the tips of the horns the lightning flashed.

First Man asked the Water Buffalo why she had come and why she had sent the flood. She said nothing. Then the Coyote drew the two babies from his coat and said that it was, perhaps, because of them.

The Turquoise Boy took a basket and filled it with turquoise. On top of the turquoise he placed the blue pollen, tha'di'thee do tlij, from the blue flowers, and the yellow pollen from the corn; and on top of these he placed the pollen from the water flags, tquel aqa'di din; and again on top of these he placed the crystal, which is river pollen. This basket he gave to the Coyote who put it between the horns of the Water Buffalo. The Coyote said that with this sacred offering he would give back the male child. He said that the male child would be known as the Black Cloud or Male Rain, and that he would bring the thunder and lightning. The female child he would keep. She would be known as the Blue, Yellow, and White Clouds or Female Rain. She would be the gentle rain that would moisten the earth and help them to live. So he kept the female child, and he placed the male child on the sacred basket between the horns of the Water Buffalo. And the Water Buffalo disappeared, and the waters with her.

After the water sank there appeared another person. They did not know him, and they asked him where he had come from. He told them that he was the badger, nahashch'id, and that he had been formed where the Yellow Cloud had touched the Earth. Afterward this Yellow Cloud turned out to be a sunbeam.

PART 1: CREATION MYTHS

THE FIFTH WORLD

First Man was not satisfied with the Fourth World. It was a small barren land; and the great water had soaked the earth and made the sowing of seeds impossible. He planted the big Female Reed and it grew up to the vaulted roof of this Fourth World. First Man sent the newcomer, the badger, up inside the reed, but before he reached the upper world water began to drip, so he returned and said that he was frightened.

At this time there came another strange being. First Man asked him where he had been formed, and he told him that he had come from the Earth itself. This was the locust. He said that it was now his turn to do something, and he offered to climb up the reed.

The locust made a headband of a little reed, and on his forehead he crossed two arrows. These arrows were dressed with yellow tail feathers. With this sacred headdress and the help of all the Holy Beings the locust climbed up to the Fifth World. He dug his way through the reed as he digs in the earth now. He then pushed through mud until he came to water. When he emerged he saw a black water bird swimming toward him. He had arrows crossed on the back of his head and big eyes.

The bird said: "What are you doing here? This is not your country." And continuing, he told the locust that unless he could make magic he would not allow him to remain.

The black water bird drew an arrow from the back of his head, and shoving it into his mouth drew it out of his nether extremity. He inserted it underneath his body and drew it out of his mouth.

"That is nothing," said the locust. He took the arrows from his headband and pulled them both ways through his body, between his shell and his heart. The bird believed that the locust possessed great medicine, and he swam away to the East, taking the water with him.

Then came the blue water bird from the South, and the yellow water bird from the West, and the white water bird from the North, and everything happened as before. The locust performed the magic with his arrows; and when the last water bird had gone he found himself sitting on land.

The locust returned to the lower world and told the people that the beings above had strong medicine, and that he had had great difficulty getting the best of them.

Now two dark clouds and two white clouds rose, and this meant that two nights and two days had passed, for there was still no sun. First Man again sent the badger to the

THE CREATION OR AGE OF BEGINNING

upper world, and he returned covered with mud, terrible mud. First Man gathered chips of turquoise which he offered to the five Chiefs of the Winds who lived in the uppermost world of all. They were pleased with the gift, and they sent down the winds and dried the Fifth World.

First Man and his people saw four dark clouds and four white clouds pass, and then they sent the badger up the reed. This time when the badger returned he said that he had come out on solid earth. So First Man and First Woman led the people to the Fifth World, which some call the Many Colored Earth and some the Changeable Earth. They emerged through a lake surrounded by four mountains. The water bubbles in this lake when anyone goes near.

Now after all the people had emerged from the lower worlds First Man and First Woman dressed the Mountain Lion with yellow, black, white, and grayish corn and placed him on one side. They dressed the Wolf with white tail feathers and placed him on the other side. They divided the people into two groups. The first group was told to choose whichever chief they wished. They made their choice, and, although they thought they had chosen the Mountain Lion, they found that they had taken the Wolf for their chief. The Mountain Lion was the chief for the other side. And these people who had the Mountain Lion for their chief turned out to be the people of the Earth. They were to plant seeds and harvest corn. The followers of the Wolf chief became the animals and birds; they turned into all the creatures that fly and crawl and run and swim.

And after all the beings were divided, and each had his own form, they went their ways.

This is the story of the Four Dark Worlds and the Fifth, the World we live in. Some medicine men tell us that there are two worlds above us, the first is the World of the Spirits of Living Things, the second is the Place of Melting into One.

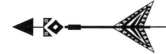 

How Kemush Created the World
(Klamath)

As told by Katharine Berry Judson

In the time that was, Kemush, Old Man of the Ancients, slept in Yamsi, Lodge of the North Wind. Hard had been his work. Kemush had made the world. He had sprung quickly from the ashes of the northern lights and made the world at the call of Morning Star. At first Kaila, the earth, had been flat and bare. Then Kemush planted in the valleys the grass, and camas roots, iba and ipo roots. On Molaiksi, Steepness, he had set Kapka, the pine, Wako, the white pine, and Ktalo, the juniper. On the rivers and lakes Kemush placed Weks, the mallard, and Waiwash, the white goose. Mushmush, the white-tail deer, Wan, the red fox, and Ketchkatch, the little gray fox, ran through the forest. Koil, the mountain sheep, and Luk, the grizzly bear, Kemush set on Kta-iti, place of rocks. So made Kemush the earth. And all the earth was new except Shapashkeni, the rock, where was built the lodge of Sun and Moon.

So Kemush slept while the day was young. Then came Wanaka, the sun halo, and called to the sleeping one, Old Man of the Ancients. Kemush rose from the door of the lodge. Together they followed the trail of Shel, the sun, until they reached the edge of the dark. But Maidu, the Indian, was not yet created.

Then Kemush, with his daughter, Evening Sky, went to the Place of the Dark, to the lodges of the Munatalkni. Five nights in a great circle about a vast fire they danced with the spirits of the dark. The spirits were without number, like the leaves on the trees. But when Shel called to the world, the spirits became dry bones.

On the fifth day, when the sun was new, Kemush rose and put the dry bones into a sack. Then as he followed the trail of Shel to the edge of the world, he threw away the bones. He threw them away two by two. To Kta-iti, place of steepness, he threw two. To Kuyani Shaiks, the crawfish trail, to Molaiksi, steepness of snow, and to Kakasam Yama, mountain of the great blue heron, to each he threw two bones. Thus people were created. The dry bones became Maidu, the Indian, Aikspala, the people of the chipmunks, and last of all, Maklaks, the Klamath Indian. Then Kemush followed the trail of Shel, the sun, climbing higher and higher. At the top of the trail he built his lodge. Here still lives Kemush, Old Man of the Ancients, with his daughter Evening Sky, and Wanaka, the sun halo.

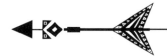 

How the World Was Made
(Cherokee)

As told by Katharine Berry Judson

The earth is a great floating island in a sea of water. At each of the four corners there is a cord hanging down from the sky. The sky is of solid rock. When the world grows old and worn out, the cords will break, and then the earth will sink down into the ocean. Everything will be water again. All the people will be dead. The Indians are much afraid of this.

In the long time ago, when everything was all water, all the animals lived up above in Galun'lati, beyond the stone arch that made the sky. But it was very much crowded. All the animals wanted more room. The animals began to wonder what was below the water and at last Beaver's grandchild, little Water Beetle, offered to go and find out. Water Beetle darted in every direction over the surface of the water, but it could find no place to rest. There was no land at all. Then Water Beetle dived to the bottom of the water and brought up some soft mud. This began to grow and to spread out on every side until it became the island which we call the earth. Afterwards this earth was fastened to the sky with four cords, but no one remembers who did this.

At first the earth was flat and soft and wet. The animals were anxious to get down, and they sent out different birds to see if it was yet dry, but there was no place to alight; so the birds came back to Galun'lati. Then at last it seemed to be time again, so they sent out Buzzard; they told him to go and make ready for them. This was the Great Buzzard, the father of all the buzzards we see now. He flew all over the earth, low down near the ground, and it was still soft. When he reached the Cherokee country, he was very tired; his wings began to flap and strike the ground. Wherever they struck the earth there was a valley; whenever the wings turned upwards again, there was a mountain. When the animals above saw this, they were afraid that the whole world would be mountains, so they called him back, but the Cherokee country remains full of mountains to this day. When the earth was dry and the animals came down, it was still dark. Therefore they got the sun and set it in a track to go every day across the island from east to west, just overhead. It was too hot this way. Red Crawfish had his shell scorched a bright red, so that his meat was spoiled. Therefore the Cherokees do not eat it.

Then the medicine men raised the sun a handsbreadth in the air, but it was still too hot. They raised it another time; and then another time; at last they had raised it seven handsbreadths so that it was just under the sky arch. Then it was right and they left it so. That is why the medicine men called the high place "the seventh height." Every day the sun goes along under this arch on the underside; it returns at night on the upper side of the arch to its starting place.

There is another world under this earth. It is like this one in every way. The animals, the plants, and the people are the same, but the seasons are different. The streams that come down from the mountains are the trails by which we reach this underworld. The springs at their head are the doorways by which we enter it. But in order to enter the other world, one must fast and then go to the water, and have one of the underground people for a guide. We know that the seasons in the underground world are different, because the water in the spring is always warmer in winter than the air in this world; and in summer the water is cooler.

We do not know who made the first plants and animals. But when they were first made, they were told to watch and keep awake for seven nights. This is the way young men do now when they fast and pray to their medicine. They tried to do this. The first night, nearly all the animals stayed awake. The next night several of them dropped asleep. The third night still more went to sleep. At last, on the seventh night, only the owl, the panther, and one or two more were still awake. Therefore, to these were given the power to see in the dark, to go about as if it were day, and to kill and eat the birds and animals which must sleep during the night.

Even some of the trees went to sleep. Only the cedar, the pine, the spruce, the holly, and the laurel were awake all seven nights. Therefore they are always green. They are also sacred trees. But to the other trees it was said, "Because you did not stay awake, therefore you shall lose your hair every winter."

PART 1: CREATION MYTHS

After the plants and the animals, men began to come to the earth. At first there was only one man and one woman. He hit her with a fish. In seven days a little child came down to the earth. So people came to the earth. They came so rapidly that for a time it seemed as though the earth could not hold them all.

The Making of Lakes and Mountains
(Haida)

As told by Katharine Berry Judson

Once the Bears stole a woman. Now she wanted to escape, and she remembered to do as she was told. When she combed her hair, she gathered the combings together. She prepared some hair oil and she made ready also a whetstone and some red ochre.

Then the woman went out to get wood. Bear was watching her. He went with her. So she piled much wood upon him and tied the bundle. Now she took a little wood herself and ran to the house with it. She threw it down outside. Then she took the things she had made ready and ran away.

After the woman had gone on awhile, the one who watched her came and called out. After she had run awhile longer, she heard them making a great noise in pursuit. When they got very close to her, she poured out some of the hair oil. It became a big lake. And after she had run on awhile longer, she broke off a piece of the whetstone. It became a mountain. Now after she had run on again, snowbirds almost surrounded her. Then she poured out some red ochre and the birds all went back to it and painted their faces with it.

Now she ran on again, and after a while when they had almost overtaken her, she threw down the hair combings. They at once became a mass of fallen trees. And while the Bears struggled through these, she went on a long distance.

When she was almost overtaken again, she broke off part of the whetstone and put it in the ground. It became a great mountain. Then as she ran on, she threw down her hair combings and again they became great masses of fallen trees.

Now as she ran on, she saw they had almost overtaken her. She stuck the whole comb into the ground. "Become a mountain!" she said. It became a great mass of mountains which they could not cross. They had to go around. Then again the snowbirds almost came

PART 1: CREATION MYTHS

up with her. She poured out all her red ochre and they began again to paint their faces. When again she heard the noise of pursuit, she stuck the remainder of the whetstone in the ground. It became a great mountain. And as the birds pursued her, she poured out all the hair oil, and put combings around it, and it became a large lake with masses of fallen trees about it. She ran on.

Then she ran to the shore of the great sea. A man in a canoe paddled near her. She cried, "Let me go with you!" At first he paid no attention to her, then he said, "Get in." He let her get into his canoe.

Just at that moment, in a great crowd, the Bears came after her. They crowded about the shore and then began to swim out to her. The man put a carved club into the water, and this club of itself killed all the Bears. The man said to her, "Look out here," and the woman saw the Bears were all dead.

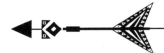 

Pokoh, the Old Man
(Pai Ute)

As told by Katharine Berry Judson

Pokoh, Old Man, they say, created the world. Pokoh had many thoughts. He had many blankets in which he carried around gifts for men. He created every tribe out of the soil where they used to live. That is why an Indian wants to live and die in his native place. He was made of the same soil. Pokoh did not wish men to wander and travel, but to remain in their birthplace.

Long ago, Sun was a man, and was bad. Moon was good. Sun had a quiver full of arrows, and they are deadly. Sun wishes to kill all things.

Sun has two daughters (Venus and Mercury) and twenty men kill them; but after fifty days, they return to life again.

Rainbow is the sister of Pokoh, and her breast is covered with flowers.

Lightning strikes the ground and fills the flint with fire. That is the origin of fire. Some say the beaver brought fire from the east, hauling it on his broad, flat tail. That is why the beaver's tail has no hair on it, even to this day. It was burned off.

There are many worlds. Some have passed and some are still to come. In one world the Indians all creep; in another they all walk; in another they all fly. Perhaps in a world to come, Indians may walk on four legs; or they may crawl like snakes; or they may swim in the water like fish.

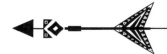 

Old Man Above and the Grizzlies
(Shasta)

As told by Katharine Berry Judson

A long time ago, while smoke still curled from the smoke hole of the tepee, a great storm arose. The storm shook the tepee. Wind blew the smoke down the smoke hole. Old Man Above said to Little Daughter: "Climb up to the smoke hole. Tell Wind to be quiet. Stick your arm out of the smoke hole before you tell him." Little Daughter climbed up to the smoke hole and put out her arm. But Little Daughter put out her head also. She wanted to see the world. Little Daughter wanted to see the rivers and trees, and the white foam on the Bitter Waters. Wind caught Little Daughter by the hair. Wind pulled her out of the smoke hole and blew her down the mountain. Wind blew Little Daughter over the smooth ice and the great forests, down to the land of the Grizzlies. Wind tangled her hair and then left her cold and shivering near the tepees of the Grizzlies.

Soon Grizzly came home. In those days Grizzly walked on two feet, and carried a big stick. Grizzly could talk as people do. Grizzly laid down the young elk he had killed and picked up Little Daughter. He took Little Daughter to his tepee. Then Mother Grizzly warmed her by the fire. Mother Grizzly gave her food to eat.

Soon Little Daughter married the son of Grizzly. Their children were not Grizzlies. They were men. So the Grizzlies built a tepee for Little Daughter and her children. White men call the tepee Little Shasta.

At last Mother Grizzly sent a son to Old Man Above. Mother Grizzly knew that Little Daughter was the child of Old Man Above, but she was afraid. She said: "Tell Old Man Above that Little Daughter is alive."

Old Man Above climbed out of the smoke hole. He ran down the mountain side to the land of the Grizzlies. Old Man Above ran very quickly. Wherever he set his foot the snow melted. The snow melted very quickly and made streams of water. Now Grizzlies stood in line to welcome Old Man Above. They stood on two feet and carried clubs. Then Old Man Above saw his daughter and her children. He saw the new race of men. Then Old Man Above became very angry. He said to Grizzlies: "Never speak again. Be silent. Neither shall ye stand upright. Ye shall use your hands as feet. Ye shall look downward." Then Old Man Above put out the fire in the tepee. Smoke no longer curls from the smoke hole. He fastened the door of the tepee. The new race of men he drove out. Then Old Man Above took Little Daughter back to his tepee.

That is why grizzlies walk on four feet and look downward. Only when fighting they stand on two feet and use their fists like men.

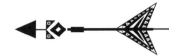 

The Naming of Creation
(Nez Percé)

As told by Katharine Berry Judson

Coyote was chief of all the animals. Now, he told them that the tribes of men were coming near, one and all. Everything he told them came true. Then he said, "To-morrow the people will come out of the ground. I will name them and they will spread out."

Then he named them; he named them until he had named them all. And the people came out, but Coyote had no name for himself. Many people came out. Then he named himself Coyote. Thus came people, — not we alone, but all people.

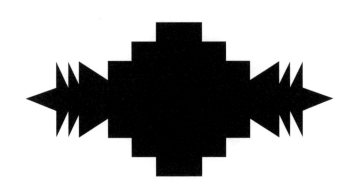

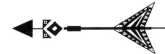 

The Gifts of the Sky God
(Chitimacha)

As told by Katharine Berry Judson

Long, long ago, many Indians started to reach the Sky-world. They walked far to the north until they came to the edge of the sky, where it is fitted down over the Earth-plain. When they came to this place, they tried to slip through a crack under the edge, but the Sky-cover came down very tightly and quickly, and crushed all but six. These six had slipped through into the Sky-land.

Then these men began to climb up, walking far over the sky floor. At last they came to the lodge of Kutnakin. They stayed with him as his guests. At last they wished to go back to their own lodges on the Earth-plain.

Kutnakin said, "How will you go down to the Earth-plain?"

One said, "I will go down as a squirrel." So he started to spring down from the Sky-land. He was dashed to pieces.

Kutnakin said to the next, "How will you go down to the Earth-plain?"

And this man also went as an animal. And so the next one also. They were dashed to pieces. Then the others saw that they were crushed by their fall.

Therefore the fourth said, "I will go down as a spider." And he spun a long line down which he climbed safely to earth.

The fifth said, "I will go down as an eagle," and he spread his wings and circled through the air until he alighted on a tree branch.

The last one said, "I will go down as a pigeon," and so he came softly to earth.

Now each one brought back a gift from Kutnakin. The one who came back as a spider had learned how to howl and sing and dance when people were sick. He was the first medicine man. But one Indian had died while these six men were up in the Sky-land. He died before the shaman came down to earth as a spider. Therefore death came among the

PART 1: CREATION MYTHS

Indians. Had the shaman come back to earth in time to heal this Indian, there would have been no death.

The one who came back as an eagle taught men how to fish. And the pigeon taught the Indians the use of wild maize.

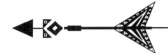 

The Flood
(Miwok)

As told by Edward Winslow Gifford

Prairie Falcon told his people to prepare. He said, "Get ready, Eagle. Get ready, Flicker. Get ready, Dove. Get ready, Woodpecker. Get ready, Quail. Get ready, Kingbird. Get ready, Hummingbird. We are going. We are going. We are going, going toward the north. Hurry, prepare, for we must go at once, must go at once, must go at once." Thus he spoke, when he told his people to prepare "We shall take the people. We shall take the people to the place where my father always goes."

Prairie Falcon said to Eagle, "Tell everyone, Eagle. Tell everyone. Eagle. Have your people prepare. Tell California Jay to come. Tell Coyote to come. Tell Hummingbird to come. We will go to the top of the great mountain."

Eagle said, "We shall follow our chief to the great mountain. We will go there, so that we may see how the world fares. I hear that a flood approaches. We are all going together. Do not say 'I shall stay home.' We are all going. Do not say 'I am sick.' Do not be lazy. We are all going, going toward the north. We will arrive there. We will see different sorts of people." Thus spoke the chief, when he told his people to prepare.

Prairie Falcon said, "We are all going. Do not stay behind. Take Chief Eagle for a guide. He knows the way. Hurry, the water comes. Do not stay at home, for you will drown. We are all going. We will try to escape from the flood." Thus spoke Prairie Falcon to Eagle. He continued to Eagle, "I do not think that the water will cover the great mountain. If we arrive there before it overtakes us, I think we shall be saved."

They hurried. "The water is just coming over the bluff," said Coyote to Chief Prairie Falcon. Coyote saw the water coming over the bluff. Flicker became frightened and fainted. They called Hummingbird to save Flicker's life.

PART 1: CREATION MYTHS

Coyote said, "I am the only one who will drown, as I can not run fast enough. One of my legs is cut off." They all went, except Coyote. He could not walk. He stayed on a big log as the water neared him. The water reached him and he floated with the log. Meanwhile, the people gained the mountain top. The water overwhelmed everything, making great caverns in the mountains. Coyote on his log drifted hither and thither and finally stranded in a different country. The water subsided after drowning all human beings.

Eagle said to Rattlesnake, "The flood washed us to this mountain top." Rattlesnake repeated this to his wife, saying, "The water washed those people to our mountain."

The water rose a second time. It rose higher than ever, and it washed down the great mountain where the Rattlesnakes lived. Eagle sent Dove into the air to survey the water for another mountain, where they might take refuge. Then he sent Hummingbird on a similar quest. Hummingbird found dry land, returned, and told Prairie Falcon.

"Hurry, let us go before the water overtakes us," said Prairie Falcon to his people, "for the water still rises." They went, taking Rattlesnake with them. On the way Rattlesnake bit Flicker, who was carrying him. They dropped Rattlesnake in the water, and he had to swim. He swam back to his home, which the water had not quite covered. After he arrived there, the water rose higher and completely covered the mountain. Rattlesnake was forced to swim again, but as he could not find land, he became exhausted and was drowned.

Water flooded the entire world. At last Prairie Falcon and Eagle and their people arrived at a piece of dry land. There they found green fruit. Hummingbird told them not to eat the fruit. Then they sent Dove to survey the water and discover how humanity fared. Dove reported that all human beings were dead.

Prairie Falcon and his people were starving upon their piece of dry land. Prairie Falcon again sent forth Dove and Hummingbird with orders to bring back some earth. He told them to obtain mud. He instructed Hummingbird not to suck the flowers and Dove not to eat the weed seed. "Do not forget to bring mud," he said, "Do not eat the weed seed and do not suck the flowers." The water had subsided. Prairie Falcon said, when he sent Dove and Hummingbird, "Do not forget to bring mud. Do not forget to bring mud." Thus he spoke to Dove and Hummingbird. Then the two went to obtain mud. This occurred after all human beings were dead, after they had been drowned and after the great mountains had been changed. Then Dove and Hummingbird went.

Part 2:
Nature Origin Myths

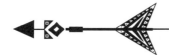 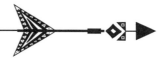

Kana'tĭ and Selu: The Origin of Game and Corn
(Cherokee)

As told by James Mooney

When I was a boy this is what the old men told me they had heard when they were boys.

Long years ago, soon after the world was made, a hunter and his wife lived at Pilot knob with their only child, a little boy. The father's name was Kana'tĭ (The Lucky Hunter), and his wife was called Selu (Corn). No matter when Kana'tĭ went into the wood, he never failed to bring back a load of game, which his wife would cut up and prepare, washing off the blood from the meat in the river near the house. The little boy used to play down by the river every day, and one morning the old people thought they heard laughing and talking in the bushes as though there were two children there. When the boy came home at night his parents asked him who had been playing with him all day. "He comes out of the water," said the boy, "and he calls himself my elder brother. He says his mother was cruel to him and threw him into the river." Then they knew that the strange boy had sprung from the blood of the game which Selu had washed off at the river's edge.

Every day when the little boy went out to play the other would join him, but as he always went back again into the water the old people never had a chance to see him. At last one evening Kana'tĭ said to his son, "Tomorrow, when the other boy comes to play, get him to wrestle with you, and when you have your arms around him hold on to him and call for us." The boy promised to do as he was told, so the next day as soon as his playmate appeared he challenged him to a wrestling match. The other agreed at once, but as soon as they had their arms around each other, Kana'tĭ's boy began to scream for his father. The old folks at once came running down, and as soon as the Wild Boy saw them he struggled

PART 2: NATURE ORIGIN MYTHS

to free himself and cried out, "Let me go; you threw me away!" but his brother held on until the parents reached the spot, when they seized the Wild Boy and took him home with them. They kept him in the house until they had tamed him, but he was always wild and artful in his disposition, and was the leader of his brother in every mischief. It was not long until the old people discovered that he had magic powers, and they called him I'năge-utăsûñ'hĭ (He-who-grew-up-wild).

Whenever Kana'tĭ went into the mountains he always brought back a fat buck or doe, or maybe a couple of turkeys. One day the Wild Boy said to his brother, "I wonder where our father gets all that game; let's follow him next time and find out." A few days afterward Kana'tĭ took a bow and some feathers in his hand and started off toward the west. The boys waited a little while and then went after him, keeping out of sight until they saw him go into a swamp where there were a great many of the small reeds that hunters use to make arrow shafts. Then the Wild Boy changed himself into a puff of bird's down, which the wind took up and carried until it alighted upon Kana'tĭ's shoulder just as he entered the swamp, but Kana'tĭ knew nothing about it. The old man cut reeds, fitted the feathers to them and made some arrows, and the Wild Boy—in his other shape—thought, "I wonder what those things are for?" When Kana'tĭ had his arrows finished he came out of the swamp and went on again. The wind blew the down from his shoulder, and it fell in the woods, when the Wild Boy took his right shape again and went back and told his brother what he had seen. Keeping out of sight of their father, they followed him up the mountain until he stopped at a certain place and lifted a large rock. At once there ran out a buck, which Kana'tĭ shot, and then lifting it upon his back he started for home again. "Oho!" exclaimed the boys, "he keeps all the deer shut up in that hole, and whenever he wants meat he just lets one out and kills it with those things he made in the swamp." They hurried and reached home before their father, who had the heavy deer to carry, and he never knew that they had followed.

A few days later the boys went back to the swamp, cut some reeds, and made seven arrows, and then started up the mountain to where their father kept the game. When they got to the place, they raised the rock and a deer came running out. Just as they drew back to shoot it, another came out, and then another and another, until the boys got confused and forgot what they were about. In those days all the deer had their tails hanging down

KANA'TĬ AND SELU: THE ORIGIN OF GAME AND CORN

like other animals, but as a buck was running past the Wild Boy struck its tail with his arrow so that it pointed upward. The boys thought this good sport, and when the next one ran past the Wild Boy struck its tail so that it stood straight up, and his brother struck the next one so hard with his arrow that the deer's tail was almost curled over his back. The deer carries his tail this way ever since. The deer came running past until the last one had come out of the hole and escaped into the forest. Then came droves of raccoons, rabbits, and all the other four-footed animals—all but the bear, because there was no bear then. Last came great flocks of turkeys, pigeons, and partridges that darkened the air like a cloud and made such a noise with their wings that Kana'tĭ, sitting at home, heard the sound like distant thunder on the mountains and said to himself, "My bad boys have got into trouble; I must go and see what they are doing."

So he went up the mountain, and when he came to the place where he kept the game he found the two boys standing by the rock, and all the birds and animals were gone. Kana'tĭ was furious, but without saying a word he went down into the cave and kicked the covers off four jars in one corner, when out swarmed bedbugs, fleas, lice, and gnats, and got all over the boys. They screamed with pain and fright and tried to beat off the insects, but the thousands of vermin crawled over them and bit and stung them until both dropped down nearly dead. Kana'tĭ stood looking on until he thought they had been punished enough, when he knocked off the vermin and made the boys a talk. "Now, you rascals," said he, "you have always had plenty to eat and never had to work for it. Whenever you were hungry all I had to do was to come up here and get a deer or a turkey and bring it home for your mother to cook; but now you have let out all the animals, and after this when you want a deer to eat you will have to hunt all over the woods for it, and then maybe not find one. Go home now to your mother, while I see if I can find something to eat for supper."

When the boys got home again they were very tired and hungry and asked their mother for something to eat. "There is no meat," said Selu, "but wait a little while and I'll get you something." So she took a basket and started out to the storehouse. This storehouse was built upon poles high up from the ground, to keep it out of the reach of animals, and there was a ladder to climb up by, and one door, but no other opening. Every day when Selu got ready to cook the dinner she would go out to the storehouse with a basket and bring it back full of corn and beans. The boys had never been inside the storehouse, so wondered

PART 2: NATURE ORIGIN MYTHS

where all the corn and beans could come from, as the house was not a very large one; so as soon as Selu went out of the door the Wild Boy said to his brother, "Let's go and see what she does." They ran around and climbed up at the back of the storehouse and pulled out a piece of clay from between the logs, so that they could look in. There they saw Selu standing in the middle of the room with the basket in front of her on the floor. Leaning over the basket, she rubbed her stomach—*so*—and the basket was half full of corn. Then she rubbed under her armpits—*so*—and the basket was full to the top with beans. The boys looked at each other and said, "This will never do; our mother is a witch. If we eat any of that it will poison us. We must kill her."

When the boys came back into the house, she knew their thoughts before they spoke. "So you are going to kill me?" said Selu. "Yes," said the boys, "you are a witch." "Well," said their mother, "when you have killed me, clear a large piece of ground in front of the house and drag my body seven times around the circle. Then drag me seven times over the ground inside the circle, and stay up all night and watch, and in the morning you will have plenty of corn." The boys killed her with their clubs, and cut off her head and put it up on the roof of the house with her face turned to the west, and told her to look for her husband. Then they set to work to clear the ground in front of the house, but instead of clearing the whole piece they cleared only seven little spots. This is why corn now grows only in a few places instead of over the whole world. They dragged the body of Selu around the circle, and wherever her blood fell on the ground the corn sprang up. But instead of dragging her body seven times across the ground they dragged it over only twice, which is the reason the Indians still work their crop but twice. The two brothers sat up and watched their corn all night, and in the morning it was full grown and ripe.

When Kana'tĭ came home at last, he looked around, but could not see Selu anywhere, and asked the boys where was their mother. "She was a witch, and we killed her," said the boys; "there is her head up there on top of the house." When he saw his wife's head on the roof, he was very angry, and said, "I won't stay with you any longer; I am going to the Wolf people." So he started off, but before he had gone far the Wild Boy changed himself again to a tuft of down, which fell on Kana'tĭ's shoulder. When Kana'tĭ reached the settlement of the Wolf people, they were holding a council in the townhouse. He went in and sat down with the tuft of bird's down on his shoulder, but he never noticed it. When the Wolf

KANA'TĬ AND SELU: THE ORIGIN OF GAME AND CORN

chief asked him his business, he said: "I have two bad boys at home, and I want you to go in seven days from now and play ball against them." Although Kana'tĭ spoke as though he wanted them to play a game of ball, the Wolves knew that he meant for them to go and kill the two boys. They promised to go. Then the bird's down blew off from Kana'tĭ's shoulder, and the smoke carried it up through the hole in the roof of the townhouse. When it came down on the ground outside, the Wild Boy took his right shape again and went home and told his brother all that he had heard in the townhouse. But when Kana'tĭ left the Wolf people he did not return home, but went on farther.

The boys then began to get ready for the Wolves, and the Wild Boy—the magician—told his brother what to do. They ran around the house in a wide circle until they had made a trail all around it excepting on the side from which the Wolves would come, where they left a small open space. Then they made four large bundles of arrows and placed them at four different points on the outside of the circle, after which they hid themselves in the woods and waited for the Wolves. In a day or two a whole party of Wolves came and surrounded the house to kill the boys. The Wolves did not notice the trail around the house, because they came in where the boys had left the opening, but the moment they went inside the circle the trail changed to a high brush fence and shut them in. Then the boys on the outside took their arrows and began shooting them down, and as the Wolves could not jump over the fence they were all killed, excepting a few that escaped through the opening into a great swamp close by. The boys ran around the swamp, and a circle of fire sprang up in their tracks and set fire to the grass and bushes and burned up nearly all the other Wolves. Only two or three got away, and from these have come all the wolves that are now in the world.

Soon afterward some strangers from a distance, who had heard that the brothers had a wonderful grain from which they made bread, came to ask for some, for none but Selu and her family had ever known corn before. The boys gave them seven grains of corn, which they told them to plant the next night on their way home, sitting up all night to watch the corn, which would have seven ripe ears in the morning. These they were to plant the next night and watch in the same way, and so on every night until they reached home, when they would have corn enough to supply the whole people. The strangers lived seven days' journey away. They took the seven grains and watched all through the darkness until

PART 2: NATURE ORIGIN MYTHS

morning, when they saw seven tall stalks, each stalk bearing a ripened ear. They gathered the ears and went on their way. The next night they planted all their corn, and guarded it as before until daybreak, when they found an abundant increase. But the way was long and the sun was hot, and the people grew tired. On the last night before reaching home they fell asleep, and in the morning the corn they had planted had not even sprouted. They brought with them to their settlement what corn they had left and planted it, and with care and attention were able to raise a crop. But ever since the corn must be watched and tended through half the year, which before would grow and ripen in a night.

As Kana'tĭ did not return, the boys at last concluded to go and find him. The Wild Boy took a gaming wheel and rolled it toward the Darkening land. In a little while the wheel came rolling back, and the boys knew their father was not there. He rolled it to the south and to the north, and each time the wheel came back to him, and they knew their father was not there. Then he rolled it toward the Sunland, and it did not return. "Our father is there," said the Wild Boy, "let us go and find him." So the two brothers set off toward the east, and after traveling a long time they came upon Kana'tĭ walking along with a little dog by his side. "You bad boys," said their father, "have you come here?" "Yes," they answered, "we always accomplish what we start out to do—we are men." "This dog overtook me four days ago," then said Kana'tĭ, but the boys knew that the dog was the wheel which they had sent after him to find him. "Well," said Kana'tĭ, "as you have found me, we may as well travel together, but I shall take the lead."

Soon they came to a swamp, and Kana'tĭ told them there was something dangerous there and they must keep away from it. He went on ahead, but as soon as he was out of sight the Wild Boy said to his brother, "Come and let us see what is in the swamp." They went in together, and in the middle of the swamp they found a large panther asleep. The Wild Boy got out an arrow and shot the panther in the side of the head. The panther turned his head and the other boy shot him on that side. He turned his head away again and the two brothers shot together—*tust, tust, tust!* But the panther was not hurt by the arrows and paid no more attention to the boys. They came out of the swamp and soon overtook Kana'tĭ, waiting for them. "Did you find it?" asked Kana'tĭ. "Yes," said the boys, "we found it, but it never hurt us. We are men." Kana'tĭ was surprised, but said nothing, and they went on again.

KANA'TĬ AND SELU: THE ORIGIN OF GAME AND CORN

After a while he turned to them and said, "Now you must be careful. We are coming to a tribe called the Anăda'dûñtăskĭ ("Roasters," i. e., cannibals), and if they get you they will put you into a pot and feast on you." Then he went on ahead. Soon the boys came to a tree which had been struck by lightning, and the Wild Boy directed his brother to gather some of the splinters from the tree and told him what to do with them. In a little while they came to the settlement of the cannibals, who, as soon as they saw the boys, came running out, crying, "Good, here are two nice fat strangers. Now we'll have a grand feast!" They caught the boys and dragged them into the townhouse, and sent word to all the people of the settlement to come to the feast. They made up a great fire, put water into a large pot and set it to boiling, and then seized the Wild Boy and put him down into it. His brother was not in the least frightened and made no attempt to escape, but quietly knelt down and began putting the splinters into the fire, as if to make it burn better. When the cannibals thought the meat was about ready they lifted the pot from the fire, and that instant a blinding light filled the townhouse, and the lightning began to dart from one side to the other, striking down the cannibals until not one of them was left alive. Then the lightning went up through the smoke-hole, and the next moment there were the two boys standing outside the townhouse as though nothing had happened. They went on and soon met Kana'tĭ, who seemed much surprised to see them, and said, "What! are you here again?" "O, yes, we never give up. We are great men!" "What did the cannibals do to you?" "We met them and they brought us to their townhouse, but they never hurt us." Kana'tĭ said nothing more, and they went on.

PART 2: NATURE ORIGIN MYTHS

He soon got out of sight of the boys, but they kept on until they came to the end of the world, where the sun comes out. The sky was just coming down when they got there, but they waited until it went up again, and then they went through and climbed up on the other side. There they found Kana'tï and Selu sitting together. The old folk received them kindly and were glad to see them, telling them they might stay there a while, but then they must go to live where the sun goes down. The boys stayed with their parents seven days and then went on toward the Darkening land, where they are now. We call them Anisga'ya Tsunsdi' (The Little Men), and when they talk to each other we hear low rolling thunder in the west.

After Kana'tï's boys had let the deer out from the cave where their father used to keep them, the hunters tramped about in the woods for a long time without finding any game, so that the people were very hungry. At last they heard that the Thunder Boys were now living in the far west, beyond the sun door, and that if they were sent for they could bring back the game. So they sent messengers for them, and the boys came and sat down in the middle of the townhouse and began to sing.

At the first song there was a roaring sound like a strong wind in the northwest, and it grew louder and nearer as the boys sang on, until at the seventh song a whole herd of deer, led by a large buck, came out from the woods. The boys had told the people to be ready with their bows and arrows, and when the song was ended and all the deer were close around the townhouse, the hunters shot into them and killed as many as they needed before the herd could get back into the timber.

Then the Thunder Boys went back to the Darkening land, but before they left they taught the people the seven songs with which to call up the deer. It all happened so long ago that the songs are now forgotten—all but two, which the hunters still sing whenever they go after deer.

Origin of the Buffalo
(Teton)

As told by Katharine Berry Judson

In the days of the grandfathers, buffaloes lived under the earth. In the olden times, they say, a man who was journeying came to a hill where there were many holes in the ground. He entered one of them. When he had gone inside he found buffalo chips and buffalo tracks on all sides. He found also buffalo hairs where the buffaloes had rubbed against the walls. These were the real buffaloes and they lived under the ground. Afterwards some of them came to the surface of the earth and lived there. Then the herds on the earth increased.

These buffaloes had many lodges and there they raised their children. They did many strange things. Therefore when a man escapes being wounded by an enemy, people say he has seen the buffaloes in his dreams, and they have helped him.

Men who dream of the buffaloes act like them and dance the buffalo-bull dance. Then the man who acts the buffalo has a real buffalo inside of him, people say, a little hard ball near the shoulder blade; and therefore he is very hard to kill. No matter how often he is wounded, he does not die.

People know that the buffaloes live in earth lodges; so they never dance the buffalo dance vainly.

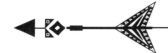 

The Coming of the Salmon
(Bella Coola)

As told by Katharine Berry Judson

A long time ago, a man named Winwina lived on the Bella Coola River, and he often sat in front of his house looking at the river. One day he thought, "I wish fish would ascend this river." At that time not a single salmon visited the Bella Coola River. He thought much about it.

One night Winwina had a dream. He dreamed that with the help of all the animals he had made war upon the Salmon People and had defeated them.

At once Winwina invited all the animals to his house, and told them his dream. When they came, he said, "I wish something. You shall help me obtain what I desire."

Mink said, "What are we to do?" Mink always talked a great deal.

Winwina said, "I want to go to Mialtoa. There is not a single salmon in this river. Let us make war upon the Salmon People. I shall certainly take some slaves and we will place them in this river."

Mink sputtered. He said, "I'm glad *you're* speaking in regard to this matter. I asked my father, Sun, to give us salmon and I think he gave you the dream you have just told us."

But all the tribes agreed. The animals all wanted to start at once.

Winwina asked a person to make a canoe for them. He at once made a self-moving canoe. In the third moon after the winter solstice the canoe was completed.

At once Winwina started. With him went the clouds, the birds, and all the animals. When they passed the village of Bella Bella, Cormorant was sitting on the beach. He asked to be taken along as passenger. So they followed the trail of Sun for a long time.

At last they reached the country of the Salmon People. The country was a great plain, and there were no trees at all. A large sun was shining in the sky. Soon the warriors saw the Salmon village and they sent Raven out to spy. Raven was not gone very long. When

THE COMING OF THE SALMON

he returned, he said, "The Salmon People play on the beach every evening." Mink at once said, "That would be a good time to carry them off."

Crane said, "I will carry away Sockeye Salmon."

Winwina said, "I will carry off the Humpback Salmon."

Kingfisher said, "And I will look after the Dog Salmon."

Raven said, "You can depend upon me for the Silver Salmon."

Fish Hawk said, "I will capture the Salmon Trout and Olachen." Fish Hawk was undertaking a good deal, but the olachen and salmon trout were not so large, nor so warlike as the Salmon People.

Cloud said, "I will capture the Spring Salmon."

But Cormorant said, after everyone else had spoken, "Well, I'm only a passenger. I'll take whatever I can get."

Mink answered, "I won't tell what I am going to take! Now start! The Salmon People can not see you, just as we can not see ghosts."

At once they went on the warpath. They each seized a boy and a girl of the various Salmon tribes, and the Salmon People could not see them at all. They only saw that their children were fainting, as though their ghosts had gone away.

Then the bird and animal warriors went back to the canoe with their slaves. They were about to start home, when someone said, "Let us go and see what is beyond this country of the Salmon People."

The canoe at once went on, and they came to the Berry Country. One of the birds went ashore and picked up a great many of the Berry People and put them in the canoe. Then they returned home. For seven moons they had remained in the Land of the Salmon People.

When they passed Bella Bella, Cormorant said, "This is my town. I will go ashore here."

The birds and animals traveled on, and came to the mouth of the Bella Coola River. There they threw all their Salmon slaves into the water. The Salmon people jumped and began to ascend the river. Then Winwina arose in his canoe and told each one—the silver salmon, the hump-back salmon—at what season he was to arrive. Ever since that time there have been salmon in the Bella Coola River.

PART 2: NATURE ORIGIN MYTHS

Winwina also scattered the Berry People all over the mountains, and through the valleys, and told each one at what season it was to ripen.

After all this was done, Winwina invited everyone to his house. He gave them a great feast.

Origin of the Saguaro and Palo Verde Cacti
(Pima)

As told by Katharine Berry Judson

Once upon a time an old Indian woman had two grandchildren. Every day she ground wheat and corn between the grinding stones to make porridge for them. One day as she put the water-olla on the fire outside the house to heat the water, she told the children not to quarrel because they might upset the olla. But the children began to quarrel. They upset the olla and spilled the water and their grandmother spanked them.

Then the children were angry and ran away. They ran far away over the mountains. The grandmother heard them whistling and she ran after them and followed them from place to place, but she could not catch up with them.

At last the older boy said, "I will turn into a saguaro, so that I shall live forever and bear fruit every summer."

The younger said, "Then I will turn into a palo verde and stand there forever. These mountains are so bare and have nothing on them but rocks, I will make them green."

The old woman heard the cactus whistling and recognized the voice of her grandson. So she went up to it and tried to take the prickly thing into her arms, but the thorns killed her.

That is how the saguaro and the palo verde came to be on the mountains and the desert.

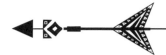 

Discovery of the Wild Rice
(Ojibwa)

As told by Katharine Berry Judson

Long ago, Wenibojó made his home with his grandmother, Nokomis. One day Nokomis said to her grandson, "Prove yourself a man. Take a long journey. Go through the great forests. Fast you. Prepare for the hardships of life."

So Wenibojó took his bow and arrow from his wigwam. He wandered out into the forest. Many days he wandered. Then at last he reached a broad lake, covered thick with heavy-headed stalks. But Wenibojó knew not that the grain was food.

So Wenibojó went back to his grandmother, Nokomis. He told her of the broad, quiet lake, with the heavy-headed stalks. So Nokomis came, and in their canoe they gathered the wild rice and sowed it in another lake.

Again Wenibojó left Nokomis. With his bow and arrow he wandered far into the forest. Then some little bushes spoke as he walked. "Sometimes they eat us," they said. Wenibojó made no answer. Again the bushes spoke, "Sometimes they eat us."

"Who are you talking to?" he asked.

"To Wenibojó," they said. So he bent down and dug up the bushes by the roots. The roots were long, like an arrow. They were good to eat, but Wenibojó had fasted too long.

After a while, Wenibojó wandered on. He was very hungry. Many bushes spoke to him. Many said, "Sometimes they eat us," but he made no answer.

One day he followed the river trail, when the sun was high. Many little bunches of straw were growing out of the water. They spoke to him. They said, "Wenibojó, sometimes they eat us."

So Wenibojó picked some of the grains from the heavy-headed stalks and ate.

"You are good to eat," he said. "What do they call you?"

"They call us *manomin*," answered the wild rice.

Then Wenibojó waded far out into the water. He beat out grains and ate many. They were good for food.

Then Wenibojó remembered the grain which Nokomis had sown, and he returned to his grandmother and the *manomin* lake.

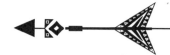 

Origin of Tobacco
(Menomini)

As told by Katharine Berry Judson

One day when Manabush was passing by a high mountain, a fragrant odor came to him from a crevice in the cliffs. He went closer. Then he knew that in the mountain was a giant who was the Keeper of the Tobacco. He entered the mouth of a cave, going through a long tunnel to the center of the mountain.

There in a great wigwam was the giant. The giant said sternly, "What do you want?"

Manabush said, "I want some tobacco."

"Come back again in one year," said the giant. "The manidoes have just been here for their smoke. They come but once a year."

Manabush looked around. He saw a great number of bags filled with tobacco. He seized one and ran out into the open air, and close after him came the giant.

Up to the mountain tops fled Manabush leaping from peak to peak. The giant came close behind him, springing with great bounds. When Manabush reached a very high peak, he suddenly lay flat on the ground; but the giant, leaping, went over him and fell into the chasm beyond.

The giant picked himself up, and began to climb up the face of the cliff. He almost reached the top, hanging to it by his hands. Manabush seized him, and drew him upwards, and dropped him down on the ground.

He said, "For your meanness, you shall become Kakuene, the jumper. You shall become the pest of those who raise tobacco." Thus the giant became a grasshopper.

Then Manabush took the tobacco, and divided it amongst his brothers, giving to each some of the seed. Therefore the Indians are never without tobacco.

Origin of Maple Sugar
(Menomini)

As told by Katharine Berry Judson

One day Manabush returned from the hunt without any food. He could find no game at all. So Nokomis gathered all their robes, and the beaded belts, and their belongings together. They built a new wigwam among the sugar maple trees.

Nokomis said, "Grandson, go into the woods and gather for me pieces of birch bark. I am going to make sugar." Manabush went into the woods. He gathered strips of birch bark, which he took back to the wigwam. Nokomis had cut tiny strips of the bark to use as thread in sewing the bark into hollow buckets. Then Nokomis went from tree to tree cutting small holes through the maple bark, so that the sap might flow. She placed a birch-bark vessel under each hole. Manabush followed her from tree to tree looking for the sap to drop. None fell. When Nokomis had finished, Manabush found all the vessels half full.

He stuck his finger into the thick syrup. It was sweet. Then he said, "Grandmother, this is all very good, but it will not do. If people make sugar so easily, they will not have to work at all. I will change all this. They must cut wood and keep the sap boiling several nights. Otherwise they will not be busy."

So Manabush climbed to the very top of a tree. He showered water all over the maples, like rain. Therefore the sugar in the tree dissolved and flows from the tree as thin sap. This is why the uncles of Manabush and their children always have to work hard when they want to make sugar.

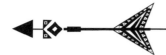

Origin of the Bear
(Cherokee)

As told by Katharine Berry Judson

Long ago, before the white man came, in the land of the Cherokees was a clan called the Ani Tsagulin. One of the boys of the clan used to wander all day long in the mountains. He never ate his food at home.

"Why do you do so?" asked his father and mother. The boy did not answer.

"Why do you do so?" they asked many days, as the boy wandered away into the hills. He did not answer them.

Then his mother saw that long brown hair covered his body. They said again, "Where do you go?" They asked, "Why do you not eat at home?"

At last the boy said, "There is plenty to eat there. It is better than the corn in the village. Soon I shall stay in the woods all the time."

His father and mother said, "No."

The boy kept saying, "It is better than here. I am beginning to be different. Soon I shall not want to live here. If you come with me you will not have to hunt, or plant corn. But first you must fast seven days."

The people began to talk about it. They said, "Often we do not have enough to eat here. There he says there is plenty. We will go with him."

So they fasted seven days. Then they left their village and went to the mountains.

Now the other tribes had heard what they had talked about in their village. At once they sent messengers. But when the messengers met them, they had started towards the mountains and their hair was long and brown. Their nature was changing. This was because they had fasted seven days. But the Ani Tsagulin would not go back to their village. They said to the others:

"We are going where there is always plenty to eat. Hereafter we shall be called *Yana*, bears. When you are hungry, come into the woods and call us, and we will give you food to eat."

So they taught these messengers how to call them and to hunt them. Because, even though they may seem to be killed, the Ani Tsagulin live forever.

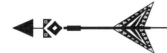

Origin of the Black Snakes
(Passamaquoddy)

As told by Charles G. Leland

Far away, very far in the north, there dwelt by the border of a great lake a man and his wife. They had no children, and the woman was very beautiful and passionate.

The lake was frozen over during the greater part of the year. One day when the woman cut away the ice, she saw in the water a bright pair of large eyes looking steadily at her. They charmed her so that she could not move. Then she distinguished a handsome face; it was that of a fine slender young man. He came out of the water. His eyes seemed brighter and more fascinating than ever; he glittered from head to foot; on his breast was a large shining silvery plate.

The woman learned that this was At-o-sis, the Serpent, but she returned his embraces and held conversation with him, and was so charmed with her lover that she not only met him more than once every day, but even went forth to see him in the night.

Her husband, noticing these frequent absences asked her why she went forth so frequently. She replied, "To get the fresh air."

The weather grew warmer; the ice left the lake; grass and leaves were growing. Then the woman waited till her husband slept, and stole out from the man whom she kissed no more, to the lover whom she fondled and kissed more than ever.

At last the husband's suspicions being fairly aroused, he resolved to watch her. To do this he said that he would be absent for three days. But he returned at the end of the first day, and found that she was absent. As she came in he observed something like silvery scales on the logs. He asked what they were. She replied, "*Brooches.*"

He was still dissatisfied, and said that he would be gone for one day. He went to the top of a hill not far distant, whence he watched her. She went to the shore, and sat there. By and by there rose up out of the lake, at a distance, what seemed to be a brightly shining

ORIGIN OF THE BLACK SNAKES

piece of ice. It came to the strand and rose from the water. It was a very tall and very handsome man, dressed in silver. His wife clasped the bright stranger in her arms, kissing him again and again.

The husband was awed by this strange event. He went home, and tried to persuade his wife to leave the place and to return to her people. This she refused to do. He departed; he left her forever. But her father and mother came to find her. They found her there; they dwelt with her. Every day she brought to them furs and meat. They asked her whence she got them. "I have another husband," she replied; "one who suits me. The one I had was bad, and did not use me well. This one brings all the animals to me." Then she sent them away with many presents, telling them not to return until the ice had formed; that was in the Fall.

When they returned she had become white. She was with young, and soon gave birth to her offspring. It consisted of many serpents. The parents went home. As they departed she said to them, "When you come again you may see me, but you will not know me."

Years after some hunters, roaming that way, remembered the tale, and looked for the wigwam. It was there, but no one was in it. But all the woods about the place were full of great black snakes, which would rise up like a human being and look one in the face, then glide away without doing any harm.

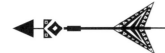 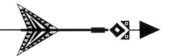

Origin of Strawberries
(Cherokee)

As told by Katharine Berry Judson

When the world was new, there was one man and one woman. They were happy; then they quarreled. At last the woman left the man and began to walk away toward the Sunland, the Eastland. The man followed. He felt sorry, but the woman walked straight on. She did not look back.

Then Sun, the great Apportioner, was sorry for the man. He said, "Are you still angry with your wife?"

The man said, "No."

Sun said, "Would you like to have her come back to you?"

"Yes," said the man.

So Sun made a great patch of huckleberries which he placed in front of the woman's trail. She passed them without paying any attention to them. Then Sun made a clump of blackberry bushes and put those in front of her trail. The woman walked on. Then Sun created beautiful service-berry bushes which stood beside the trail. Still the woman walked on.

So Sun made other fruits and berries. But the woman did not look at them.

Then Sun created a patch of beautiful ripe strawberries. They were the first strawberries. When the woman saw those, she stopped to gather a few. As she gathered them, she turned her face toward the west. Then she remembered the man. She turned to the Sunland but could not go on. She could not go any further.

Then the woman picked some of the strawberries and started back on her trail, away from the Sunland. So her husband met her, and they went back together.

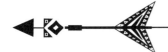 

Creation of the Killer Whale
(Tlingit)

As told by Katharine Berry Judson

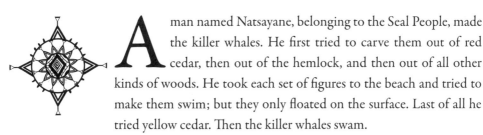

A man named Natsayane, belonging to the Seal People, made the killer whales. He first tried to carve them out of red cedar, then out of the hemlock, and then out of all other kinds of woods. He took each set of figures to the beach and tried to make them swim; but they only floated on the surface. Last of all he tried yellow cedar. Then the killer whales swam.

Natsayane on one marked white lines from the corners of its mouth back to its head. He said, "This is going to be the white-mouthed killer whale."

When Natsayane put them into the water, he said, "Go up into the inlets. Go up into the head of the bays. Hunt for seal, for halibut, and for things under the sea. Do not hurt human beings." Before this people did not know what a killer whale was.

When the Killer whale tribe start north, the Seal People say, "Here comes another battle. Here come the warriors." They say this because the killer whales are always after seals. The killer whale which always swims ahead is the red killer whale, called the "killer whale spear" because it is long and slender.

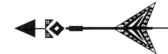 

The Maiden with Golden Hair
(Chippewa)

As told by Julia Darrow Cowles

Shawondasee lived far away in the South Land where it was always warm and bright. His father, Kabeyun, the father of the winds, had given him this part of the earth in which to dwell. The soft, warm winds of the South were given him.

But Shawondasee was not strong, and quick, and eager, like his brothers who governed the North Wind, and the West Wind. He was fat, and lazy, and sluggish. He liked to take life easily, and moved slowly, when he moved at all.

Sometimes, because he was so fat and heavy, he sighed deeply, and then his warm breath would travel far across the land to the North, and the people would cry, "What a balmy day! How soft and warm the air is!"

One day, as Shawondasee looked far away toward the North, he saw upon the prairie a beautiful maiden. Her body was tall and slender. She wore a gown of green, and her hair was a wonderful yellow, like burnished gold.

Shawondasee looked long upon her, for never had he seen a maiden like her before. The Indian maidens had hair of deepest black, like the glossy feathers of the crow, and their skins were dark.

"She is fair and beautiful," sighed Shawondasee. "I should woo her, if she were not so far away."

He stirred a little, and sighed, and the air grew warm, and a soft breeze blew. The beautiful maiden on the prairie swayed in the breeze, and her green robe fluttered.

"She is very beautiful," cried Shawondasee. "I will send her a kiss." So with his softest breath he sent a kiss to the maiden of the yellow hair, and again she bowed and swayed.

Still Shawondasee did not leave his home in the South Land to visit the maiden. He sent soft breezes to blow upon her, and the breezes carried sighs and kisses to her; but Shawondasee himself remained at home. Day after day he wished that he might win the maiden with the golden hair. Day after day he looked toward the North where she stood and waited for his coming.

Then one morning there was a change. As Shawondasee looked out upon the prairie he saw that the beautiful golden hair of the maiden he loved had turned to snowy white. For once he was startled. "What have I done?" he cried. "I have put off going to her, and now I have lost her. Her golden beauty has changed to a beauty which is not of this earth. It is now too late!"

Shawondasee heaved a mighty sigh as he spoke—a sigh that stirred all the winds of the South Land—and behold! the air was filled with the silvery white locks of the Dandelion maiden.

Far and wide they floated, and wherever one fell, there a new flower sprang up, and it was called the Dandelion.

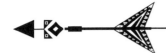 

Origin of the Violet
(Iroquois)

As told by Julia Darrow Cowles

Three wonderful deeds had the Indian youth performed: three deeds for which the older men of the tribe gave him honor.

First of all he had gone forth with his bow and arrow and, taking true aim with a strong and steady hand, had pierced the heart of the great heron flying overhead: the great heron that was the enemy of his people. Often had the bird caught the children of the tribe and carried them away to devour them. And now the young brave, who was little more than a lad, had slain the great heron.

On the second occasion he had gone forth alone, and sought out the cave of the witches. And from the cave he had brought away the roots which alone would cure his people of the great sickness which we call the plague. The journey was long and difficult, and food was scarce, but only the witches knew the secret of the roots.

When the young brave returned with the medicine and the people were made well, the old men of the tribe gave him honor, and the women of the tribe blessed him.

On the third occasion the young warrior led a band of his fellows in combat with a tribe of their enemies, and overthrew them. Those who were not killed fled in confusion. And again he was honored by all his tribe.

But now the young warrior's mind was troubled, and favor and honor no longer satisfied his heart. Among the tribe of the enemy that he had conquered, he had seen a maiden who had won his love.

Unknown to her, and hidden, he had watched as she moved about the wigwam of her father. He had followed the fleeing enemy, and had come silently to the outskirts of their village, and there he discovered the maiden who alone had stirred his heart.

ORIGIN OF THE VIOLET

"I must have her for my very own! She shall be the light of my wigwam!" he cried.

So he stayed in the forest near the village of the enemy, and there he sang all the songs that the Indian lover sings, and always they were in praise of the graceful maiden whom he loved.

So sweet and tender were the words, and so rich the music, that the birds of the forest learned to sing them after him. And so often were they repeated that even the roving animals knew the words, and wondered of whom the strange warrior sang.

One day the Indian maiden, enticed by the freshness of the woods and the caroling of the birds, wandered away to the forest alone. Unknown to her, a young Indian of her own tribe, who long had loved her, followed at a distance.

When she reached the forest she listened happily to the singing birds, and she thought she heard, too, a strong, clear voice that was different from the voice of the birds.

Farther into the woods she went, when suddenly a young brave sprang toward her, clasped her in his arms, and ran swiftly away, bearing her with him.

The maiden, looking into his face, saw that it was strong, and fearless, and loving; and with his voice he reassured her, promising that he would do her no harm. And the maiden's heart went out to him, as his had done to her.

The unseen lover of her own tribe saw what had happened and, recognizing the young brave who had stolen the maiden from him as the one who had defeated his people, was afraid. He ran back to the village to tell the men, and to get help for the pursuit.

"And you came back!" cried the men of the village in a voice of scorn. "You did not save the maiden you claim to love! Stay here at home with the women while we ride forth and overtake them!"

So the men mounted their ponies and rode away; and toward evening they came in sight of the brave young warrior, and the maiden of their tribe.

But as they drew nearer they saw that the maiden had braided the long tresses of her hair and had bound them about the neck of the young warrior who bore her in his arms. And this was the sign to them that she loved him, and wished to go with him and become his wife.

PART 2: NATURE ORIGIN MYTHS

Then the Indians of her own tribe were doubly angry, and drawing their bows they shot both the young warrior and the maiden through the heart, and returned to their own village.

And where the two fell, there sprang from the earth a new flower, the purple violet, which speaks of courage and of love.

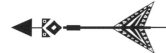 

The Corn Maidens
(Zuni)

As told by Katharine Berry Judson

After long ages of wandering, the precious Seed-things rested over the Middle at Zuni, and men turned their hearts to the cherishing of their corn and the Corn Maidens instead of warring with strange men.

But there was complaint by the people of the customs followed. Some said the music was not that of the olden time. Far better was that which of nights they often heard as they wandered up and down the river trail. Wonderful music, as of liquid voices in caverns, or the echo of women's laughter in water-vases. And the music was timed with a deep-toned drum from the Mountain of Thunder. Others thought the music was that of the ghosts of ancient men, but it was far more beautiful than the music when danced the Corn Maidens. Others said light clouds rolled upward from the grotto in Thunder Mountain like to the mists that leave behind them the dew, but lo! even as they faded the bright garments of the Rainbow women might be seen fluttering, and the broidery and paintings of these dancers of the mist were more beautiful than the costumes of the Corn Maidens.

Then the priests of the people said, "It may well be Paiyatuma, the liquid voices his flute and the flutes of his players.

"Now when the time of ripening corn was near, the fathers ordered preparation for the dance of the Corn Maidens. They sent the two Master-Priests of the Bow to the grotto at Thunder Mountains, saying, "If you behold Paiyatuma, and his maidens, perhaps they will give us the help of their customs."

Then up the river trail, the priests heard the sound of a drum and strains of song. It was Paiyatuma and his seven maidens, the Maidens of the House of Stars, sisters of the Corn Maidens.

PART 2: NATURE ORIGIN MYTHS

The God of Dawn and Music lifted his flute and took his place in the line of dancers. The drum sounded until the cavern shook as with thunder. The flutes sang and sighed as the wind in a wooded canon while still the storm is distant. White mists floated up from the wands of the Maidens, above which fluttered the butterflies of Summer-land about the dress of the Rainbows in the strange blue light of the night.

Then Paiyatuma, smiling, said, "Go the way before, telling the fathers of our custom, and straightway we will follow."

Soon the sound of music was heard, coming from up the river, and soon the Flute People and singers and maidens of the Flute dance. Up rose the fathers and all the watching people, greeting the God of Dawn with outstretched hand and offering of prayer meal. Then the singers took their places and sounded their drum, flutes, and song of clear waters, while the Maidens of the Dew danced their Flute dance. Greatly marveled the people, when from the wands they bore forth came white clouds, and fine cool mists descended.

Now when the dance was ended and the Dew Maidens had retired, out came the beautiful Mothers of Corn. And when the players of the flutes saw them, they were enamored of their beauty and gazed upon them so intently that the Maidens let fall their hair and cast down their eyes. And jealous and bolder grew the mortal youths, and in the morning dawn, in rivalry, the dancers sought all too freely the presence of the Corn Maidens, no longer holding them so precious as in the olden time. And the matrons, intent on the new dance, heeded naught else. But behold! The mists increased greatly, surrounding dancers and watchers alike, until within them, the Maidens of Corn, all in white garments, became invisible. Then sadly and noiselessly they stole in amongst the people and laid their corn wands down amongst the trays, and laid their white broidered garments thereupon, as mothers lay soft kilting over their babes. Then even as the mists became they, and with the mists drifting, fled away, to the far south Summer-land.

Then the people in their trouble called the two Master-Priests and said: "Who, now, think ye, should journey to seek our precious Maidens? Bethink ye! Who amongst the Beings is even as ye are, strong of will and good of eyes? There is our great elder brother and father, Eagle, he of the floating down and of the terraced tail-fan. Surely he is enduring of will and surpassing of sight."

"Yea. Most surely," said the fathers. "Go ye forth and beseech him."

Then the two sped north to Twin Mountain, where in a grotto high up among the crags, with his mate and his young, dwelt the Eagle of the White Bonnet.

They climbed the mountain, but behold! Only the eaglets were there. They screamed lustily and tried to hide themselves in the dark recesses. "Pull not our feathers, ye of hurtful touch, but wait. When we are older we will drop them for you even from the clouds."

"Hush," said the warriors. "Wait in peace. We seek not ye but thy father."

Then from afar, with a frown, came old Eagle. "Why disturb ye my featherlings?" he cried.

"Behold! Father and elder brother, we come seeking only the light of thy favor. Listen!"

Then they told him of the lost Maidens of the Corn, and begged him to search for them.

"Be it well with thy wishes," said Eagle. "Go ye before contentedly."

So the warriors returned to the council. But Eagle winged his way high into the sky. High, high, he rose, until he circled among the clouds, small-seeming and swift, like seed-down in a whirlwind. Through all the heights, to the north, to the west, to the south, and to the east, he circled and sailed. Yet nowhere saw he trace of the Corn Maidens. Then he flew lower, returning. Before the warriors were rested, people heard the roar of his wings. As he alighted, the fathers said, "Enter thou and sit, oh brother, and say to us what thou hast to say." And they offered him the cigarette of the space relations.

When they had puffed the smoke toward the four points of the compass, and Eagle had purified his breath with smoke, and had blown smoke over sacred things, he spoke.

"Far have I journeyed, scanning all the regions. Neither bluebird nor woodrat can hide from my seeing," he said, snapping his beak. "Neither of them, unless they hide under bushes. Yet I have failed to see anything of the Maidens ye seek for. Send for my younger brother, the Falcon. Strong of flight is he, yet not so strong as I, and nearer the ground he takes his way ere sunrise."

Then the Eagle spread his wings and flew away to Twin Mountain. The Warrior-Priests of the Bow sped again fleetly over the plain to the westward for his younger brother, Falcon.

PART 2: NATURE ORIGIN MYTHS

Sitting on an ant hill, so the warriors found Falcon. He paused as they approached, crying, "If ye have snare strings, I will be off like the flight of an arrow well plumed of our feathers!"

"No," said the priests. "Thy elder brother hath bidden us seek thee."

Then they told Falcon what had happened, and how Eagle had failed to find the Corn Maidens, so white and beautiful.

"Failed!" said Falcon. "Of course he failed. He climbs aloft to the clouds and thinks he can see under every bush and into every shadow, as sees the Sunfather who sees not with eyes. Go ye before."

Before the Warrior-Priests had turned toward the town, the Falcon had spread his sharp wings and was skimming off over the tops of the trees and bushes as though verily seeking for field mice or birds' nests. And the Warriors returned to tell the fathers and to await his coming.

But after Falcon had searched over the world, to the north and west, to the east and south, he too returned and was received as had been Eagle. He settled on the edge of a tray before the altar, as on the ant hill he settles today. When he had smoked and had been smoked, as had been Eagle, he told the sorrowing fathers and mothers that he had looked behind every copse and cliff shadow, but of the Maidens he had found no trace.

"They are hidden more closely than ever sparrow hid," he said. Then he, too, flew away to his hills in the west.

"Our beautiful Maiden Mothers," cried the matrons. "Lost, lost as the dead are they!"

"Yes," said the others. "Where now shall we seek them? The far-seeing Eagle and the close-searching Falcon alike have failed to find them."

"Stay now your feet with patience," said the fathers. Some of them had heard Raven, who sought food in the refuse and dirt at the edge of town, at daybreak.

"Look now," they said. "There is Heavy-nose, whose beak never fails to find the substance of seed itself, however little or well hidden it be. He surely must know of the Corn Maidens. Let us call him."

So the warriors went to the river side. When they found Raven, they raised their hands, all weapon less.

"We carry no pricking quills," they called. "Blackbanded father, we seek your aid. Look now! The Mother-maidens of Seed whose substance is the food alike of thy people and our people, have fled away. Neither our grandfather the Eagle, nor his younger brother the Falcon, can trace them. We beg you to aid us or counsel us."

"Ka! ka!" cried the Raven. "Too hungry am I to go abroad fasting on business for ye. Ye are stingy! Here have I been since perching time, trying to find a throatful, but ye pick thy bones and lick thy bowls too clean for that, be sure."

"Come in, then, poor grandfather. We will give thee food to eat. Yea, and a cigarette to smoke, with all the ceremony."

"Say ye so?" said the Raven. He ruffled his collar and opened his mouth so wide with a lusty kaw-la-ka—that he might well have swallowed his own head. "Go ye before," he said, and followed them into the court of the dancers.

He was not ill to look upon. Upon his shoulders were bands of white cotton, and his back was blue, gleaming like the hair of a maiden dancer in the sunlight. The Master-Priest greeted Raven, bidding him sit and smoke.

"Ha! There is corn in this, else why the stalk of it?" said the Raven, when he took the cane cigarette of the far spaces and noticed the joint of it. Then he did as he had seen the Master-Priest do, only more greedily. He sucked in such a throatful of the smoke, fire and all, that it almost strangled him. He coughed and grew giddy, and the smoke all hot and stinging went through every part of him. It filled all his feathers, making even his brown eyes bluer and blacker, in rings. It is not to be wondered at, the blueness of flesh, blackness of dress, and skinniness, yes, and tearfulness of eye which we see in the Raven to-day. And they are all as greedy of corn food as ever, for behold! No sooner had the old Raven recovered than he espied one of the ears of corn half hidden under the mantle-covers of the trays. He leaped from his place laughing. They always laugh when they find anything, these ravens. Then he caught up the ear of corn and made off with it over the heads of the people and the tops of the houses, crying.

"Ha! ha! In this wise and in no other will ye find thy Seed Maidens."

But after a while he came back, saying, "A sharp eye have I for the flesh of the Maidens. But who might see their breathing-beings, ye dolts, except by the help of the Father of

PART 2: NATURE ORIGIN MYTHS

Dawn-Mist himself, whose breath makes breath of others seem as itself." Then he flew away cawing.

Then the elders said to each other, "It is our fault, so how dare we prevail on our father Paiyatuma to aid us? He warned us of this in the old time."

Suddenly, for the sun was rising, they heard Paiyatuma in his daylight mood and transformation. Thoughtless and loud, uncouth in speech, he walked along the outskirts of the village. He joked fearlessly even of fearful things, for all his words and deeds were the reverse of his sacred being. He sat down on a heap of vile refuse, saying he would have a feast.

"My poor little children," he said. But he spoke to aged priests and white-haired matrons.

"Good-night to you all," he said, though it was in full dawning. So he perplexed them with his speeches.

"We beseech thy favor, oh father, and thy aid, in finding our beautiful Maidens." So the priests mourned.

"Oh, that is all, is it? But why find that which is not lost, or summon those who will not come?"

Then he reproached them for not preparing the sacred plumes, and picked up the very plumes he had said were not there.

Then the wise Pekwinna, the Speaker of the Sun, took two plumes and the banded wing-tips of the turkey, and approaching Paiyatuma stroked him with the tips of the feathers and then laid the feathers upon his lips.

Then Paiyatuma became aged and grand and straight, as is a tall tree shorn by lightning. He said to the father:

"Thou are wise of thought and good of heart. Therefore I will summon from Summer-land the beautiful Maidens that ye may look upon them once more and make offering of plumes in sacrifice for them, but they are lost as dwellers amongst ye."

Then he told them of the song lines and the sacred speeches and of the offering of the sacred plume wands, and then turned him about and sped away so fleetly that none saw him.

Beyond the first valley of the high plain to the southward Paiyatuma planted the four plume wands. First he planted the yellow, bending over it and watching it. When it ceased to flutter, the soft down on it leaned northward but moved not. Then he set the blue wand and watched it; then the white wand. The eagle down on them leaned to right and left and still northward, yet moved not. Then farther on he planted the red wand, and bending low, without breathing, watched it closely. The soft down plumes began to wave as though blown by the breath of some small creature. Backward and forward, northward and southward they swayed, as if in time to the breath of one resting.

"'T is the breath of my Maidens in Summer-land, for the plumes of the southland sway soft to their gentle breathing. So shall it ever be. When I set the down of my mists on the plains and scatter my bright beads in the northland, summer shall go thither from afar, borne on the breath of the Seed Maidens. Where they breathe, warmth, showers, and fertility shall follow with the birds of Summer-land, and the butterflies, northward over the world."

Then Paiyatuma arose and sped by the magic of his knowledge into the countries of Summer-land,—fled swiftly and silently as the soft breath he sought for, bearing his painted flute before him. And when he paused to rest, he played on his painted flute and the butterflies and birds sought him. So he sent them to seek the Maidens, following swiftly, and long before he found them he greeted them with the music of his songsound, even as the People of the Seed now greet them in the song of the dancers.

When the Maidens heard his music and saw his tall form in their great fields of corn, they plucked ears, each of her own kind, and with them filled their colored trays and over all spread embroidered mantles,—embroidered in all the bright colors and with the creature-songs of Summer-land. So they sallied forth to meet him and welcome him. Then he greeted them, each with the touch of his hands and the breath of his flute, and bade them follow him to the northland home of their deserted children.

So by the magic of their knowledge they sped back as the stars speed over the world at night time, toward the home of our ancients. Only at night and dawn they journeyed, as the dead do, and the stars also. So they came at evening in the full of the last moon to the Place of the Middle, bearing their trays of seed.

Glorious was Paiyatuma, as he walked into the courts of the dancers in the dusk of the evening and stood with folded arms at the foot of the bow-fringed ladder of priestly council, he and his follower Shutsukya. He was tall and beautiful and banded with his

PART 2: NATURE ORIGIN MYTHS

own mists, and carried the banded wings of the turkeys with which he had winged his flight from afar, leading the Maidens, and followed as by his own shadow by the black being of the corn-soot, Shutsukya, who cries with the voice of the frost wind when the corn has grown aged and the harvest is taken away.

And surpassingly beautiful were the Maidens clothed in the white cotton and embroidered garments of Summer-land.

Then after long praying and chanting by the priests, the fathers of the people, and those of the Seed and Water, and the keepers of sacred things, the Maiden-mother of the North advanced to the foot of the ladder. She lifted from her head the beautiful tray of yellow corn and Paiyatama took it. He pointed it to the regions, each in turn, and the Priest of the North came and received the tray of sacred seed.

Then the Maiden of the West advanced and gave up her tray of blue corn. So each in turn the Maidens gave up their trays of precious seed. The Maiden of the South, the red seed; the Maiden of the East, the white seed; then the Maiden with the black seed, and lastly, the tray of all-color seed which the Priestess of Seed-and-All herself received.

And now, behold! The Maidens stood as before, she of the North at the northern end, but with her face southward far looking; she of the West, next, and lo! so all of them, with the seventh and last, looking southward. And standing thus, the darkness of the night fell around them. As shadows in deep night, so these Maidens of the Seed of Corn, the beloved and beautiful, were seen no more of men. And Paiyatuma stood alone, for Shutsukya walked now behind the Maidens, whistling shrilly, as the frost wind whistles when the corn is gathered away, among the lone canes and dry leaves of a gleaned field.

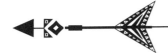 

The Course of the Sun
(Sia)

As told by Katharine Berry Judson

Sussistinnako, the spider, said to the sun, "My son, you will ascend and pass over the world above. You will go from north to south. Return and tell me what you think of it."

The sun said, on his return, "Mother, I did as you bade me, and I did not like the road."

Spider told him to ascend and pass over the world from west to the east. On his return, the sun said, "It may be good for some, mother, but I did not like it."

Spider said, "You will again ascend and pass over the straight road from the east to the west. Return and tell me what you think of it."

That night the sun said, "I am much contented. I like that road much."

Sussistinnako said, "My son, you will ascend each day and pass over the world from east to west."

Upon each day's journey the sun stops midway from the east to the center of the world to eat his breakfast. In the center he stops to eat his dinner. Halfway from the center to the west he stops to eat his supper. He never fails to eat these three meals each day, and always stops at the same points.

The sun wears a shirt of dressed deerskin, with leggings of the same reaching to his thighs. The shirt and leggings are fringed. His moccasins are also of deerskin and embroidered in yellow, red, and turkis beads. He wears a kilt of deerskin, having a snake painted upon it. He carries a bow and arrows, the quiver being of cougar skin, hanging over his shoulder, and he holds his bow in his left hand and an arrow in his right. He always wears the mask which protects him from the sight of the people of Ha-arts.

At the top of the mask is an eagle plume with parrot plumes; an eagle plume is at each side, and one at the bottom of the mask. The hair around the head and face is red like fire,

PART 2: NATURE ORIGIN MYTHS

and when it moves and shakes people can not look closely at the mask. It is not intended that they should observe closely, else they would know that instead of seeing the sun they see only his mask.

The moon came to the upper world with the sun and he also wears a mask.

Each night the sun passes by the house of Sussistinnako, the spider, who asks him, "How are my children above? How many have died to-day? How many have been born to-day?" The sun lingers only long enough to answer his questions. He then passes on to his house in the east.

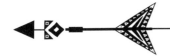 

The Quarrel of Sun and Moon
(Sioux)

As told by Katharine Berry Judson

In the days of the first grandfather, Niaba, the Moon, and Mi, the Sun, lived upon the earth. Then they quarreled.

Said Niaba: "I am out of patience with you. I gather the people but you scatter them. You cause them to be lost."

Said Mi, the Sun: "I wish for many people to grow, so I scatter them. You put them in darkness; thus you kill many with hunger." Then Mi called to the people, "Ho! Ye who are people. Many of you shall grow strong. I will look down on you from above. I will rule all your work."

Said Niaba: "And I, too, will dwell above you. I will gather you when it is dark. Assembling in full numbers, you shall sleep. I myself will rule all your work. We will walk in the trail, one after the other. I will walk behind him."

So Niaba follows Mi on the trail in the sky. Niaba is just like a woman. She always walks with a kettle on her arm.

The White Hawk
(Shawnee)

Waupee was an Indian youth, and a mighty hunter. The meaning of his name was White Hawk. He was tall, and strong as the great oaks of the forest. He was fleet of foot, and keen of sight. When he drew his bow, his arrow went swiftly to the mark.

The Chief of the tribe said, "White Hawk will provide well for the maiden he chooses as his wife. He has the flesh of every animal for food. He has the skin of every animal for his lodge and for his clothing."

But Waupee lived alone in his lodge. He loved the chase, but as yet he cared for no maiden.

One day, as he followed a deer through the forest, he went far away from his lodge; far away from his usual hunting ground. Beyond the forest he saw an open space where the grass grew green, and yellow blossoms studded it like stars in the sky.

Waupee passed swiftly through the forest until he came to the open space, and there, as he looked about, he discovered a curious thing. It was a circle, where the grass bent down as though many feet had passed lightly over it. He wondered what dancing feet could have made this circle in the grass. And he wondered still more when he looked all about and could find no trace of a footstep outside it.

"How did they come? How did they go?" questioned Waupee in amazement. "I must know more of this."

So he hid himself among the trees in the edge of the forest and waited.

He had hunted long: the drowsy insects droned about him, and at length Waupee fell asleep. Soon he was aroused by the sound of tinkling music. It was like the ringing of a silver bell.

He started up and listened. It seemed to come from the sky. He looked up; then he stood still and waited.

Directly over the circle upon the prairie grass there was descending something—Waupee knew not what. It was like a boat, but its colors were like the colors of a seashell, changing from silver to green, to pink, and to blue.

The wonderful boat came to rest in the center of the circle, and out of it stepped twelve maidens, more beautiful than any Waupee had seen before.

Taking hold of hands, they danced lightly round and round, while the silver bells kept time to their steps. Their eyes were bright as the stars, and a star rested upon the breast of each maiden. But though all were beautiful, Waupee was attracted by one alone, and she was the youngest.

"I must have this maiden for my own!" cried Waupee. He ran from the shelter of the trees and would have clasped her in his arms, but he was too late.

The startled maidens sprang into their boat, which lifted instantly and carried them away.

Waupee watched until they disappeared among the clouds. Then slowly he returned to his lodge, but he could think only of the beautiful maiden with eyes like stars, and he determined to use all his powers to win her.

The next day, at the same hour, he was again at the edge of the forest, but this time he had changed to the form of the white hawk, whose name he bore.

"I will wait until they dance," he said to himself, "and then I will fly to the maiden of my choice. I will change to my own form and clasp her in my arms."

So Waupee waited, and as before he heard music like the tinkling of silver bells, and the boat with its changing silvery colors floated down within the circle.

Out stepped the twelve maidens and began their dance.

Waupee was too eager to wait, and he flew at once from the tree. But the moment the maidens heard the sound of his wings, they sprang into their boat and were carried swiftly back to the sky.

Waupee, resuming his form as a man, sat down in the forest, and drew his blanket over his head, as the Indians do when they mourn. He feared that the maidens would nevermore return.

But after a time his courage and hope came back, and he determined that he would not give up until he had captured the maiden who had won his heart.

PART 2: NATURE ORIGIN MYTHS

On the third day he was again at the edge of the forest, and there he noticed the half-decayed stump of a tree. In and out, about the stump, a dozen field mice were playing.

"Now you must help me, little brothers," said Waupee. He lifted the stump and set it down near the magic circle in the field. The little field mice continued to play about it as before. Waupee changed himself into the form of a field mouse, and began running about with the others.

He soon heard the tinkling music, and looking up saw once more the silvery boat floating down from the sky.

When it touched the earth the star maidens sprang out and began their dance. But one of them saw the old stump.

"That was not there before!" she cried, and running from the circle she looked closely at it.

"Let us return!" said the youngest maiden, but the others replied, "But look! Here are field mice running about. Let us chase them!"

The little mice ran in all directions, and the maidens ran after them, laughing, and threatening them with their silver wands.

And the one that the youngest maiden chased ran far from the others. Then, just as the maiden reached him, and would have struck him with her wand, the little field mouse changed suddenly to the form of a man,—and it was Waupee.

He caught the maiden in his arms, and he told her how she had won his heart by her loveliness, and begged her to stay with him.

The other maidens, frightened at the sight of Waupee, sprang into their boat, and it rose and bore them away.

Then the youngest maiden wept, but Waupee comforted her, for he was strong and brave, and a mighty hunter. And her heart was won, and she went with him to the village.

So Waupee was wedded to the Star Maiden, and she was the loveliest maiden in all the tribe.

The next year Waupee and his bride were made still happier by the coming of a baby boy, and the White Hawk was the proudest father in all the tribe.

But after many moons had passed, the Star Maiden grew lonely for her father, and for the scenes of her star home in the sky. And so, one day, she took her little son by the hand

and led him to the magic circle in the grass of the prairie. In the center of the circle she placed a boat which she had woven from the grass and rushes of the meadow, and she and her little son stepped into it. Then she sang the song of the silvery bells which had been always in her heart, and the boat of woven rushes began to rise.

Up and up it went until it carried the Star Maiden and her son far away to the Sky Land.

Waupee, far away at the chase, heard the strains of the magic song and ran to the spot, but he was too late. He saw the boat with its occupants disappear among the clouds, and then he sat down upon the prairie, covered his head with his blanket, and mourned. And no one in all the tribe could comfort him.

The Star Maiden and her son were welcomed by her father, and for some time they were happy. Then the boy began to long for his father, the White Hawk, who was so strong and brave. And his mother, too, secretly longed for Waupee and the home he had made for her.

One day her father, who had noticed, said to her, "Go, my daughter, back to the Earth country. Tell your husband that I want him to visit me in the land of stars, and bring him here to dwell with you and your son. But before he comes have him shoot one of every kind of bird and beast, and bring a specimen of each to our Sky Land."

So the Star Maiden gladly took her son and stepped into her boat. Then singing the magic song which was always in her heart, they were carried back to Earth.

Waupee's heart leaped up like a deer when he heard the music of the song, and running to the magic circle he clasped his wife and his son in his strong, loving arms.

The Star Maiden gave him the message from her father, and though Waupee loved the forests and the prairies, he prepared to go to the Sky Land. He hunted day after day, and from each bird or animal that he shot he cut a wing, or a foot, or a tail, to carry with him. At last he was ready, and with the Star Maiden and their son, he stepped into the magic boat and was carried far up to the land of stars.

All the people of that far-off country gathered to greet him, and to welcome the return of the Star Maiden and her boy. Her father took the great bundle of strange objects that Waupee had brought, and he said to his people: "Come, I will let you choose! Those of you who wish to stay in the Star Land may remain as you are. The others may select one

PART 2: NATURE ORIGIN MYTHS

object from this strange bundle, and according to your choice, so shall you be in the future."

Many of the people crowded forward, and one took the tail of a deer, and immediately he was changed into a deer, and bounded away to the Earth country. Another took the claw of a bear, and at once he became a bear, and shuffled off to find his way to the Earth. And so it was with the choice of every one. Some became birds and flew away.

"Come," said Waupee, to the Star Maiden, "let me choose the wing of the White Hawk, and do you the same, and our son. Then we may visit both the Earth and the Sky, and be always together."

So they chose. And so they have lived, ever since.

Part 3: Myths about Death, Spirits, and Ghosts

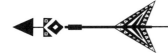

Old Woman Who Never Dies
(Mandan)

As told by Katharine Berry Judson

In the sun lives the Lord of Life. In the moon lives Old-Woman-Who-Never-Dies. She has six children, three sons and three daughters. These live in the sky. The eldest son is the Day; another is the Sun; another is Night. The eldest daughter is the Morning Star, called "The Woman Who Wears a Plume"; another is a star which circles around the polar star, and she is called "The Striped Gourd"; the third is Evening Star.

Every spring Old-Woman-Who-Never-Dies sends the wild geese, the swans, and the ducks. When she sends the wild geese, the Indians plant their corn and Old-Woman-Who-Never-Dies makes it grow. When eleven wild geese are found together, the Indians know the corn crop will be very large. The swans mean that the Indians must plant gourds; the ducks, that they must plant beans.

Indians always save dried meat for these wild birds, so when they come in the spring they may have a corn feast. They build scaffolds of many poles, three or four rows, and one above the others. On this they hang the meat. Then the old women in the village, each one with a stick, meet around the scaffold. In one end of the stick is an ear of corn. Sitting in a circle, they plant their sticks in the ground in front of them. Then they dance around the scaffolds while the old men beat the drums and rattle the gourds.

Afterwards the old women in the village are allowed to eat the dried meat.

In the fall they hold another corn feast, after the corn is ripe. This is so that Old-Woman-Who-Never-Dies may send the buffalo herds to them. Each woman carries the entire cornstalk, with the ears attached, just as it was pulled up by the roots. Then they call on Old-Woman-Who-Never-Dies and say, "Mother, pity us. Do not send the cold too

PART 3: MYTHS ABOUT DEATH, SPIRITS, AND GHOSTS

soon, or we may not have enough meat. Mother, do not let the game depart, so that we may have enough for winter."

In the fall, when the birds go south to Old-Woman, they take back the dried meat hung on the scaffolds, because Old-Woman is very fond of it.

Old-Woman-Who-Never-Dies has large patches of corn, kept for her by the great stag and by the white-tailed stag. Blackbirds also help her guard her corn patches. The corn patches are large, therefore the Old Woman has the help also of the mice and the moles. In the spring the birds go north, back to Old Man-Who-Never-Dies.

In the olden time, Old-Woman-Who-Never-Dies lived near the Little Missouri. Sometimes the Indians visited her. One day twelve came, and she offered them only a small kettle of corn. They were very hungry and the kettle was very small. But as soon as it was empty, it at once became filled again, so all the Indians had enough to eat.

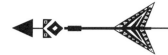 

Duration of Human Life
(Haida)

As told by Katharine Berry Judson

At one time Raven said to stones scattered about, "Get up and help me. I am tired;" so he said. The stones got up, but they were unable to stand erect. Then Raven said, "Remain stones forever!" so they did.

Now the grass on the landward side of the stones was thick, and the salmon-berry bushes were very thick indeed. Then Raven said to the salmon-berry bushes and the grass, "Get up! Get up and help me. I am tired!" Then the grass and the salmon-berry bushes both arose. They turned into human beings, and they helped Raven.

So we are salmon-berry bushes and grass. Therefore we die in a short time, because grass and salmon-berry bushes are weak. Therefore people die in just the same way the leaves fall.

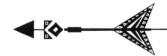 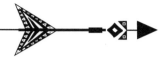

How Death Came
(Lillooet)

As told by Katharine Berry Judson

Raven was once a chief of great power and very wise. At that time people did not die. One day a man came to Raven and said, "I am not happy as things go now. Let people die so that we may weep, and then we will be happy."

Raven said, "Very well. If people wish to die, it shall be so."

The man went away and soon after his child died. He was sorry. He wept; but instead of being happy when he wept, he was very miserable. He went to Raven and asked him to stop people from dying.

Raven said, "It was too late for that now. I made it as you asked it. I cannot change things now. Henceforth people shall continue to die."

That is the reason people die. Afterward Raven was changed into a mere bird, because he let death happen. Through him it came into the world.

The Daughter of the Sun
(Cherokee)

As told by James Mooney

The Sun lived on the other side of the sky vault, but her daughter lived in the middle of the sky, directly above the earth, and every day as the Sun was climbing along the sky arch to the west she used to stop at her daughter's house for dinner.

Now, the Sun hated the people on the earth, because they could never look straight at her without screwing up their faces. She said to her brother, the Moon, "My grandchildren are ugly; they grin all over their faces when they look at me." But the Moon said, "I like my younger brothers; I think they are very handsome"—because they always smiled pleasantly when they saw him in the sky at night, for his rays were milder.

The Sun was jealous and planned to kill all the people, so every day when she got near her daughter's house she sent down such sultry rays that there was a great fever and the people died by hundreds, until everyone had lost some friend and there was fear that no one would be left. They went for help to the Little Men, who said the only way to save themselves was to kill the Sun.

The Little Men made medicine and changed two men to snakes, the Spreading-adder and the Copperhead, and sent them to watch near the door of the daughter of the Sun to bite the old Sun when she came next day. They went together and hid near the house until the Sun came, but when the Spreading-adder was about to spring, the bright light blinded him and he could only spit out yellow slime, as he does to this day when he tries to bite. She called him a nasty thing and went by into the house, and the Copperhead crawled off without trying to do anything.

So the people still died from the heat, and they went to the Little Men a second time for help. The Little Men made medicine again and changed one man into the great Uktena

PART 3: MYTHS ABOUT DEATH, SPIRITS, AND GHOSTS

and another into the Rattlesnake and sent them to watch near the house and kill the old Sun when she came for dinner. They made the Uktena very large, with horns on his head, and everyone thought he would be sure to do the work, but the Rattlesnake was so quick and eager that he got ahead and coiled up just outside the house, and when the Sun's daughter opened the door to look out for her mother, he sprang up and bit her and she fell dead in the doorway. He forgot to wait for the old Sun, but went back to the people, and the Uktena was so very angry that he went back, too. Since then we pray to the rattlesnake and do not kill him, because he is kind and never tries to bite if we do not disturb him. The Uktena grew angrier all the time and very dangerous, so that if he even looked at a man, that man's family would die. After a long time the people held a council and decided that he was too dangerous to be with them, so they sent him up to Gălûñ'lătĭ, and he is there now. The Spreading-adder, the Copperhead, the Rattlesnake, and the Uktena were all men.

When the Sun found her daughter dead, she went into the house and grieved, and the people did not die anymore, but now the world was dark all the time, because the Sun would not come out. They went again to the Little Men, and these told them that if they wanted the Sun to come out again they must bring back her daughter from Tsûsginâ'ĭ, the Ghost country, in Usûñhi'yĭ, the Darkening land in the west. They chose seven men to go, and gave each a sourwood rod a hand-breadth long. The Little Men told them they must take a box with them, and when they got to Tsûsginâ'ĭ they would find all the ghosts at a dance. They must stand outside the circle, and when the young woman passed in the dance they must strike her with the rods and she would fall to the ground. Then they must put her into the box and bring her back to her mother, but they must be very sure not to open the box, even a little way, until they were home again.

They took the rods and a box and traveled seven days to the west until they came to the Darkening land. There were a great many people there, and they were having a dance just as if they were at home in the settlements. The young woman was in the outside circle, and as she swung around to where the seven men were standing, one struck her with his rod and she turned her head and saw him. As she came around the second time another touched her with his rod, and then another and another, until at the seventh round she fell out of the ring, and they put her into the box and closed the lid fast. The other ghosts seemed never to notice what had happened.

They took up the box and started home toward the east. In a little while the girl came to life again and begged to be let out of the box, but they made no answer and went on. Soon she called again and said she was hungry, but still they made no answer and went on. After another while she spoke again and called for a drink and pleaded so that it was very hard to listen to her, but the men who carried the box said nothing and still went on. When at last they were very near home, she called again and begged them to raise the lid just a little, because she was smothering. They were afraid she was really dying now, so they lifted the lid a little to give her air, but as they did so there was a fluttering sound inside and something flew past them into the thicket and they heard a redbird cry, "*kwish! kwish! kwish!*" in the bushes. They shut down the lid and went on again to the settlements, but when they got there and opened the box it was empty.

So we know the Redbird is the daughter of the Sun, and if the men had kept the box closed, as the Little Men told them to do, they would have brought her home safely, and we could bring back our other friends also from the Ghost country, but now when they die we can never bring them back.

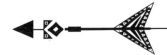 

A Visiting Ghost
(Teton)

As told by Katharine Berry Judson

Once a young brave warrior came to a great forest just at nightfall. He was alone, so he lay down at the edge of the woods. At midnight he heard a woman cry, "My son! my son!" Then he heard the breaking of twigs. Thus the warrior knew that someone was approaching. The warrior put brush on his fire, then he peeped through a hole in his blanket. A woman was approaching. She wore a skin dress with long fringe. She wore also a blanket drawn over her head. Her leggings were decorated with bead work and porcupine quills.

The woman came to where the warrior lay with his legs stretched out. She took his foot and raised it. Then she dropped it. Twice the woman did this. Then she drew a rusty knife.

The warrior sprang up.

He shouted, "What are you doing?"

Then he shot at her suddenly.

The woman ran away screaming, "Yun! yun! yun!"

When daylight came, the warrior saw he had camped near a scaffold grave. Therefore he said, "This is the ghost which came to me."

The Forked Roads
(Omaha)

As told by Katharine Berry Judson

Long ago, in the days of the grandfathers, a man died and was buried by his village. For four nights his ghost had to walk a very dark trail. Then he reached the Milky Way and there was plenty of light. For this reason, people ought to keep the funeral fires lighted for four nights, so the spirit will not walk in the dark trail.

The spirit walked along the Milky Way. At last he came to a point where the trail forked. There sat an old man. He was dressed in a buffalo robe, with the hair on the outside. He pointed to each ghost the road he was to take. One was short and led to the land of good ghosts. The other was very long; along it the ghosts went wailing.

The spirits of suicides can not travel either road. They must hover over their graves. For them there is no future life.

A murderer is never happy after he dies. Ghosts surround him and keep up a constant whistling. He is always hungry, though he eats much food. He is never allowed to go where he pleases, lest high winds arise and sweep down upon the others.

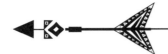 

The Death Trail
(Choctaw)

As told by Katharine Berry Judson

After a man dies, he must travel far on the death trail. It journeys to the Darkening-land, where Sun slips over the edge of the Earth-plain. Then the spirit comes to a deep, rapid stream. There are steep and rugged hills on each side, so that one may not follow a land trail. The Trail of the Dead leads over the stream, and the only bridge is a pine log. It is a very slippery log, and even the bark has been peeled off. Also on the other side of the bridge are six persons. They have rocks in their hands, and throw them at spirits when they are just at the middle of the log.

Now when an evil spirit sees the stones coming, he tries to dodge them. Therefore he slips off the log. He falls far into the water below, where are evil things. The water carries him around and around, as in a whirlpool, and then brings him back again among the evil things. Sometimes evil spirit climbs up on the rocks and looks over into the country of the good spirits. But he can not go there.

Now the good spirit walks over safely. He does not mind the stones and does not dodge them. He crosses the stream and goes to a good hunting land. It is more beautiful there than on the Earth-plain. There are no storms. The sky is always blue, and the grass is green, and there are many buffaloes. Therefore there is always feasting and dancing.

The Spirit Land
(Arapahoe)

As told by Katharine Berry Judson

The spirit world is toward the Darkening Land, higher up, and separated from the world of living by a great lake. Now when the spirits came back to this world [in the ghost-dance excitement] Crow was their leader. That is because Crow is black; his color is the same as that of the Darkening Land. Crow was followed by all the Indians. But when they reached the edge of the Shadow Land, below them was a great sea.

Far away, toward the Sunrise Land were their people in the world of living. So Crow took a pebble in his beak. He dropped it into the water, and it became a mountain, towering up to the shadow land. So the Indians came down the mountain side to the edge of the water.

Then Crow took some dust in his bill. He flew out and dropped it into the water, and it became solid land. It stretched between the spirit land and the world of living.

Then Crow flew out again, with blades of grass in his beak. He dropped these upon the new made land. At once the earth was covered with green grass.

Again Crow flew out with twigs in his beak, and he dropped these upon the new earth. At once it was covered with a forest of trees.

Again he flew back to the base of the mountain. Then he called all the spirit Indians together. Now he is coming to help the living Indians. He has already passed the sea. He is now on the western edge of the world of living.

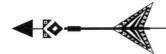

The Ghost Land
(Tlingit)

As told by Katharine Berry Judson

The young wife of a chief's son died and the young man was so sorrowful he could not sleep. Early one morning he put on his fine clothes and started off. He walked all day and all night. He went through the woods a long distance, and then to a valley. The trees were very thick, but he could hear voices far away. At last he saw light through the trees and then came to a wide, flat stone on the edge of a lake.

Now all the time this young man had been walking in the Death Trail. He saw houses and people on the other side of the lake. He could see them moving around. So he shouted, "Come over and get me." But they did not seem to hear him. Upon the lake a little canoe was being paddled about by one man, and all the shore was grassy. The chief's son shouted a long while but no one answered him. At last he whispered to himself, "Why don't they hear me?"

At once a person across the lake said, "Someone is shouting." When he whispered, they heard him.

The voice said also, "Someone has come up from Dreamland. Go and bring him over."

When the chief's son reached the other side of the lake, he saw his wife. He was very happy to see her again. People asked him to sit down. They gave him something to eat, but his wife said, "Don't eat that. If you eat that you will never get back." So he did not eat it.

Then his wife said, "You had better not stay here long. Let us go right away." So they were taken back in the same canoe. It is called Ghost's Canoe and it is the only one on that lake. They landed at the broad, flat rock where the chief's son had stood calling. It is called Ghost's Rock, and is at the very end of the Death Trail. Then they started down the

THE GHOST LAND

trail, through the valley and through the thick woods. The second night they reached the chief's house.

The chief's son told his wife to stay outside. He went in and said to his father, "I have brought my wife back."

The chief said, "Why don't you bring her in?"

The chief laid down a nice mat with fur robes on it for the young wife. The young man went out to get his wife, but when he came in, with her, they could see only him. When he came very close, they saw a deep shadow following him. When his wife sat down and they put a marten skin robe around her, it hung about the shadow just as if a person were sitting there. When she ate, they saw only the spoon moving up and down, but not the shadow of her hands. It looked very strange to them.

Afterward the chief's son died and the ghosts of both of them went back to Ghost Land.

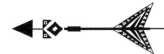 

The Memaloose Islands
(Klickitat)

As told by Katharine Berry Judson

Long ago, before the white man came, a young chief and a maiden loved one another. Suddenly the chief went over the spirit trail. But he could find no rest in the land of the spirits. The maiden also grieved for him. Then a vision came to the maiden. It told her to go to the land of the spirits.

The maiden told her father of the vision and they both obeyed. The father made ready a canoe, placed her in it and they paddled up Great River to the spirit island. Through the darkness, as they neared the death island, they heard singing and the tom-tom of the dance drum. Four spirit people met them on the shore. The maiden landed but the father returned. At the great dance house the maiden met her lover, more beautiful than on earth. All night long they danced. Then when morning came and the robins chirped, the dancers fell asleep.

The maiden slept, but not soundly. When the sun was high, she awoke. All around her were skeletons and skulls. Her lover, with grinning teeth, was gazing upon her. The maiden was in the island of the dead. Struck with horror, she ran to the shore. At last she found an old boat and paddled herself across Great River to the Indian village.

But her father was frightened. She had been to the spirit land. Therefore, if she returned, evil would fall upon the tribe. That night again the father made ready a canoe and paddled across the river to the memaloose island. Through the darkness, they heard singing and the tom-tom of the dance drum.

In course of time a baby, half human, half spirit, was born. The spirit lover wished his mother to see it. He sent a messenger to her, telling her to come to the island by night. He told her, when she arrived, not to look at the baby until it was ten days old. After the old woman reached the memaloose island, she became impatient. She lifted the cloth from

THE MEMALOOSE ISLANDS

the baby's face. She lifted just one little corner and looked at the baby's face. Therefore the baby died. Thus the spirit people became displeased. They said that never again should living people visit the land of those who had gone by the spirit trail.

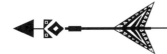 

The Ghost's Resentment
(Dakota)

As told by Katharine Berry Judson

Long, long ago, a Dakota died and his parents made a death lodge for him on the bluff. In the lodge they made a grave scaffold, on which they laid the body of their son.

Now in that same village of Dakotas lived a young married man. His father lived with him, and there were two old men who used to visit the father and smoke with him, and talk with him about many things.

One night the father of the young man said, "My friends, let us go to the death scaffold and cut off summer robes for ourselves from the tent skins."

The young man said, "No! Do not do so. It was a pity the young man died, and as his parents had nothing else to give up for him they made the death lodge and left it there."

"What use can he get from the tent?" asked the father. "We have no robes, so we wish to use part of the tent skins for ourselves."

"Well, then," said the young man. "Go as you have said and we shall see what will happen."

The old men arose without saying a word and went to the lodge on the bluff. As soon as they were gone, the young man said, "Oh, wife, get my piece of white clay. I must scare one of those old men nearly to death."

But the woman was unwilling, saying, "Let them alone. They have no robes. Let them cut off robes for themselves."

But as the husband would not stop talking about it, the wife got the piece of white clay for him. He whitened his whole body and his face and hands. Then he went to the lodge in a course parallel to that taken by the old men. He went very quickly and reached there before they did.

He climbed the scaffold and lay on it, thrusting his head out through the tent skins just above the doorway.

THE GHOST'S RESENTMENT

At last the old men approached, ascending the hill, and talking together in a low tone. The young man lay still, listening to them. When they reached the lodge, they sat down.

The leader said, "Fill your pipe, friends. We must smoke this last time with our friend up there."

"Yes, your friend has spoken well. That should be done," answered one of them.

So he filled the pipe. He drew a whiff, and when the fire glowed, he turned the pipestem toward the seam of the skins above the doorway. He looked up towards the sky, saying, "Ho, friend, here is the pipe. We must smoke with you this last time. And then we must separate. Here is the pipe."

As he said this, he gazed above the doorway and saw a head looking out from the tent.

"Oh! My friends!" he cried. "Look at this place behind you."

When the two looked, they said, "Really! Friends, it is he!" And all fled.

Then the young man leaped down and pursued them. Two of them fell to the ground in terror, but he did not disturb them, going on in pursuit of his father. When the old man was overtaken, he fell to the ground. He was terrified. The young man sat astride of him. He said, "You have been very disobedient! Fill the pipe for me!"

The old man said, "Oh! My grandchild! Oh! My grandchild!" hoping that the ghost would pity him. Then he filled the pipe as he lay stretched there and gave it to his son.

The young man smoked. When he stopped smoking, the old man said, "Oh! My grandchild! Oh! My grandchild! Pity me, and let me go. We thought we must smoke with you this last time, so we went to the place where you were. Oh! My grandchild, pity me."

"If that be so, arise and extend your hands to me in entreaty," said the young man.

The old man arose and did so, saying continually, "Oh! My grandchild! Oh! My grandchild!"

It was as much as the young man could do to keep from laughing. At length he said, "Well! Begone! Beware lest you come again and go around my resting place very often! Do not visit it again!" Then he let the old man go.

On returning to the burial lodge, he found the two old men still lying where they had fallen. When he approached them, they slipped off, with their heads covered, as they were terrified, and he let them go undisturbed. When they had gone, the young man hurried home. He reached there first and after washing himself, reclined at full length.

He said to his wife, "When they return, be sure not to laugh. Make an effort to control yourself. I came very near making them die of fright."

When the old men returned, the young people seemed to be asleep. The old men did not lie down; all sat in silence, smoking together until daylight. When the young man arose in the morning, the old men appeared very sorrowful.

Then he said, "Give me one of the robes that you and your friends cut off and brought back. I, too, have no robe at all."

His father said, "Why! We went there, but we did not get anything at all. We were attacked. We came very near being killed."

To this the son replied, "Why! I was unwilling for this to happen, so I said, 'Do not go,' but you paid no attention to me, and went. But now you think differently and you weep."

When it was night, the young man said, "Go again and make another attempt. Bring back a piece for me, as I have no robe at all."

The old men were unwilling to go again, and they lost their patience, as he teased them so often.

The Ghost Bride
(Pawnee)

As told by George Bird Grinnell

In a place where we used to have a village, a young woman died just before the tribe started on the hunt. When she died they dressed her up in her finest clothes, and buried her, and soon after this the tribe started on the hunt.

A party of young men had gone off to visit another tribe, and they did not get back until after this girl had died and the tribe had left the village. Most of this party did not go back to the village, but met the tribe and went with them on the hunt. Among the young men who had been away was one who had loved this girl who had died. He went back alone to the village. It was empty and silent, but before he reached it, he could see, far off, someone sitting on top of a lodge. When he came near, he saw that it was the girl he loved. He did not know that she had died, and he wondered to see her there alone, for the time was coming when he would be her husband and she his wife. When she saw him coming, she came down from the top of the lodge and went inside. When he came close to her, he spoke and said, "Why are you here alone in the village?" She answered him, "They have gone off on the hunt. I was sulky with my relations, and they went off and left me behind." The man wanted her now to be his wife, but the girl said to him, "No, not yet, but later we will be married." She said to him, "You must not be afraid. To-night there will be dances here; the ghosts will dance." This is an old custom of the Pawnees. When they danced they used to go from one lodge to another, singing, dancing and hallooing. So now, when the tribe had gone and the village was deserted, the ghosts did this. He could hear them coming along the empty streets, and going from one lodge to another. They came into the lodge where he was, and danced about, and whooped and sang, and sometimes they almost touched him, and he came pretty near being scared. The next day, the young man persuaded the girl to go on with him, and follow the tribe, to

PART 3: MYTHS ABOUT DEATH, SPIRITS, AND GHOSTS

join it on the hunt. They started to travel together, and she promised him that she would surely be his wife, but not until the time came. They overtook the tribe; but before they got to the camp, the girl stopped. She said, "Now we have arrived, but you must go first to the village, and prepare a place for me. Where I sleep, let it be behind a curtain. For four days and four nights I must remain behind this curtain. Do not speak of me. Do not mention my name to anyone."

The young man left her there and went into the camp. When he got to his lodge, he told a woman, one of his relations, to go out to a certain place and bring in a woman, who was waiting there for him. His relative asked him, "Who is the woman?" And to avoid speaking her name, he told who were her father and mother. His relation, in surprise, said, "It can not be that girl, for she died some days before we started on the hunt."

When the woman went to look for the girl she could not find her. The girl had disappeared. The young man had disobeyed her, and had told who she was. She had told him that she must stay behind a curtain for four days, and that no one must know who she was. Instead of doing what she had said, he told who she was, and the girl disappeared because she was a ghost. If he had obeyed the girl, she would have lived a second time upon earth. That same night this young man died in his sleep.

Then the people were convinced that there must be a life after this one.

Journey to the World of Souls
(Wyandot)

As told by Father Brébeuf and recounted by Marius Barbeau

A man having lost one of his sisters, whom he loved above all the rest, and having wept for some time after her death, resolved to seek her, in whatever part of the world she might be; and he traveled twelve days toward the setting Sun, where he had learned the Village of souls was, without eating or drinking. At the end of this time, his sister appeared to him in the night, with a dish of meal cooked in water, after the fashion of the country, which she gave to him, and disappeared at the moment he wished to put his hand on her and stop her.

He went on, and journeyed three whole months, hoping always to succeed in claiming her. During all this time she never failed to show herself every day and to render him the same service that she had at first—increasing in this way his desire, without giving it any other consolation than the little nourishment which she brought him. The three months expired; he came to a river, which presented great difficulty to him at first, for it was very rapid and did not appear fordable.

There were, indeed, some fallen trees thrown across it; but this bridge was so shaky that he did not dare to trust himself to it. What should he do? There was on the other side a piece of cleared land, which made him think there must be some inhabitants near. In fact, after looking in all directions he perceived, on the outskirts of the wood, a little Cabin. He calls several times. A man appears and shuts himself up immediately in his Cabin; this gives him great joy, and he resolves to cross.

Having successfully accomplished this, he goes straightaway to this cabin, but finds the door closed; he calls, he beats on the door. He is told to wait, and first to pass in his arm, if he wishes to enter; the other one is much astonished to see a living body. He opens to

PART 3: MYTHS ABOUT DEATH, SPIRITS, AND GHOSTS

him, and asks him where he was going and what his purpose was, as this country was only for souls.

"I know that well," says this Adventurer, "and that is why I came here to seek the soul of my sister."

"Oh indeed," replies the other one, "well and good; come, take courage, you will be presently in the Village of souls, where you will find what you desire. All the souls are now gathered in a Cabin, where they are dancing to heal Aataentsic, who is sick. Don't be afraid to enter; stay, there is a pumpkin, you can put into it the soul of your sister."

He takes it, and at the same time bids good-bye to his host, very glad of so fortunate a meeting. On his departure, he asks the host his name, "Be satisfied," says the other, "that I am he who keeps the brains of the dead."

So he goes away and reaches the Village of souls. He enters the Cabin of Aataentsic, where he finds that they are indeed dancing for the sake of her health; but he can not yet see the soul of his sister, for the souls were so startled at the sight of the man that they vanished in a moment, so that he remained all day the master of the Cabin.

In the evening, as he was seated by the fire, they returned; but they showed themselves at first only at a distance. Approaching slowly, they began again to dance; he recognized his sister amid the troop, he endeavored even to seize her, but she fled from him. He withdrew some distance, and at last chose his time so well that she could not escape him. Nevertheless, he made certain of his prey only by securing her well; for he had to struggle against her all night, and in the contest she grew so little that he put her without difficulty into the pumpkin.

Having corked her in well, he immediately returns by way of the house of his host, who gives him his sister's brains in another pumpkin, and instructs him in all he must do to resuscitate her.

"When thou reachest home," he says to him, "go to the cemetery, take the body of thy sister, bear it to thy cabin, and make a feast. When all thy guests are assembled carry it on thy shoulders, and take a walk through the cabin holding the two pumpkins in thy hands; thou wilt no sooner have resumed thy place than thy sister will come to life again, provided thou givest orders that all keep their eyes lowered, and that no one shall look at what thou art doing, else everything will go wrong."

Soon the man returns to his village; he takes the body of his sister, makes a feast, carries out, in due order, all the directions given him, and indeed, he already felt motion in the half-decayed corpse; but, when he was two or three steps from his place, one curious person raised his eyes; at that moment the soul escaped, and there remained to him only the corpse in his arms, which he was constrained to bear to the tomb whence he had taken it.

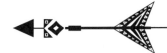

Chinook Ghosts
(Chinook)

As told by Katharine Berry Judson

The ghosts wanted to buy a wife. They bought Blue Jay's sister, Ioi. They came in the evening and on the next morning Ioi had disappeared. Now Blue Jay was a wise bird, a foe to magic. After a year Blue Jay said, "I am going to search for Ioi."

Blue Jay asked all the trees, "Where do people go when they die?"

They did not answer. Then Blue Jay asked all the birds, "Where do people go when they die?" They did not answer.

At last Blue Jay said to his wedge, "Where do people go when they die?"

Wedge said, "Pay me and I will tell you."

Blue Jay paid him, and Wedge took him on a journey. They arrived at a large village. The last lodge was very large. Smoke was rising only from this lodge. There Blue Jay found Ioi.

When Ioi saw Blue Jay, she said, "Where did you come from?"

Blue Jay said, "I am not dead. Wedge brought me here. Are you dead?"

Then Blue Jay opened all the lodges and he saw that they were full of bones. He saw a skull and bones close to Ioi. He said, "What are you going to do with that skull?"

Ioi said, "That is my husband."

When it grew dark, the bones became alive. Blue Jay asked, "Where did all these people come from?"

Ioi said, "Do you think they are people? They are ghosts."

After some time, Ioi said to him, "Go with those people fishing with a dip net."

He went with a young boy. The people spoke always in very low tones and he did not understand them. Ioi told him to speak in low tones. When they were going fishing in their canoe, another canoe came down the river. The people in it were singing. Blue Jay began to sing, too, and at once the boy became a skeleton. Blue Jay stopped singing and the boy became a ghost again. When Blue Jay spoke in loud tones, the boy always became a skeleton.

The ghosts caught leaves and branches in the dip net. These branches and leaves were their trout and salmon. Blue Jay shouted often and all the ghosts became skeletons.

One day when all the ghosts were bones, Blue Jay changed their skulls. He put children's skulls on old people. Therefore the ghosts disliked him. They told Ioi to send him back. But he did not know in what to go. Their canoes were full of holes and covered with moss.

So Ioi sent Blue Jay home, but he did not follow her directions. Therefore he died and became a ghost. He returned to the ghost land and found all the bones were real men. The leaves and branches were real salmon and trout, and all their canoes were new.

Part 4: Myths about the Weather

 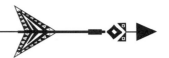

How the Seasons Came to Be
(Ojibwa)

As told by Julia Darrow Cowles

There was once a little boy who wanted above everything else to become a mighty hunter.

His father, whose name was Ojeeg, the Fisher, was the mightiest hunter of his tribe, and Omeme wanted to be like his father.

Often he went out into the forest with the little bow and arrows which his father had made for him, to hunt the small creatures of the woods. But it was too cold for him to stay long; for in those days there were no seasons, only cold and snow day after day, moon following moon.

So little Omeme often came back to the lodge with fingers stiff and numb. As he shivered and held his fingers over the fire of the lodge, he cried, "There is nothing for Omeme to shoot. The birds fly up to the sun for warmth. The little creatures hide in the forest: they hide far down beneath the snow blanket. It is cold. Omeme can get no game."

One day Omeme met a squirrel in the forest, and the squirrel said, "Do not shoot me, Omeme. I will tell you a great secret."

Then Omeme said, "I will not shoot you. Tell me your secret."

And the squirrel said, "Away up in the Sky Land it is always warm. There is no frost, no snow. If we could have some of the warmth of the Sky Land, we should not always be cold. There would be good hunting for Omeme. There would be plenty for us all to eat."

"But the Sky Land is far away," said Omeme.

"Yes," replied the squirrel, "but Ojeeg is mighty. Could he not go to the Sky Land and bring away some of its warmth?"

"My father is mighty," answered Omeme. "I will ask him."

He ran home, for he had grown cold while listening to the squirrel's secret. Ojeeg was in the lodge.

PART 4: MYTHS ABOUT THE WEATHER

"Oh, my father," exclaimed Omeme, "all we little creatures are so cold! The squirrel tells me there is warmth in the Sky Land. Could you not go there and bring some of its warmth to the earth?"

Ojeeg was silent for a long, long time. He loved Omeme dearly. He was sorry that Omeme was cold. But the journey to the Sky Land was long. It was full of dangers.

At length Ojeeg said, "The earth *is* cold. I will hold a council with my neighbors."

So Ojeeg, the Fisher, called together his neighbors, the Otter, the Beaver, the Badger, the Lynx, and the Wolverine. Long and earnestly they considered the matter, and at length they decided to undertake the journey to the Sky Land.

Upon a given day they started. It was a great adventure, and Ojeeg felt sure that he would never return to his lodge, and never again would he see the little Omeme.

For a long, long distance they traveled and at last, tired and spent with hunger, they reached the top of a very high mountain. So high it was that the sky seemed almost to rest upon it.

There they found meat and a fire, as though some traveler had left them. So they rested and were refreshed.

Then Ojeeg said to the Otter, "Now we will try to gain entrance to the Sky Land. It is just above us. Jump, and see if you can not break through, and we will follow."

The Otter tried, but he could not jump high enough, and he fell, and slid all the way down to the foot of the mountain. So he gave up and returned to his home.

Then Ojeeg said to the Beaver, "Jump, and see if you can not do better than the Otter." The Beaver jumped; but neither could he jump high enough, and he too fell, and slid all the way down to the bottom of the mountain. So the Beaver gave up, and returned to his home.

Then Ojeeg said to the Badger, "Jump. Let us see if you can not do better than the Otter and the Beaver."

The Badger jumped; but neither could he jump high enough, and back he slid to the bottom of the mountain. So the Badger gave up, and returned to his home.

Then Ojeeg said to the Lynx, "Surely you are stronger than the Otter, and the Beaver, and the Badger, and you can jump farther. Try, and see if you can not break through into the Sky Land, and we will follow."

The Lynx jumped; but neither could he break through the Sky, though he made a deep scratch upon it with one of his sharp claws; and back he slid to the bottom of the mountain. So the Lynx gave up, and returned to his home.

Then said Ojeeg to the Wolverine, "You are stronger and more agile than the others. Jump, and see if you cannot break through, and I will follow you. Do your best. You must not fail me."

The Wolverine prepared for a mighty jump. He sprang upward, and touched the Sky just where the Lynx's claw had scratched it. He broke it, and sprang through the opening.

After him sprang Ojeeg, and now they two were in the Sky Land.

It was a beautiful country. There was no snow. The winds blew softly; the air was balmy; and all about them were flowers, and grass, and singing birds.

Ojeeg stamped hard with his foot, and a great hole was made where he stamped. Down through the hole rushed the singing birds, and the warm air of the Sky Land.

Down went Spring, and after Spring went Summer, and after Summer went Fall. But just as Fall disappeared, Ojeeg heard a great noise and shouting, for the people of the Sky Land were coming. He knew that they would punish him for his daring.

The Wolverine slipped through the hole and followed Fall; but before Ojeeg could follow, the Sky people came, and the hole was closed.

Ojeeg ran, but the arrows of the Sky people were swift, and overtook him.

So Ojeeg gave up his life, but he had sent warmth to all the creatures of the earth, and since that time his people have had the four seasons, instead of one unbroken season of bitter cold and snow.

The little Omeme was proud of the mighty deed of his father. He was cold no more: and he grew up to be a mighty hunter, as his father the great Ojeeg had been before him.

And when the Indians look up at the stars and see the constellation of the fish, they say, "That is Ojeeg, the Fisher, who gave the summer to his people."

As-ai-yahal
(Tillamook)

As told by Katharine Berry Judson

As-ai-yahal, the god, lived far up in the country. A long time ago he traveled all over the world. He came down the river and arrived at Natahts. There he gathered clams and mussels. He made a fire and roasted them. When he opened them, he found two animals in each shell. After he had roasted them he began to eat and soon had enough. That made him angry and he said, "Henceforth there shall be only one animal in each shell."

The god came to Tillamook Bay and then went up the river. He had to cross it far up because he had no canoe and the river was deep. He met a number of women who were digging roots. He asked, "What are you doing there?" They replied, "We are digging roots." He said, "I do not like that." He took the roots away and sent them to Clatsop. Ever since that time there have been no roots at Tillamook while at Clatsop they are very plentiful. He went on and came to a river full of salmon which were clapping their fins. He caught one of them, threw it ashore, stepped on it, and flattened it. It became a flounder. Ever since then flounders have been plentiful at Tillamook while there have been no salmon there.

As-ai-yahal traveled on and came to a house in which he saw people lying around the fire.

He asked, "What is the matter? Are you sick?"

"No," they replied, "we are starving. East Wind wants to kill us. The river, sea, and beach are frozen over and we can not get any food."

Then he said, "Can't you make East Wind stop blowing so you can secure food?"

He went out of the house and far up the river, which was frozen over. It was so slippery he could hardly stand. He went up the river to meet East Wind and to conquer him.

Before he came to the house of East Wind, he took up some pieces of ice which he threw into the river, saying, "Henceforth it shall not be as cold as it is now. Winter shall be a little cold but not very much so. You shall become herring." The ice at once became herring and swam down the river.

As-ai-yahal went on until he reached the house of East Wind. He entered and whistled. He was trembling with cold, but did not go near the fire. He said, "I am so warm I can not go near the fire." Then he told East Wind he came from a house where they were drying herring.

East Wind said, "Don't say so. It is winter now. There will be no herring for a long time to come."

As-ai-yahal replied, "Don't you believe me? There are plenty of herring outside." He took an icicle which he warmed at the fire. "Look how quickly it boils," he said to East Wind as the ice melted. He made East Wind believe that the melting ice was a herring.

Then East Wind ceased to blow, the ice began to melt, and the people had plenty of food. Until then, it had been winter all the year; now we have both summer and winter.

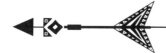

Chinook Wind
(Yakama)

As told by Katharine Berry Judson

Once five brothers lived on Great River. They were the Chinook brothers and they caused the warm wind to blow. There were five other brothers who lived on Great River. They lived at Walla Walla, the meeting of the waters. They caused the cold wind to blow. Now the grandparents of all these brothers lived at Umatilla, the place of wind-drifted sands.

Walla Walla brothers and Chinook brothers were always fighting. They made the winds to sweep over the country, they blew down trees and raised great clouds of dust, they froze the rivers and thawed them so as to make floods. It was very hard for the people.

At last Walla Walla brothers said to Chinook brothers: "We will wrestle with you. Whoever falls down shall have his head cut off. Thus he shall be dead." So Coyote was made judge. He was also to cut the heads off those who fell down.

Now Coyote secretly told the grandparents of Chinook brothers to throw oil on the ground. Then their sons would not fall. Coyote also secretly told the grandparents of Walla Walla brothers to throw ice on the ground. Then their sons would not fall. The oil and the ice made the ground very slippery. But the Walla Walla grandparents had thrown ice on the ground last. So Chinook brothers fell down. First one fell and then another, until all fell down. Then Coyote cut off their heads.

Now the oldest Chinook brother had a baby son. The baby's mother taught him he must revenge his father and uncles. So Young Chinook grew very strong. At last he felt himself very strong. He could pull up large fir trees and throw them around like weeds.

Then Young Chinook went up Great River. Wherever he went he pulled up large fir trees and threw them around like weeds. In the valley of the Yakima he turned aside and went to sleep by Setas, the creek. The mark of his sleeping-place can still be seen on the mountain side.

Then Young Chinook came back to the Great River and went to Umatilla, the place of wind-drifted sands. Here he found his grandparents very cold and hungry. Walla Walla brothers caused the northeast wind to blow all the time. They also stole their fish, when they were returning to the shore. Always they stole the fish.

Young Chinook said: "We will go fishing now." So grandfather started out to fish. Young Chinook lay down in the bottom of the boat. When the boat was full of fish, grandfather started back for the shore. Then Walla Walla brothers started out from the shore to rob grandfather. But they could not catch the boat. Every time Walla Walla brothers came near the boat, it would shoot ahead. So grandfather reached the shore with his fish. Then Young Chinook took his grandparents to the river and bathed them. All the straw and grass and bark which he washed off became trout. That is how trout came to be in Great River.

Now Walla Walla brothers knew that Young Chinook was alive. They sent a messenger to him. They said: "We will wrestle with you. Whoever falls down shall have his head cut off. Thus he shall be dead." So Coyote was made judge. He was also to cut off the heads of those who fell down.

Now Coyote secretly told the grandparents of Walla Walla brothers to throw ice on the ground. Coyote also secretly told the grandparents of Young Chinook to throw oil on the ground. But he told them to throw oil last. So Young Chinook wrestled with Walla Walla brothers, one after another. So the Walla Walla brothers fell to the ground. First one fell and then another, until four had fallen. Then Coyote cut off their heads. The fifth one yielded without wrestling. So Coyote let him live. But Coyote said: "You must blow only lightly. You must never freeze people again."

To Young Chinook, Coyote said: "You shall blow hardest only at night. You shall blow first on the mountain ridges to warn the people."

Thus now winter is only a little cold.

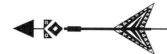 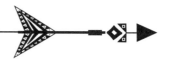

The Hill Giant
(Inuit)

As told by Evelyn Wolfson

Darkness covered the frozen tundra the night Taku slipped out the long underground entrance of the house she had shared for many years with her cruel young husband. Tired of being beaten, Taku was leaving and never coming back.

Taku pulled her caribou-skin anorak up around her face and headed west. She traveled for many days and nights, going out of her way to avoid houses and villages, fearing someone might see her and take her home. When she was sure all signs of human life were behind her, Taku slowed down.

Then, a cold wind began to whip her face, and she stopped to look for shelter. A series of large and small hills off in the distance gave her renewed energy, and she began to run toward them. At last Taku reached the smallest hill and made a clearing between two short ridges. She snuggled into the deep snow and fell sound asleep.

The following day, Taku continued to trek along the hills, and in the evening, she nestled down beside two small round hills. Each day, Taku climbed higher and higher along the hilly ridges until one morning a great booming voice awoke her: "Who are you? Humans never visit me. What are you doing here?"

Taku trembled with fright. She told the invisible voice her sad story and how she had been forced to run away from her husband's constant beatings.

"You may call me Kinak," said the voice. "My great body spreads out over the tundra, and I have allowed you to sleep between my toes and knees, on my chest, and now on my face. But you must never again sleep so close to my mouth or I will be forced to breathe on you and blow you away."

Taku trembled. "I did not realize I was traveling on the body of a giant," said the young wife. "I will leave right away."

THE HILL GIANT

The giant heaved a sigh. "You do not have to leave. Build a house in the thickest part of my beard, far away from my mouth. But go quickly. I must take a breath and clear my lungs right now."

Taku had barely settled in the giant's beard when a fierce wind roared out over the hills and heavy snow swirled across the tundra. While she waited for something more to happen, a dark cloud appeared in the sky and moved slowly toward her. When it was directly overhead, Taku recognized the outline of the giant's huge fist. The shadow lingered for a moment, then a freshly killed caribou dropped down beside her. Taku was so hungry she thanked the giant out loud. "Thank you. Thank you," she yelled into the sky. Taku quickly gathered hairs from the giant's beard, built a fire with the hairs, and ate heartily. She was pleased to be living with a giant who could stretch his arm toward the land and capture a caribou, or simply reach toward the sea and bring her seals and walruses.

Taku lived happily with the giant for many years. She ate well and fashioned fine clothing for herself from the many animals he brought. She had never been so happy and content.

But one day, the giant called out to her. "Taku?" he asked. "Are you listening to me? I am tired of lying in one place. I must turn over. It is time for you to go home."

Taku trembled with fear. Her husband would surely inflict severe punishment on her for staying away so long. "I would like very much to go home," she said, "but I know my husband will beat me for staying away for so long."

"Do not worry," said Kinak. "I will protect you. If you are ever in danger, just call my name and I will come. But before you leave, you must cut both ears from each of the animal skins in storage and put them in a container to take home."

Taku did as she was told without asking Kinak for a reason.

"Now crouch down in front of my mouth and I will send you home," said Kinak.

Again, Taku did as she was told. The giant took a deep breath and WHOOSH, he expelled a powerfully strong wind that blew the young wife far out over the tundra. And before long, Taku landed in her old village. She walked slowly toward the house she had shared with her cruel husband, placed the container of animal ears in the storage shed outside the house, and went inside. To Taku's surprise, her husband greeted her with great

PART 4: MYTHS ABOUT THE WEATHER

joy. He told her he had mourned her death and believed he would never see her again. Taku's fears disappeared, and she settled back into her old household routines.

The next day, when Taku's husband went out to the storage shed, he found piles of fine well-tanned animal hides, one for every ear in Taku's container. The large quantity of fine furs would make Taku's husband a very rich man, and thus one of the village leaders.

Taku's husband was so pleased with his new status in the village that he forgot all about beating his wife.

Then one day Taku's husband told his wife he wanted a child. "What will become of us if we remain childless into our old age? Who will take care of us?" he argued. And that evening Taku's husband dipped a feather in oil and drew the form of a baby boy on his wife's abdomen.

Before long, Taku gave birth to a handsome little boy whom she named Kinak, in memory of the kind giant. Little Kinak soon grew up to be handsome and strong. But while her son was maturing into a fine young man, her husband was reverting back to his old ways. One day, Taku's husband got so angry when his food was not prepared on time that he picked up his spear and rushed toward her, intending to strike her.

Taku ran out of the house shouting, "Kinak. Kinak. Help!" Her husband, who believed she was calling their son, ignored her cries and chased her out through the long passageway.

Once outside, a fierce wind blew down from the north, picked up the angry husband, and whisked him off into the clear blue summer sky, never to be seen again.

Taku was pleased never to see her husband, and thrilled to have her young son all to herself. But young Kinak soon developed a cruel and fierce temper. Every day he bragged to his mother that he had killed a hunting companion. Often, the cocky young man boasted of having killed more than one.

"You are endangering both of our lives," Taku said to her son. "The families of your victims will seek revenge. They will kill both of us," she warned.

So Kinak behaved properly for some time thereafter, and nothing more was said about his evil deeds. Then, one day when he returned home from hunting, he told his mother he had killed his companion after a quarrel. Kinak's mother heaved a heavy sigh. "You are hated and feared in the village," she said at last. "Soon there will only be women and children living among us. It will be better for all of us if you go away and do not return."

THE HILL GIANT

Then Taku turned and walked away.

Some months later, after Kinak had filled his mother's storage racks with meat and skins, he said, "I have provided you with food and hides. Now I will go."

Kinak traveled north in the direction his mother had taken many years before. When he came upon the series of hills where his mother had lived for many years, he immediately climbed the highest one. No sooner had he reached the top when he heard the booming voice of the giant. "Who are you?" the giant asked the young man who was standing too close to his mouth. When Kinak the giant learned that the young man was the son of his friend Taku he smiled. "You may settle down on my face," said the giant. "But you must never climb onto my lips. If you do, evil will befall you."

Taku's son thanked the giant and settled down on his long wiry beard. But he was not accustomed to being told what to do, and soon he became restless. Finally, the bold young man decided to find out why the giant was so protective of his lips. It took a long time for the young man to make his way through the giant's thick tangled beard, but eventually he landed on the cleft of Kinak's deep chin. After he had caught his breath, Taku's son stepped up onto the giant's lower lip and looked over the edge. WHOOSH. A blast of ice-cold air whirled up out of the opening, picked up the surprised young man, and hurled him into the air. Round and round he spun until, eventually, he disappeared off into space.

Taku and her son were the last humans to visit the hill giant. But Kinak the giant still lives in the north and breathes out fierce winds and snow in winter to remind the people of his presence.

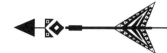
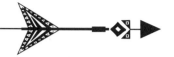

Mink's War with the Southeast Wind
(Kwakiutl)

As told by Katharine Berry Judson

Mink called all his friends together—Deer, Raccoon, Young Raccoon, and Canoe-Calking, the Raven. The four friends went in at once to the council.

Mink said, "Oh, friends, my reason for calling you is that I wish to make war on Southeast Wind." Thus he said. Deer thanked Mink for what he said. They said they would ask Halibut, Sea Bear, Devilfish, and Merman to go along. Mink and all these people lived at Crooked Beach. Southeast Wind was blowing hard all the time, and therefore these people had no way of getting anything to eat.

Therefore they all went to the house of Devilfish and Halibut, for these two lived together. They asked them to join in war on Southeast Wind. They agreed at once. Sea Bear and Merman also agreed.

In the morning, when daylight came, they started in their canoe. In one day they expected to reach Southeast Wind's house. They went southward from Crooked Beach. They were already sailing close to the southeast wind. The wind blew hard. It did not detain them. When evening came, they discovered the house of Southeast Wind. Then Mink said, "Let us stop at this cove and consider how we may conquer him." Then they held a council.

Now Mink said, "Oh, friend Halibut! Lie down flat outside of the door of Southeast Wind. When he comes out of his door, he will step on you, and slip on you, and come stumbling down into our canoe, where we will hold him." Then Deer said the wrong thing. He said they should go to Southeast Wind's house while it was not yet dark. They indeed tried to, but they could not, because of the strong wind. When night came, it was calmer. So they started at once, and stopped on the beach right in front of the house. Halibut at once went and lay down flat just outside of the door. Soon Southeast Wind came to the door and stepped upon Halibut. At once he slipped; he could not stand up. He slipped right down into Mink's canoe. Then Devilfish caught hold of him, and Sea Bear and Merman. Now they held Southeast Wind.

Then Southeast Wind said, "Oh, Born-to-be-the-Sun, tell me what you intend to do with me!" He said that to Mink. He saw that Mink was a great warrior.

Mink answered, "I am doing this because you do not let our world be calm." Southeast Wind answered quickly, "Oh, Chief, now your world shall always be calm, and your sea shall always be smooth." So he spoke to Mink.

Mink said, "Don't give us too much. I do not say that it is good when our world is always calm." Thus he spoke.

Then Southeast Wind said, "It shall not blow in your world for four days." Thus he said. Then those who held him let him go at once, because Southeast Wind was very much afraid of Born-to-be-the-Sun.

Therefore the southeast wind does not blow all the time, on account of what Mink did. This is the end.

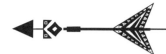 

Origin of the Winds
(Inuit)

As told by Katharine Berry Judson

A long time ago a man and his wife had no children. So one night the man went out of the house to find a solitary tree that grew on the tundra. First he saw a long track of bright light, like that made by the moon shining on the snow. It led across the tundra. So far, far along the trail of bright light traveled the man until he saw a beautiful tree, all alone, shining in the bright light. He took out his hunting knife, cut off part of the trunk, and went home again over the bright trail.

When the man reached home, he carved a boy doll from the wood and his wife made fur clothes for it. Then the man carved little wood dishes from the scraps of wood. The wife set the doll on the bench opposite the entrance, in the place of honor. She placed before it food and water.

That night, when all was dark, they heard low whistling sounds. The woman said, "Do you hear that? It was the doll." When they made a light, they saw that the doll had eaten the food and drunk the water. They saw that its eyes moved.

In the morning, the doll was gone. The man and his wife could not find it, but they saw the tracks of the boy doll leading away from the door. The tracks followed the direction of the trail of light which the man had followed the night before. So the man and his wife went into the house.

But Doll followed the bright path until he came to the edge of day, where the sky comes down to the earth. There were holes in the sky wall covered with gut-skin.

In the east, Doll saw the gut-skin cover over the hole in the sky wall bulging inward. Doll stopped and said, "It is very quiet in here. I think a little wind will make it better." Doll drew his knife and cut the cover loose about the edge of the hole. A strong wind blew through, bringing with it a live reindeer. Looking through the hole, Doll saw another world, just like the earth. Then he drew the cover loosely over the hole, and said to East Wind, "Sometimes blow hard, sometimes lightly. Sometimes do not blow at all."

Doll walked along the sky wall to another opening at the southeast. The gut-skin cover bulged inward. Then Doll cut the cover loose at the edges, and a great gale swept in. It brought reindeer, trees, and bushes. Then Doll fastened the cover lightly and said "Sometimes blow hard, sometimes lightly. Sometimes do not blow at all."

Then Doll came to a hole in the south, and the gut-skin cover bulged inward. He cut the edges loose and a hot wind rushed in. It brought rain, and spray from the great salt sea which lay beyond the sky hole on that side. Then Doll closed the opening lightly and said to South Wind, "Sometimes blow hard, sometimes lightly. Sometimes do not blow at all."

Doll walked along the sky wall to the west. There he saw another opening, covered by gut-skin. So he cut the edges loose, and West Wind swept in, bringing with him rain, with sleet and spray from the gray ocean. Then Doll fastened the edges of the gut-skin loosely, and said to West Wind, "Sometimes blow hard, sometimes lightly. Sometimes do not blow at all."

So Doll passed along the sky wall to the northwest. When he cut the edges of the gut-skin covering, a blast of cold wind rushed in, bringing snow and ice. Doll became cold; he almost froze. Therefore Doll closed the hole quickly, saying, "Sometimes blow hard, sometimes lightly. Sometimes do not blow at all."

Again Doll went along the sky wall to the north, but it became so cold he had to leave it. So he went toward the center of the earth, away from the sky wall, until he saw the opening to the north. Then he went to the hole in the sky wall, but so great was the cold that Doll feared to cut the strings. He waited. Then he cut the strings quickly. The terrible North Wind swept in, bringing with him great masses of snow and ice. North Wind strewed the snow and ice all over the earth plain. Then Doll closed the hole very quickly, yet he fastened it loosely. He said to North Wind, "Sometimes blow hard, sometimes lightly. Sometimes do not blow at all."

Then Doll traveled into the midst of the earth plain. He looked up and saw the sky arch, resting upon long, slender poles, like a tepee, but of beautiful blue material. Then Doll went back to the village where he was made.

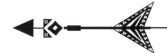 

Capture of Wind
(Chilcotin)

As told by Katharine Berry Judson

A long time ago there was a chief who had many sons. In those days Wind used to blow furiously all the time, and the chief told one of his sons to capture Wind. The son made a snare and placed it in a tree. Then next morning, when he went to that tree, he found in the snare a small boy with a fat body and streaming hair. Now that boy was Wind. The chief's son kept him for some time, then he let him go free when Wind promised he would not blow so hard. Only once in a while could he blow hard, said the chief's son, and Wind agreed. So now he is free, and he does not blow nearly so hard as he used to.

Keeper of the Winds
(Algonquin)

As told by Julia Darrow Cowles

Mudjekeewis, father of the four winds of heaven, had three sons. Their names were Wabun, Kabibonokka, and Shawondasee. Mudjekeewis said to the chiefs of his people, "You have named me Kabeyun, the West Wind, and have given to me all the four winds of the heavens. I will appoint my three sons to be keepers of the north wind, the east wind, and the south wind."

So to Kabibonokka he gave the north wind, to Wabun he gave the east wind, and to Shawondasee he gave the south wind.

Wabun was a hunter. He liked to rise early and to leap upon the mountains in pursuit of the wild deer. He liked to shoot with his bow and arrows. He was glad that the east wind had been given to him, for he loved to watch the heavens in the early morning when the sun shot its first rays across the mountain tops where he hunted. He said to Mudjekeewis, "I am most grateful, my father, that the east wind has been given into my keeping. When I hunt in the early morning I will shoot away the clouds of darkness with my silver arrows; I will chase away the shadows."

So Wabun cared for the east wind, and each morning he painted the sky with wonderful colors. He sent his silver arrows down to the earth to waken the people, and to light up the lakes and meadows.

At last Wabun grew lonely in his home in the eastern sky, and he began to watch day by day for a beautiful maiden who walked upon the prairie gathering grasses for her baskets. And Wabun wooed her with his soft breezes, and with sweet flowers, and with the songs of birds. And when he had won her heart he changed her into a beautiful star, which he set in his home in the heavens.

PART 4: MYTHS ABOUT THE WEATHER

Kabibonokka, the second son, was very different from Wabun. He was cold and cruel, and he was glad that the north wind had been given to him. When he sent his winds across the earth the leaves upon the trees turned to crimson and gold, and were very lovely, but they whirled and twisted in the wind and said to each other, "Our days will soon be at an end. We shall soon turn dry and brown and fall to the earth. Kabibonokka laughs when we put on our beautiful colors."

Then Kabibonokka sent icy blasts, and the waters of the lakes froze, and the snows fell, and the winds came through the door of the tepee, and life became hard for the people. And Kabibonokka laughed, and his laugh was like the whistling of the wind through the bare treetops. The fish were deep beneath the frozen waters; the snow covered the tracks of the animals of the forest. Food was scarce, and hard to obtain.

Only the bravest of the Indians could fish and hunt when the north wind blew its coldest. Shingebis was one of these, and he never lacked for fish or fuel.

"I will get the best of Shingebis," said Kabibonokka, and so one morning he went to Shingebis' tepee. And Shingebis asked him to eat with him, and he gave him a meal of fish. And Kabibonokka ate greedily. But the warmth of Shingebis' tepee was too great for him, and he had to go away. As he left he tried to put out the tepee fire, but Shingebis blew upon it and it burned more brightly, so that Kabibonokka had to hasten. In revenge he froze the waters more deeply, but Shingebis only laughed, for no weather was too cold for him to find fish for his dinner.

But the Indians did not love Kabibonokka, for he was cold and cruel.

Shawondasee was not like either of his brothers. He was fat and lazy. He loved to lie upon green banks under shady trees. He loved the sweet flowers, and the warmth of the South Land. He was far too lazy to send strong winds such as came from the North Land. His breezes were soft and traveled slowly, and they were sweet with the perfume of southern groves and meadows.

Shawondasee, like his brother Wabun, saw a beautiful maiden that he loved. Do you remember the story? Her hair was of golden yellow, and she nodded and swayed in the breeze. Her home was in the meadows, and Shawondasee looked for her day by day, and wafted sweet odors and fair flowers to her, and he won her love, even as Wabun won the love of the prairie maiden. But he was too sluggish to go himself to win her, and to bring her to his home in the South Land. Instead he said to himself each morning, "To-day I will go and seek the golden-haired maiden, and bring her to my home," but each day he was too indolent.

The days went by, and at last the golden hair of the maiden turned silvery white, and when Shawondasee saw this he heaved a great sigh, so great a sigh that it reached even to the maiden, and lo, all the silver white of her hair was scattered over the meadow!

So Shawondasee still lives alone in the South Land, and sends gentle sighing breezes to the meadows of the North.

The Children of Cloud
(Pima)

As told by Katharine Berry Judson

When the Hohokam dwelt on the Gila River and tilled their farms around the great temple which we call Casa Grande, there was a beautiful young woman in the pueblo who had two twin sons. Their father was Cloud, and he lived far away.

One day the boys came to their mother, as she was weaving mats. "Who is. our father?" they asked. "We have no one to run to when he returns from the hunt, or from war, to shout to him."

The mother answered: "In the morning, look toward the sunrise and you will see a white Cloud standing upright. He is your father."

"Can we visit our father?" they asked.

"Yes," said their mother. "You may visit him, but you must make the journey without stopping. First you will reach Wind, who is your father's eldest brother. Behind him you will find your father."

The boys traveled four days and came to the house of Wind.

"Are you our father?" they asked.

"No, I am your Uncle," answered Wind." Your father lives in the next house. Go on to him."

They traveled on to Cloud. But Cloud drove them away. He said, "Go to your uncle Wind. He will tell you something." But Wind sent them back to Cloud again. Thus the boys were driven away from each house four times.

Then Cloud said to them, "Prove to me you are my sons. If you are, you can do what I do."

THE CHILDREN OF CLOUD

The younger boy sent chain lightning across the sky with sharp, crackling thunder. The elder boy sent the heat lightning with its distant rumble of thunder.

"You are my children," said Cloud. "You have power like mine."

But again he tested them. He took them to a house nearby where a flood of rain had drowned the people. "If they are my sons," he said, "they will not be harmed."

Then Cloud sent the rain and the storm. The water rose higher and higher, but the two boys were not harmed. The water could not drown them. Then Cloud took them to his home and there they stayed a long, long time.

But after a long time, the boys wished to see their mother again. Then Cloud made them some bows and arrows differing from any they had ever seen, and sent them to their mother. He told them he would watch over them as they traveled but they must speak to no one they met on their way.

So the boys traveled to the setting sun. First they met Raven. They remembered their father's command and turned aside so as not to meet him. Then they met Roadrunner, and turned aside to avoid him. Next came Hawk and Eagle.

Eagle said, "Let's scare those boys." So he swooped down over their heads until they cried from fright.

"We were just teasing you," said Eagle. "We will not do you any harm." Then Eagle flew on.

Next they met Coyote. They tried to avoid him, but Coyote ran around and put himself in their way. Cloud was watching and he sent down thunder and lightning. And the boys sent out their magic thunder and lightning also, until Coyote was frightened and ran away.

Now this happened on the mountain top, and one boy was standing on each side of the trail. After Coyote ran away, they were changed into mescal—the very largest mescal ever known. The place was near Tucson. This is the reason why mescal grows on the mountains, and why thunder and lightning go from place to place—because the children did. That is why it rains when we gather mescal.

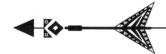

The Thunder People
(Passamaquoddy)

As told by Julia Darrow Cowles

Once upon a time a young Indian warrior was hunting with his bow and arrows. He followed far after a fleet deer, until he found himself standing upon a great rock, high above the plains.

The clouds were gathering thickly. The sky was black with clouds. The Indian youth was far away from his lodge.

Again he saw the deer, and he drew his bow. But as he did so the deer was changed into the form of a maiden, standing against the rock.

The youth dropped his bow in wonder. He looked at the maiden. In the distance he heard the voice of the thunder.

"Who are you?" he asked in amazement.

And the maiden answered, "I am the sister of the Thunder Men. Will you come with me and visit our home?" The youth consented, and the maiden struck the great rock against which she had stood.

There was a flash, like a flash of lightning, and the rock opened and made a passage for them.

The maiden led the way, and the youth followed; and when they had passed through the rock, they came into a strange country—to the home of the Thunder Maiden. The floors and walls were of clouds, and the clouds were of every shade, from silver gray to the deepest purple black. They were soft to walk upon, and smooth as the smoothest velvet. And their changing shades were more wonderful than any artist could paint.

The maiden's robes were of trailing silver, and her hair was black as midnight.

She led the youth to her father, who sat upon a throne formed from the deepest purple clouds. His hair and beard were white like the mists that float across the sky. But his robe was black, with here and there a dash of brilliant gold.

"Welcome, my son," said the old man. "Have you come to dwell among us?"

The youth looked at the beautiful maiden, and he answered, "Yes, my father."

So he became one of the Thunder People.

After a time the brothers of the maiden returned home. And when they saw the youth and knew that he had come to dwell among them, they proposed a game of ball.

Now their balls were big and black, and very heavy; and they did not throw them, but rolled them back and forth across the clouds. And the noise was very great.

When the father of the Thunder Men saw that the youth was strong, and could roll the ball well, he said, "You shall go with my sons to-morrow. You shall see greater sport than this."

In the morning, when the Thunder Men put on their great purple wings, the maiden brought forth another pair and fastened them upon the shoulders of the youth. Then they all flew away to the south. They carried bows, and their arrows were of gold.

Their wings made a mighty roaring and crashing as they flew, and the people on the earth said, "Listen, how the thunder roars and crashes!"

Then they shot their golden arrows from their bows, and the earth people cried, "See, how the lightning flashes across the sky!" And some of the earth people ran and hid, for they were afraid.

But the old man of the Thunder World had said to his sons: "Shoot your arrows only at the great bird of the south, which is our enemy. Destroy not the people of the earth. And fly not too low. Touch not the trees, for they are our friends."

So they flew about for a time, taking care where they sent their arrows. And when they had grown tired of their sport, they flew back to their home in the clouds and took off their great purple wings.

For many moons the youth enjoyed the company of the Thunder Maiden, and took part in the sports of her brothers. But at last there took possession of him a great longing to visit again his brothers and sisters of the earth. He longed to chase the deer in the forest, to follow his chief in battle, to smell the fire of his lodge.

He told his longing to the old man of the Thunder World, and the old man said he should have his way. So for the last time the Thunder Maiden fastened his purple wings to his shoulders, handed him the golden arrows, and bade him good-bye. Then away he flew with the Thunder Men.

PART 4: MYTHS ABOUT THE WEATHER

Closer and closer to the earth they went, and the people covered their ears to keep out the crash and roar of the thunder; and they covered their eyes to keep out the sight of the dazzling, flashing lightning.

"Oh, what a storm!" cried the earth people, as they looked toward a hill outside their village where the noise seemed most deafening, and the glare seemed most blinding.

And there, on the hill, the Thunder Men left their Indian brother; then, with many a rumble and flash, they flew away back to their home in the clouds.

When the people looked again, the storm had lifted, and a warrior was seen descending from the hill to the village. They recognized him as the youth who had been lost for many, many moons.

As they sat together around the fire of the lodge, the youth told them the tale that I have told you, of the Thunder People who dwell in the purple clouds.

Bear and the Fawns
(Miwok)

As told by Edward Winslow Gifford

"Sister-in-law, let us get clover. I like clover," Bear said to Deer. Then Deer replied, "Yes, we will eat clover." Bear said, "We will leave these girls (Fawns) at home. They always follow you." She told the Fawns, "We go to eat clover. Clover is high enough to eat now, I think. You girls stay at home until we return."

Bear said to her sister-in-law, "Let's go. We will be back tonight." Then they went below to eat clover.

After they had gone below, Bear said, "Let's sit down and rest." Then she continued, "Examine my head, examine my head. I must have lice on my head." Deer replied, "Yes, yes, come here and I will look for lice." Then she found lice on Bear's head. She found large frogs on Bear's head. When she found the frogs, she picked them off and threw them away. Bear asked her, "What is it that you throw away? Are you throwing away my lice?" Deer replied, "No, you hear the leaves dropping." Bear said, "Take them all out. I have many lice."

Then Deer removed them all. Bear asked, "What are you throwing away?" Deer replied, "I throw away nothing. You hear pinecones dropping from the tree." Bear said, "I think that you throw away my lice." Deer retorted, "No, those are pinecones dropping from the trees."

"Remove them all, then," said Bear; "remove them all. My head feels light, since you have finished picking the lice from it." Deer threw away the frogs, threw away large frogs.

Bear said to Deer, "Let me examine your head." Deer said, "All right." Bear examined Deer's head and said, "There are many." Deer's lice were wood-ticks and Bear proceeded to take them from Deer's head.

Then Bear said, "There are many. I do not think I can get them all by picking. You have many. Let me chew these lice and your hair with them. That is the only way I can remove

PART 4: MYTHS ABOUT THE WEATHER

them. You have many lice. I do not think that I have removed them all. There are many. Stoop and I will chew your hair. Do not be afraid. Stoop and let me try."

Then Deer stooped. She thought Bear's intentions were good. Bear examined her hair for a while, and then chewed. Instead of chewing Deer's hair. Bear bit her neck, killing her.

Bear ate all of Deer, except the liver, which she took home. She placed the liver in a basket and put clover on top of it. Then she went home. She proceeded homeward after sundown, carrying the clover in the basket with the liver in the bottom of the basket.

Arriving at home, she told the Fawns to eat the clover. She said to them, "Your mother has not come yet; you know she is always slow. She always takes her time in coming home." Thus spoke Bear to the Fawns, when she arrived at home.

The Fawns ate the clover. After they had eaten it, they saw the liver in the bottom of the basket. The younger one found it. She told the older one, "Our aunt killed our mother. That is her liver." The older Fawn said to her younger sister, "Our aunt took her down there and killed her. We had better watch, or she will kill us, too."

They continued to eat the clover after finding the liver. Then the younger one said, "What shall we do? I fear she will kill us, if we stay here. We had better go to our grandfather. Get ready all of our mother's awls. Get all of the baskets. Get ready and then we will go. We will go before our aunt kills us. She killed our mother. I think it is best for us to go."

"Do not forget to take the awls," said the older Fawn, for she was afraid of being overtaken by Bear. The Fawns started with the baskets and awls, leaving one basket behind. Their aunt, Bear, was not at home when they left. When she returned, she looked about, but saw no Fawns. Then Bear discovered their tracks and set out to follow them. After she had tracked them a short distance, the basket, left at home, whistled. Bear ran back to see if the Fawns had returned. In the meantime the Fawns proceeded on their journey, throwing awls and baskets in different directions. Again, Bear started from the house. As she proceeded the awls whistled. Bear, thinking that the Fawns were whistling, left the trail in search of them.

The Fawns said, "We go to our grandfather."

As Bear followed them along the trail, the baskets and awls whistled and delayed her. Whenever Bear heard the whistles, she became angry and ran in the direction from which the sound proceeded. She of course saw nothing and returned to the trail.

She heard a whistle in the direction of the stream. She ran toward it, but when she arrived there, saw nothing.

When she did not find the girls she became angry. She said, "Those girls are making fun of me." Then she shouted, "Where are you, girls? Why don't you meet me?" The awls only whistled in response and Bear ran toward the sound. Then she became still angrier and said to herself, "If I capture you girls, I will eat you. If I find you girls, I will eat you."

Bear continued to track the Fawns. She found the trail easily and saw their tracks upon it. She said, "I have found the marks that will lead me to them." She followed the marks upon the trail. "If I catch them, I shall eat them." She heard more whistling and that, enraged her. Then she jumped on to a tree and bit a limb in two. It made her furious to hear the whistling. She said to herself, "If I ever catch those girls, I shall eat them." The baskets continued to whistle on both sides of the trail, making her very angry, and retarding her progress. The Fawns had many baskets.

They followed the long trail until they arrived at a river. Bear was far behind. On the opposite side of the river they saw their grandfather, Daddy Longlegs. They told him that Bear had eaten their mother and that they wanted to cross the river in order to escape from her. Their grandfather extended his leg across the river so that they might walk across on it. Then they crossed on their grandfather's leg. In the meantime Bear continued to track them. She still followed false leads because of the whistling of the baskets and awls. The following of false leads delayed her.

The Fawns said to their grandfather, Daddy Longlegs, "Do not let her cross the river. She follows us." Bear was still coming along the trail. The baskets, the soap-root brushes, and the awls continued to whistle, causing her delay. The Fawns had many baskets, soap-root brushes, and awls.

After the Fawns had crossed the river, Bear arrived at the bank. She asked Daddy Longlegs, "Did the girls come by this place?" He replied, "Yes." Then Bear told Daddy Longlegs, "The girls ran away from me." Daddy Longlegs asked, "Where is their mother?" Bear replied, "Their mother is sick. That is why she did not come, and that is why I seek the girls. She told me to bring them back."

Bear then asked Daddy Longlegs to put his leg across the river, so that she might cross. He said, "All right," and stretched his leg across the river. Then Bear walked on Daddy

PART 4: MYTHS ABOUT THE WEATHER

Longlegs' leg. When she reached the middle, Daddy Longlegs gave a sudden spring and threw her into the air. She fell into the river, and had to swim to the opposite shore.

She found again the track of the Fawns. Wherever the track was plain she ran rapidly to make up for the time lost. The numerous awls, which the Fawns had thrown to each side of the trail, whistled as before.

"Hurry, sister, we near our grandfather's (Lizard's) house," said the older Fawn to the younger. Bear became exceedingly angry and shouted in her rage.

"Hurry, she comes; hurry, sister, she comes. We would not like to have her catch us before we reached our grandfather's," said the older Fawn. Then the Fawns threw awls and baskets to each side of the trail anew. As they approached their grandfather's house. Bear gained upon them. As Bear saw them nearing their grandfather's she shouted again in her anger.

The Fawns at last arrived at their grandfather's assembly house and asked him to open the door. The grandfather told the Fawns, "My door is on the north side of the house." The Fawns ran to the north side, but found no door. Then they called again, "Hurry, grandfather, open the door." He said, "My door is on the east side of the house." Then they ran to the east side, but found no door. Then they ran around the house. They found no door. They called again to their grandfather. He said, "My door is at the top of the house. Come in through the top."

The Fawns climbed to the top of the house and entered through the smoke hole. Their grandfather asked why they had come to see him. The Fawns told him, "Bear killed our mother." The grandfather asked. "Where is Bear?"

The Fawns said, "Bear took our mother down to the clover. She ate mother there. Then she returned to the house and told us to eat the clover which she brought. While we were eating the clover from the basket, we found the liver of our mother in the bottom under the clover, found our mother's liver at the bottom of the basket. The clover was on top of it." Thus spoke the Fawns to their grandfather. He asked them again, "Where is Bear?"

The Fawns replied, "She follows us. She comes. Yes, she comes."

Then Lizard, their grandfather, threw two large white stones into the fire. The Fawns sat by and watched him while he heated the two white stones. While he heated the stones. Bear came. She had followed the tracks of the Fawns to their grandfather's assembly house.

Bear said to herself, "I think they went to their grandfather's." Meanwhile Lizard heated the white stones.

After looking around the assembly house. Bear called to Lizard, "Did the Fawns come here." Lizard said, "Yes. Why?" "Well. I wish to take them home." said Bear. Lizard asked. "Why do you wish to take them home?" Then Bear replied. "I wish to take them home to their mother. Where is your door?"

Lizard told her that the door was on the north side of the assembly house. She ran to the north side, but found no door. She called again, "Where is the door?" "It is on the west side of my assembly house," said Lizard. Bear was very angry, but she ran to the west side of the house. She found no door there, so she asked again. Lizard said, "It is on the east side of my assembly house." Again she found no door, and she became exceedingly angry and asked him crossly, "Where is the door?" Lizard replied, "Run around the assembly house and you will find it." She ran around the house four times, but to no avail. In more of a rage than ever, she asked Lizard. "Where is your door?" Then Lizard told her that it was at the top of the assembly house. Bear climbed to the top and found the opening.

Upon finding the opening, she shouted and said, "I shall eat those girls." Lizard only laughed. Bear asked how she should enter. Lizard said, "Shut your eyes tight and open your mouth wide, then you enter the quicker."

Bear shut her eyes tight and shoved her head through the smoke hole with her mouth wide open. Lizard called to her, "Wider." Then Lizard threw those two white stones, which he had heated, and threw one of them into her mouth. It rolled into her stomach. He threw the second one. It remained in her mouth. Bear rolled from the top of the assembly house dead.

Lizard told his granddaughters, "She is dead." Then Lizard went outside and skinned Bear. After skinning her, he dressed the hide well. He cut it into two pieces, making one small piece and one large piece.

He gave the large hide to the older Fawn and the small hide to the younger. He said to them, "Take care of those hides." Then he told the older Fawn to run and discover what sort of a sound the hide made when she ran. The older Fawn ran and the sound was very loud. Then Lizard told the younger Fawn to run. Her hide made a fairly loud sound, but not so loud as that of the older Fawn.

PART 4: MYTHS ABOUT THE WEATHER

Old Lizard laughed, saying, "The younger one is stronger than the older." Then he told them to run together. He pointed to a large tree and told them to try their strength against the tree. The older one tried first. She ran against it, splintering it a little. Then the younger girl ran against the tree at its thickest part. She smashed it to pieces.

Lizard laughed again and said, "You are stronger than your sister." Then he told both to run together. They ran about and kicked the tree all day long. Lizard returned home and, upon arriving there, said, "The girls are all right. I think I had better send them above."

The Fawns said to Lizard, "We are going home." Lizard asked them not to go. He said, "I shall get you both a good place. I am going to send you girls above." Then the girls went up. They ran around above and Lizard heard them running. He called them Thunders. He said, "I think it is better for them to stay there. They will be better off there." Lizard closed the door of his assembly house. Rain began to fall. The girls ran around on the top, and rain and hail fell.

How the Hunter Destroyed Snow
(Menomini)

As told by Katharine Berry Judson

Once a hunter with his wife and two children lived in a tepee. Each day the hunter went out for game. He was a good hunter and he brought back much game.

But one day, after Fall had gone and winter had come, the hunter met Kon, Snow, who froze his feet badly. Then the hunter made a large wooden bowl and filled it with Kon. He buried it in a deep hole where the midday sun could shine down upon it, and where Snow could not run away. Then he covered the hole with sticks and leaves so that Snow would be a prisoner until summer.

Now when midsummer came, and everything was warm, the hunter came back to this hole and pulled away the sticks and leaves. He let the midday sun shine down upon Kon so that he melted. Thus the hunter punished Kon.

But when Fall came again, one day the hunter heard someone say to him, when he was in the forest: "You punished me last summer, but when winter comes I will show you how strong I am."

The hunter knew it was Kon's voice. He at once built another tepee, near the one in which he lived, and filled it full of firewood.

At last winter came again. When the hunter was in the forest one day, he heard Kon say: "Now I am coming to visit you, as I said I should. In four days I shall be at your tepee."

When the hunter returned home, he made ready more firewood; he built a fire at the two sides of the tepee. After four days, everything became frozen. It was very cold. The hunter kept up the fires in the tepee. He took out all the extra fur robes to cover his wife and children. The cold became more severe. It was hard not to freeze.

On the fifth day, towards night, the hunter looked out from his tepee upon a frozen world. Then he saw a stranger coming. He looked like any other stranger, except that he had a very large head and an immense beard. When he came to the tepee, the hunter asked him in. He at once came in, but he would not go near either of the fires. This puzzled the hunter, and he began to watch the stranger.

It became colder and colder after the stranger had come into the tepee. The hunter added more wood to each of the fires until they roared. The stranger seemed too warm. The hunter added more wood, and the stranger became warmer and warmer. Then the hunter saw that as he became warm, he seemed to shrink. At last his head and body were quite small. Then the hunter knew who the stranger guest was. It was Kon, the Cold. So he kept up his fires until Kon melted altogether away.

Part 5:
"Why?" Myths

Why the Sun is Bright
(Lillooet)

As told by Katharine Berry Judson

Once a whole village moved away. They were angry with a boy, so they left him behind with his grandmother. Now it looked as though they would starve. Grandmother said, "Snare small animals. Shoot the birds." So the boy snared rabbits and squirrels and many small animals. He shot many birds with bright plumage. Grandmother cooked the animals and birds, but she made him a robe from the skins of the birds. The robe was very large and bright. The boy wore it when he went to spear fish.

Now Sun, when he followed the trail in the Sky Land, saw the robe when the boy was spearing fish. He saw that robe many times. One day Sun left the trail and came to visit the boy. Sun always dressed in a goatskin robe, with long fringe.

Sun said to the boy, "I will exchange blankets with you." The boy looked at the goatskin robe, and said, "Oh, no!"

Sun said, "You do not know the value of my robe. It can catch more fish than you can spear." Sun placed the fringe of his blanket in the water, and at once a fish caught on each tip of the fringe. When the boy saw that, he exchanged blankets at once.

Before Sun traded for the boy's robe of birds' plumage, he was pale, and his light was like the light of the moon. Therefore people could look at him. Now he became bright and dazzling as he is today, because of his bright robe. People can no longer look at him.

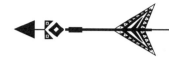 

Why the Moon is Pale
(Wyandot)

As told by Katharine Berry Judson

Now Small Turtle made Sun out of lightning when she climbed up into the sky. She also made Moon for his wife. Moon was smaller than Sun, but she was very bright. Then the animals bored a hole through the edge of the earth so that Sun and Moon could pass through at night, and begin their trail again at the east.

Small Turtle never meant Sun and Moon to travel together. But one day Moon ran into the hole at the edge of the earth much too soon. She also ran in ahead of her husband, Sun. Sun was very angry. Moon stayed under the earth for a long while. Small Turtle went after her one day to see what was the matter. She found Moon small and pale because of Sun's anger. Then Small Turtle tried to make her large again. Moon would grow larger for a while, and then remember Sun's anger, and fade away again, until she was only a strip. She does so even today. That is why Moon is so pale, and why she keeps changing as she does.

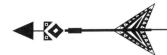 

Why James Bay is Salt
(Cree)

As told by Alanson Skinner

One day Wolverine killed a skunk out in the forest. Skunk discharged his fluid in Wolverine's face and blinded him. Wolverine tried to reach the water to wash it off. Every time he came to a tree he would ask it what kind it was. At length, he came to some driftwood, and from this he concluded that he was near the sea. Finally, he reached the sea and washed skunk's fluid out of his eyes, and it is this fluid that makes the sea salt.

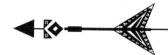 

Why Lightning Strikes the Trees
(Thompson River)

As told by Katharine Berry Judson

Thunder Bird was angry with people and tried to drown the whole world, but he could not make the water rise high enough, so some of the people escaped. Then Thunder Bird shot arrows at them. He really did hurt many, but all the people ran away and hid in a cave.

Then Turtle came out. He shouted out to Thunder Bird, "You can not kill people. Your arrows fly wild. Shoot at the trees and rocks; perhaps you can hit them." Turtle mocked Thunder.

Thunder said, "Oh, yes, I do strike people. I have killed many of them!"

Turtle said at once, "Well, then, prove it by killing me." So he drew his shell down tight and moved about very carelessly, not hiding at all, while Thunder shot many arrows at him. They only glanced off his thick shell.

Then Thunder Bird believed that he really could not hit people, so now he shoots his arrows at trees and rocks. But if people stand under a tree in a storm, it is likely that Thunder will hit them.

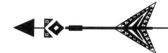 

Why the Aspen Leaves are Never Still
(Blackfoot)

As told by Julian Darrow Cowles

"Why are the leaves on the aspen tree never still, Grandmother?" asked one of the Indian children of the old basket weaver. "I have watched them so many times, and they always talk together."

"You are right, my daughter. When there is no breath in the heavens, the aspen leaves still talk."

"Is there a story about the aspen tree, grandmother?" asked the little girl. "Will you tell it to me, if there is?"

"Yes daughter," replied the old woman, "there is a story about the aspen tree which it is good that you should hear."

Taking her basket upon her knees and continuing her weaving, the grandmother told her story:

"Many, many moons ago there was a young warrior who was lonely in his father's lodge, and he said to himself, 'I will seek a maiden to wed, and make ready a lodge of my own.'

"So he watched the maidens of the village, and he found two sisters who seemed so modest, and kind, and good, that he knew not which of them to choose.

"When he went to their father's lodge, he was kindly treated by both. They gave him words of welcome, they smiled upon him, and they prepared food and set it before him. Both could weave fine baskets for the lodge, and make rich embroidery of quills.

"Many times the young brave went to the lodge, but he could not tell which maiden would make the better wife. And at last he said to himself, 'I will try magic. I will get the medicine man to help me.'

PART 5: "WHY?" MYTHS

"So he visited the lodge of the Medicine Man, and after a time there came away from the Medicine Man's lodge an old man, bent, and leaning upon a stick. He walked feebly, and his garments were ragged. His hair was white, and his chin quivered with age.

"The old man went to the lodge of the two maidens and begged a bit of food. The younger sister asked him to come inside the lodge and rest. Then she prepared some nourishing food and gave to him, and while he ate it she noticed that his feet were barely covered with pieces of skins tied about the ankle. She hastened to finish the moccasins that she was embroidering, and gave them to him, so that his feet should not be bruised with walking.

"The older sister looked on with scorn, and made unkind remarks. She asked her sister why she should spend time upon a forlorn old man who could never repay her. She laughed at his ragged garments and at his quivering chin and feeble knees. Then in a sharp voice she bade him begone before her lover should come from the hunt.

"The old man went away, after thanking the younger sister for her kindness.

"A short time later, the young warrior came to the door of the lodge, bearing upon his shoulders a deer which he had shot. Both sisters smiled at him and bade him enter. He passed the older sister without a glance, and laid the deer at the feet of the younger.

"As they looked down at the deer, both sisters discovered that the young man had upon his feet the moccasins that the younger sister had just given to the strange old man.

"'I seek a maiden to be the light of my lodge,' he said, 'and by magic I have found that one. I was the old man who came hither for shelter and comfort, and so I learned how to escape a sharp tongue and bitter words.

"'But the Medicine Man's charm has not yet finished its work,' he added. 'I do not want another to suffer the fate I have so narrowly escaped.'

"He took the younger sister by the hand and led her from the lodge. The older sister followed, and as she stepped outside, her feet became rooted to the ground, and she was turned into an aspen tree.

"The younger sister became the light of the young warrior's lodge; but the aspen tree, like the older sister, while beautiful to look upon, has since that day had a whispering and unruly tongue."

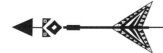

Why There are No Snakes on Takhoma
(Cowlitz)

As told by Katharine Berry Judson

A long, long time ago, Tyhee Sahale became angry with the people. Sahale ordered a medicine man to take his bow and arrow and shoot into the cloud which hung low over Takhoma. The medicine man shot the arrow, and it stuck fast in the cloud. Then he shot another into the lower end of the first. Then he shot another into the lower end of the second. He shot arrows until he had made a chain which reached from the cloud to the earth. The medicine man told his klootchman and his children to climb up the arrow trail. Then he told the good animals to climb up the arrow trail. Then the medicine man climbed up himself. Just as he was climbing into the cloud, he looked back. A long line of bad animals and snakes were also climbing up the arrow trail. Therefore the medicine man broke the chain of arrows. Thus the snakes and bad animals fell down on the mountain side. Then at once it began to rain. It rained until all the land was flooded. Water reached even to the snow line of Takhoma. When all the bad animals and snakes were drowned, it stopped raining. After a while the waters sank again. Then the medicine man, and his klootchman, and the children climbed out of the cloud and came down the mountain side. The good animals also climbed out of the cloud. Thus there are now no snakes or bad animals on Takhoma.

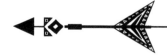 

Why the Mole Lives Underground
(Cherokee)

As told by James Mooney

A man was in love with a woman who disliked him and would have nothing to do with him. He tried every way to win her favor, but to no purpose, until at last he grew discouraged and made himself sick thinking over it. The Mole came along, and finding him in such low condition asked what was the trouble. The man told him the whole story, and when he had finished the Mole said: "I can help you, so that she will not only like you, but will come to you of her own will." So that night the Mole burrowed his way underground to where the girl was in bed asleep and took out her heart. He came back by the same way and gave the heart to the man, who could not see it even when it was put into his hand. "There," said the Mole, "swallow it, and she will be drawn to come to you and can not keep away." The man swallowed the heart, and when the girl woke up she somehow thought at once of him, and felt a strange desire to be with him, as though she must go to him at once. She wondered and could not understand it, because she had always disliked him before, but at last the feeling grew so strong that she was compelled to go herself to the man and tell him she loved him and wanted to be his wife. And so they were married, but all the magicians who had known them both were surprised and wondered how it had come about. When they found that it was the work of the Mole, whom they had always before thought too insignificant for their notice, they were very jealous and threatened to kill him, so that he hid himself under the ground and has never since dared to come up to the surface.

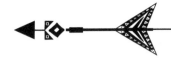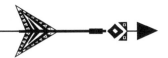

Why the Blackbird has Red Wings
(Chitimacha)

As told by Katharine Berry Judson

One day an Indian became so angry with everyone that he set the sea marshes on fire because he wanted to burn up the world.

A little blackbird saw it. He flew up into a tree and shouted, "*Ku nam wi cu! Ku nam wi cu!* The world and all is going to burn."

The man said, "If you do not go away, I will kill you." But the bird only kept shouting, "Ku nam wi cu! The world and all is going to burn."

Then the Indian threw a shell and hit the little bird on the wings, making them bleed. That is how the red-winged blackbird came by its red wings.

Now when people saw the marshes burning, they quickly ran down and killed game which had been driven from it by the fire. Then they said to the angry man,

"Because you put fire in those tall weeds, the deer and bear and other animals have been driven out and we have killed them. You have aided us by burning them."

Nowadays when the red-winged blackbird comes around the house, he still shouts, *Ku nam wi cu*, so they say.

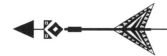 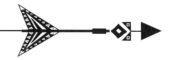

Why the Birds have Sharp Tails
(Biloxi)

As told by Katharine Berry Judson

Once upon a time, they say, the world turned over. Then the waters rose very high and many people died. A woman took two children and lodged in a tree. She sat there waiting for the waters to sink, for she had no way of reaching the ground.

When the woman saw the Ancient of Red-headed Buzzards, she called to him, "Help me to get down and I will give you one of the children." He assisted her, but she did not give him the child.

The waters were so deep that the birds were clinging by their claws to the clouds, but their tails were under water. That is why their tails are always sharp. One of these birds was the Ancient of Yellowhammers. Therefore its tailfeathers are sharp at the ends. The large Red-headed Woodpecker was there, too, and the Ivory-billed Woodpecker, and that is why their tails have their present shape.

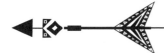 

Why the Squirrel Coughs
(Algonquin)

As told by Julia Darrow Cowles

A great trickster was Manabozho. He loved to play jokes upon his friends of the forest. One day he invited them all to a feast in his wigwam. And everyone came, from the woodpecker and the tiny mouse, to the great moose with branching horns.

It was a time of scarcity of food, and all were glad to be asked to a banquet. But the meat that Manabozho had ready for his guests, he had prepared by magic—though of that no one knew except himself.

When all had assembled, Manabozho gave to each a portion of meat. The woodpecker was the first to taste of his, and as he took the delicious looking morsel in his mouth, it turned to ashes on his tongue, so that he was choked and began to cough. But the meat looked so good, and he was so hungry that he tasted again, and again it turned to ashes and choked him.

Every guest had the same experience. The little mouse, the otter, the badger, the fox, the wolf, and even the moose tasted his portion and it turned to ashes on his tongue.

In vain the guests tried to be courteous and to stifle their coughing, but it grew worse and worse as first one and then another ate of the meat.

At length there was such a deafening noise in the wigwam, caused by the chorus of coughing and strangling from so many throats great and small, that Manabozho picked up a club in pretended anger. Threatening them with it, he drove them out of doors, where he changed them all to squirrels.

And that, the Indians tell us, is the reason that the squirrel coughs.

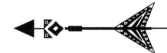 

Why the Frogs Croak
(Algonquin)

As told by Julia Darrow Cowles

"Mo-o-o-o-re, mo-o-o-o-re!" croaked a big frog in the marshes. "'Tis enough, 'tis enough, 'tis enough!" answered a smaller frog.

But the big frog called again, "Mo-o-o-o-re, mo-o-o-o-re!" And again the smaller frog answered, "'Tis enough! 'Tis enough!"

"What is it the frogs are quarreling about, grandmother?" asked a little Indian girl, and the grandmother replied, "About the water, I suppose."

"Why do they quarrel about the water? Is it a story, grandmother?"

"Yes," said the grandmother, "it is a story. Listen and I will tell it to you!

"In the long-time-ago all the waters of the land were tied up. The Indian people grew thirsty, and more thirsty. Their fields were drying up. The flowers withered. The people said, 'We shall die!'

"Then there came to one of the villages the giant, Rabbit, and he said, 'What is this I hear about the waters being tied up?'

"The Chief answered, 'For many days there has been no water. The streams are empty. No little rivers come down the mountain side. Our corn is drying up. Our people's throats are parched.'

"The giant, Rabbit, said, 'I will go into the mountains and see who has tied up the water.' Then he strode away, taking such great steps that he was out of sight in a moment.

"Up the mountain went the giant, and when he came to the top he found a tribe of men there, and they had tied up the water so that it stood in great pools which had grown green and slimy, because it was no longer fresh.

"'What are you doing with the water?' asked the Rabbit, and his voice rolled down the mountain like thunder. 'Do you not know that the tribes below you are dying for want of it?'

"The Chief of the strange tribe came out to answer the Rabbit. He was fat and ugly, and his back was covered with green slime from the pool.

"'We need the water for ourselves. It was running away down the mountain, so we stopped it,' said the Chief.

"Rabbit reached out and caught the Chief by the back of his neck and shook him. The giant's grasp was strong, and the Chief's eyes bulged from his head, and he swelled up till he was puffed out all over, from trying to get his breath.

"'So shall you look, you and all your tribe, hereafter,' said Rabbit, holding him off and looking at him. Then he threw him into the green pool, and all his tribe with him.

"After that Rabbit untied the water, and all the little streams began to flow down the mountain. Our people, at the foot of the mountain, saw them coming, and they gave thanks to the Great Spirit, because he had helped the giant, Rabbit, to give them water again, that they might live.

"The tribe at the top of the mountain became frogs, as you see them now, and they have traveled to many parts of the land; but wherever they go they keep on quarreling about the water, as you have heard them this day."

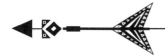 

Why the Oaks and Sumachs Redden
(Fox)

As told by Katharine Berry Judson

Once upon a time, long ago, when it was winter, so they say, it snowed for the first time. And while the very first snow lay on the ground, so they say, three men went early in the morning to hunt for game.

In a thick growth of shrub on a side hill, a bear had entered in. They could see the trail in the snow. One went in after him, and started him going in flight.

"Away from The-place-whence-comes-the-cold he is making fast!" he called to the others.

But the one who had gone round by way of The-place-from-whence-comes-the-cold, cried, "In the direction From-whence-comes-the-source-of-midday is he hurrying away." Thus he said.

The third, who had gone round by way of The-place-whence-comes-the-source-of-midday, cried out, "Towards-the-place-where-the-sun-falls-down is he hastening."

Back and forth for a long while did they keep the bear fleeing from one to another. After a while, one of the hunters who was coming behind looked down. Behold! The earth below was green. For it is really true, so they say, that up into the Sky-land were they led away by the bear. While they were chasing him about the dense growth of shrubs, that was surely the time that up into the Sky-land they went.

Then quickly he called, "Oh, Union-of-rivers, let us turn back. Truly into the Sky-land is he leading us away." So he called to Union-of-rivers, but no answer did he receive from that one.

Now Union-of-rivers, who went running between the man ahead and the man behind, had a little puppy, Hold-tight.

Now in the Fall, they overtook the bear. Then they slew him. After they had slain him, many boughs of an oak did they cut, also of sumach. So with the bear lying on top of the boughs, they skinned him, and cut up the meat. Then they began to scatter the pieces in all directions.

Towards The-place-whence-comes-the-dawn-of-day they hurled the head. In winter, when dawn is nearly breaking, stars appear which are that head, so they say.

Also to the east flung they his backbone. In winter time, certain stars lie close together. These are the backbone, so they say.

And it has also been told of the bear and the hunters that the group of four stars in front are the bear and the three hunters. And between the front star and the star behind, a tiny little star hangs. That is the little dog, Hold-tight, which was the pet of Union-of-rivers.

And so often as Fall comes, the oaks and sumachs redden at the leaf because their boughs were stained with the blood of the bear.

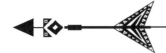 

Why the Possum's Tail is Bare
(Cherokee)

As told by Katharine Berry Judson

Possum used to have a long, bushy tail and he was so proud of it that he combed it out every morning and sang about it at the dance. Now Rabbit had had no tail since Bear pulled it off because he was jealous. Therefore he planned to play a trick on Possum.

The animals called a great council. They planned to have a dance. It was Rabbit's business to send out the news. One day as he was passing Possum's house, he stopped to talk.

"Are you going to the council?" he asked.

"Yes, if I can have a special seat," said Possum. "I have such a handsome tail I ought to sit where everyone can see me."

Rabbit said, "I will see that you have a special seat. And I will send someone to comb your tail for the dance." Possum was very much pleased.

Rabbit at once went to Cricket, who is an expert hair cutter; therefore the Indians call him the barber. He told Cricket to go the next morning and comb Possum's tail for the dance. He told Cricket just what to do.

In the morning, Cricket went to Possum's house. Possum stretched himself out on the floor and went to sleep, while Cricket combed out his tail and wrapped a red string around it to keep it smooth until night. But all the time, as he wound the string around, he was snipping off the hair closely. Possum did not know it.

When it was night, Possum went to the council and took his special seat. When it was his turn to dance, he loosened the red string from his tail and stepped into the middle of the lodge.

The drummers began to beat the drum. Possum began to sing, "See my beautiful tail."

Every man shouted and Possum danced around the circle again, singing, "See what a fine color it has." They all shouted again, and Possum went on dancing, as he sang, "See how it sweeps the ground."

Then the animals all shouted so that Possum wondered what it meant. He looked around. Every man was laughing at him. Then he looked down at his beautiful tail. It was as bare as a lizard's tail. There was not a hair on it.

He was so astonished and ashamed that he could not say a word. He rolled over on the ground and grinned, just as he does today when taken by surprise.

Why the Deer's Teeth are Blunt
(Cherokee)

As told by James Mooney

The Rabbit felt sore because the Deer had won the horns, and resolved to get even. One day soon after their race he stretched a large grapevine across the trail and gnawed it nearly in two in the middle. Then he went back a piece, took a good run, and jumped up at the vine. He kept on running and jumping up at the vine until the Deer came along and asked him what he was doing?

"Don't you see?" says the Rabbit. "I'm so strong that I can bite through that grapevine at one jump."

The Deer could hardly believe this, and wanted to see it done. So the Rabbit ran back, made a tremendous spring, and bit through the vine where he had gnawed it before. The Deer, when he saw that, said, "Well, I can do it if you can." So the Rabbit stretched a larger grapevine across the trail, but without gnawing it in the middle. The Deer ran back as he had seen the Rabbit do, made a spring, and struck the grapevine right in the center, but it only flew back and threw him over on his head. He tried again and again, until he was all bruised and bleeding.

"Let me see your teeth," at last said the Rabbit. So the Deer showed him his teeth, which were long like a wolf's teeth, but not very sharp.

"No wonder you can't do it," says the Rabbit; "your teeth are too blunt to bite anything. Let me sharpen them for you like mine. My teeth are so sharp that I can cut through a stick just like a knife." And he showed him a black locust twig, of which rabbits gnaw the young shoots, which he had shaved off as well as a knife could do it, in regular rabbit fashion. The Deer thought that just the thing. So the Rabbit got a hard stone with rough edges and filed and filed away at the Deer's teeth until they were worn down almost to the gums.

WHY THE DEER'S TEETH ARE BLUNT

"It hurts," said the Deer; but the Rabbit said it always hurt a little when they began to get sharp; so the Deer kept quiet.

"Now try it," at last said the Rabbit. So the Deer tried again, but this time he could not bite at all.

"Now you've paid for your horns," said the Rabbit, as he jumped away through the bushes. Ever since then the Deer's teeth are so blunt that he can not chew anything but grass and leaves.

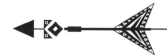

Why Brother Bear Wears a Stumpy Tail
(Ojibwa)

As told by Julia Darrow Cowles

In times long past Brother Bear was a famous fisherman. He had a large stock of patience, and great good nature. He was never in a hurry.

Brother Bear was honest as he was slow, and always ready to believe what others told him, and so he was often imposed upon by the slyer animals—Brother Fox, for instance.

One day as Brother Fox was walking beside a stream, he saw a group of plump little animals slip into the water and disappear from sight.

"Young otters, I do believe!" cried Brother Fox, smacking his lips. "What a meal they would make!" Then he sat down beside the stream and began to think. He did want those otters so badly! He could not think of anything else that would taste half so good. But how to get them! That was the question.

Presently, while he was thinking, along came Brother Bear shuffling down the path with a load of nuts and honey.

"Good morning, Brother Bear," said Brother Fox. "I see you have a load of excellent food—excellent for you, I mean. My tribe never eats nuts or honey. But perhaps you would not mind adding a bit of tender meat to your load."

"Meat? No, indeed," replied Brother Bear. "But where am I to find it?"

"Why," said Brother Fox with his craftiest smile, "there are some young otters in this stream. I just saw them slip into the water. It seems to me that they would make very good eating for you and your family."

Brother Bear smacked his lips. "But how am I to get them?" he asked.

"I am no fisherman, as you well know," said Brother Fox, "but you are a famous fisherman. Why can you not fish for them?"

Brother Bear thought for a moment. "But I have no bait," he said.

"That is true," replied Brother Fox, "but I will tell you what to do. Just go out upon that log that lies near the shore and drop your fine long tail into the water. I feel sure the otters will think your tail good bait, and when one comes to nibble it, you can jerk up your tail and just whip the otter over to the shore. I will guard your game for you until you finish fishing."

"Very good," agreed Brother Bear, "I will try that."

So Brother Bear laid down his load of nuts and honey, made his way to the log, and climbed upon it. Then he let his fine long tail drop down into the water—for this was in times long past, you must remember, when the tails of the bears were long—and then he closed his eyes and sat very still.

Presently he felt a nibble at his tail, and he whipped it up, as Brother Fox had told him. Sure enough, a fine young otter went flying across to the bank where Brother Fox lay waiting behind a bush.

"That was pretty well done!" thought Brother Bear, as he dropped his tail into the water again and waited. Presently he felt another nibble, and another otter went flying across to the bank. And soon it was followed by a fish, and then by another fish.

"What a fine dinner I shall take home to my family," thought Brother Bear to himself, as he began trying to count the number of times his tail had been nibbled, and he had sent something flying across for Brother Fox to guard.

While he was trying to count, North Wind came along and saw him sitting there with his eyes closed, and his tail hanging down in the water.

"I shall have to play a trick on Brother Bear, I do believe!" chuckled North Wind to himself, and he sent a cold breath over the water, so that it became quite still. Then he sent another breath, and a cold, shining crust formed all across its top. After that he sent another breath, and another, and the cold, shining crust grew thicker and thicker.

Presently Brother Bear stopped trying to count and opened his eyes. "Brother Fox," he called, "there seems to be no more game in the river. I have not felt a nibble for a long time."

But Brother Fox was just finishing a nice bone, and he called back earnestly, "Oh, be patient, Brother Bear! I am sure you will catch more game if you wait a little longer."

Why the Baby Says "Goo"
(Algonquin)

As told by Julia Darrow Cowles

Many, many moons ago there lived among the Red people a warrior who was greatly respected and admired by all his tribe.

When an enemy came to attack them, this warrior was always the first to resist. His arm was strong, and his arrows went true and straight to the mark. He had gone alone on many a daring hunt, and had contended with the fiercest beasts of the forest and slain them. But greatest of all, he had fought alone with mighty giants, and overcome them, so that his tribe was rid of their evil magic. It was no wonder that the people thought him great.

But then, as so often follows, the warrior became puffed up with thoughts of his own courage and power, and he was filled with pride, and boastings.

"There is no one, among men or beasts," he said, "who does not fear me. All men obey me. They tremble at the sound of my voice."

Now there was in the tribe of this warrior an old grandmother to whom age had given great wisdom. And she thought within her heart, "Our warrior is becoming puffed up. He thinks too well of himself. It would be good for him to be humbled." So among the women she said, "There is one whom I know, who is greater than the mighty warrior. *He* would not tremble at his voice, nor obey his word."

This saying was repeated to the men of the tribe, and in time it came to the ears of the great warrior himself. Immediately he went to the lodge of the grandmother.

"What is this, that I hear?" he enquired. "Show me who it is that will not obey my voice! Tell me his name!"

"His name is Wasis," replied the grandmother, "and he sits inside my lodge."

The warrior threw back the hanging of deer skin covering the entrance of the lodge, and strode within. There, upon the ground, sucking a piece of maple sugar, sat Wasis, the baby. The warrior looked at him in surprise. He knew nothing about babies, having been too busy all his life with battles and adventures to pay any attention to the little people of the tribe. But here was just a tiny fellow. It would be no trouble to get him to obey!

So without any ado, the warrior said, "Ho, baby, come here to me!"

The baby looked at him, but did not move. He repeated his command. The baby stopped sucking his maple sugar long enough to say "Goo, goo," but he did not move.

Then the warrior said, "I will show him that I am to be feared, and then he will obey me." So he began a war dance, and uttered fierce war cries, and Wasis opened his mouth and sent forth such piercing yells and shrieks, that the warrior stopped in amazement. And when he had stopped the baby began sucking his maple sugar again.

"Ho, baby, come here to me!" he repeated once more, but at that the baby again opened his mouth and cried so lustily that the great warrior covered his ears and ran from the lodge. "It is worse than the war cries of the Frost Giants!" he exclaimed.

"Did he obey you?" asked the grandmother.

"No," said the warrior. "He is a little fellow, but he is mightier than I."

"Yes," answered the grandmother, "Wasis, the baby, conquers us all, and no one can resist him."

And the baby, left alone in the lodge with his maple sugar, stopped now and then to say, "Goo, goo!" For had he not conquered the mighty warrior, the great brave of the tribe?

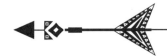 

Why the Turkey Gobbles
(Cherokee)

As told by James Mooney

The Grouse used to have a fine voice and a good halloo in the ballplay. All the animals and birds used to play ball in those days and were just as proud of a loud halloo as the ball players of to-day. The Turkey had not a good voice, so he asked the Grouse to give him lessons. The Grouse agreed to teach him, but wanted pay for his trouble, and the Turkey promised to give him some feathers to make himself a collar. That is how the Grouse got his collar of turkey feathers. They began the lessons and the Turkey learned very fast until the Grouse thought it was time to try his voice. "Now," said the Grouse, "I'll stand on this hollow log, and when I give the signal by tapping on it, you must halloo as loudly as you can." So he got upon the log ready to tap on it, as a Grouse does, but when he gave the signal the Turkey was so eager and excited that he could not raise his voice for a shout, but only gobbled, and ever since then he gobbles whenever he hears a noise.

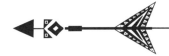 

Why the Wolves Help in War
(Dakota)

As told by Katharine Berry Judson

Once upon a time an Indian found a wolf den, and began digging into it to get the cubs.

Wolf Mother appeared, barking. She said, "Pity my children," but he paid no attention to her. So she ran for her husband.

Wolf Father soon appeared. He barked. Still the man dug into the den. Then Wolf Father sang a beautiful song. He sang, "O man, pity my children, and I will teach you one of my arts." He ended with a howl which caused a fog. When the Wolf Father howled again, the fog disappeared.

The man thought, "These animals have mysterious gifts." So he tore up his red blanket into small pieces. He tied a piece around the neck of each of the wolf cubs, as a necklace. Then he painted them with red paint and put them back into the den.

Wolf Father was very grateful. He said, "When you go to war hereafter, I will go with you. I will bring about whatever you wish." Then the man went away.

After a while the man went on the warpath. Just as he came in sight of the village of the enemy, a large wolf met him.

Wolf said, "By and by I will sing. Then you shall steal their horses when they least suspect danger."

So the man stopped on a hill close to the village. And the wolf sang. After that he howled, making a high wind arise. The horses fled to the forest, but many stopped on the hillside. When the wolf howled again, the wind died down and a mist arose. So the man on the warpath took as many horses as he pleased.

Part 6:
Myths about Heroes and Tricksters

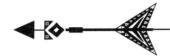 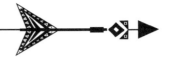

How the Rabbit Stole the Otter's Coat
(Cherokee)

As told by James Mooney

The animals were of different sizes and wore coats of various colors and patterns. Some wore long fur and others wore short. Some had rings on their tails, and some had no tails at all. Some had coats of brown, others of black or yellow. They were always disputing about their good looks, so at last they agreed to hold a council to decide who had the finest coat.

They had heard a great deal about the Otter, who lived so far up the creek that he seldom came down to visit the other animals. It was said that he had the finest coat of all, but no one knew just what it was like, because it was a long time since anyone had seen him. They did not even know exactly where he lived—only the general direction; but they knew he would come to the council when the word got out.

Now the Rabbit wanted the verdict for himself, so when it began to look as if it might go to the Otter he studied up a plan to cheat him out of it. He asked a few sly questions until he learned what trail the Otter would take to get to the council place. Then, without saying anything, he went on ahead and after four days' travel he met the Otter and knew him at once by his beautiful coat of soft dark-brown fur. The Otter was glad to see him and asked him where he was going. "O," said the Rabbit, "the animals sent me to bring you to the council; because you live so far away they were afraid you mightn't know the road." The Otter thanked him, and they went on together.

They traveled all day toward the council ground, and at night the Rabbit selected the camping place, because the Otter was a stranger in that part of the country, and cut down bushes for beds and fixed everything in good shape. The next morning they started on

PART 6: MYTHS ABOUT HEROES AND TRICKSTERS

again. In the afternoon the Rabbit began to pick up wood and bark as they went along and to load it on his back. When the Otter asked what this was for the Rabbit said it was that they might be warm and comfortable at night. After a while, when it was near sunset, they stopped and made their camp.

When supper was over the Rabbit got a stick and shaved it down to a paddle. The Otter wondered and asked again what that was for.

"I have good dreams when I sleep with a paddle under my head," said the Rabbit.

When the paddle was finished the Rabbit began to cut away the bushes so as to make a clean trail down to the river. The Otter wondered more and more and wanted to know what this meant.

Said the Rabbit, "This place is called Di'tatlâski'yĭ [The Place Where it Rains Fire]. Sometimes it rains fire here, and the sky looks a little that way to-night. You go to sleep and I'll sit up and watch, and if the fire does come, as soon as you hear me shout, you run and jump into the river. Better hang your coat on a limb over there, so it won't get burnt."

The Otter did as he was told, and they both doubled up to go to sleep, but the Rabbit kept awake. After a while the fire burned down to red coals. The Rabbit called, but the Otter was fast asleep and made no answer. In a little while he called again, but the Otter never stirred. Then the Rabbit filled the paddle with hot coals and threw them up into the air and shouted, "It's raining fire! It's raining fire!"

The hot coals fell all around the Otter and he jumped up. "To the water!" cried the Rabbit, and the Otter ran and jumped into the river, and he has lived in the water ever since.

The Rabbit took the Otter's coat and put it on, leaving his own instead, and went on to the council. All the animals were there, every one looking out for the Otter. At last they saw him in the distance, and they said one to the other, "The Otter is coming!" and sent one of the small animals to show him the best seat. They were all glad to see him and went up in turn to welcome him, but the Otter kept his head down, with one paw over his face. They wondered that he was so bashful, until the Bear came up and pulled the paw away, and there was the Rabbit with his split nose. He sprang up and started to run, when the Bear struck at him and pulled his tail off, but the Rabbit was too quick for them and got away.

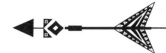 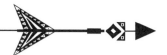

Rabbit and the Turkeys
(Omaha)

As told by Katharine Berry Judson

Rabbit was going somewhere. At length he reached a place where there were wild Turkeys.

"Come," said Rabbit. "I will sing dancing songs for you."

Turkeys went to him saying, "Oho! Rabbit will sing dancing songs for us!"

"When I sing for you, you larger ones must go around the circle next to me. Beware lest you open your eyes. Should one of you open his eyes, your eyes shall be red," said Rabbit.

Then he began to sing:

"Alas for the gazer! Eyes red! Eyes red! Spread out your tails! Spread out your tails!"

Whenever a large Turkey came near, Rabbit seized it and put it in his bag. While he was putting in a Turkey, another one opened his eyes a little, and exclaimed, "Why! He has captured nearly all of us large ones!"

Off they all flew with a whirring sound.

Rabbit took home those he had in his bag, saying to his grandmother, "Do not look at what is in that bag! I have brought it home on my back and I wish you to guard it!"

Then he went out to cut spits on which to roast the Turkeys. When the old woman was alone, she thought, "What could he have brought home on his back?" So she untied the bag, and when she looked in out flew all the Turkeys, hitting their wings hard against the grass lodge, and flying out the smoke hole. The old woman barely killed one by hitting it. At length Rabbit came home.

"Oh I have inflicted a severe injury on my grandchild," she said.

"Really," he answered. "Grandmother, I told you not to look at it."

But that is why Turkeys have red eyes.

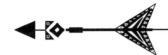 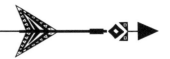

How Rabbit Caught the Sun in a Trap
(Omaha)

As told by Katharine Berry Judson

Once upon a time Rabbit dwelt in a lodge with no one but his grandmother. It was his custom to go hunting very early in the morning. But no matter how early in the morning he went, a person with a very long foot had been along, leaving a trail. Rabbit wished to know him.

"Now," he thought, "I will go in advance of that person." Having risen very early in the morning, he departed, but again it happened that the person had been along, leaving a trail. Then Rabbit went home.

"Grandmother," he said, "though I arrange for myself to go first, a person goes ahead of me every time. Grandmother, I will make a snare and I will catch him."

"Why should you do it?" she asked.

"I hate the person," he said.

Again Rabbit departed. And again had the footprints gone along. So Rabbit lay waiting for night to come. Then he made a noose of a bowstring, setting it where the footprints were commonly seen.

Next morning Rabbit reached the place very early, to see what he had caught in his trap. And it happened that he had caught the Sun. Running very fast, he went homewards to tell about it.

"Grandmother," he said, "I have caught something or other but it scares me. Grandmother, I wished to take away my bowstring, but I was scared every time."

So he went there again with a knife. This time he got very near it.

"You have done wrong. Why have you done it? Come and untie me," said the Sun.

The Rabbit, although he went to untie him, kept going past him a little on one side. Then he made a rush with his head bent down and his arm stretched out, and cut the bowstring with his knife. And the Sun rose into the sky. But Rabbit had the hair between his shoulders scorched yellow by the heat of the Sun as he stooped and cut the bowstring. Then Rabbit arrived at his lodge.

"I am burnt. Oh, grandmother! the heat has left nothing of me," he said.

Grandmother said, "Oh, my grandchild! I think the heat has left to me nothing of him!"

From that time Rabbit has always had a singed spot upon his back, between his shoulders.

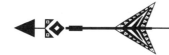 

How Rabbit Killed the Giant
(Omaha)

As told by Katharine Berry Judson

When Rabbit was going on a journey, he came to a certain village. The people said, "Halloo! Rabbit has come as a visitor."

On meeting him, they said, "Whom did you come to see?"

"Why, I will go to the lodge of anyone," said Rabbit.

"But the people have nothing to eat," they said. "The Giant is the only one who has anything to eat. You ought to go to his lodge."

Yet, the Rabbit passed on to the end lodge and entered it.

"Friend, we have nothing to eat," said the host.

"Why, my friend," said Rabbit, "when there is nothing, people eat anything they can get."

At length the Giant invited Rabbit to a feast.

"Oh ho!" called the man whose lodge Rabbit had entered. "Friend, you are invited. Hasten!"

Now all the people were afraid of the Giant. No matter what animal anyone killed, the Giant kept all of the meat.

Rabbit arrived at the lodge of the Giant. As he entered, the host said, "Oh! Pass around to that side." But Rabbit leaped over and took a seat. At length food was given him. He ate it very rapidly but left some which he hid in his robe. Then he pushed the bowl aside.

"Friend," he said to the Giant, "here is the bowl." Then he said, "Friend, I must go." He sprang past the fireplace at one leap, at the second leap his feet touched the chest of the Giant's servant, and with another leap he had gone.

When Rabbit reached the lodge where he was visiting, he gave his host the food he had not eaten. The man and his wife were glad to eat it, since they had been without food.

HOW RABBIT KILLED THE GIANT

Next morning, the crier passed through the village, commanding the people to be stirring.

They said, "The Giant is the one for whom they are to kill game." So they all went hunting. They scared some animals out of a dense forest and shot at them. Rabbit went thither very quickly. He found Giant had reached there before him and taken all the game. When Rabbit heard shooting in another place, he went thither, but again found the Giant was before him.

"This is provoking!" thought Rabbit.

When some persons shot at game in another place Rabbit noticed it, and went thither immediately, reaching the spot before the Giant.

"Friend," he said to the man who had killed the deer, "let us cut it up."

The man was unwilling. He said, "No, friend, the Giant will come by and by."

"Pshaw, friend," said Rabbit. "When one kills animals, he cuts them up and then makes an equal distribution of the pieces," said the Rabbit.

Still the man refused, fearing the Giant. So Rabbit rushed forward and seized the deer by the feet.

When he had only slit the skin, the Giant arrived.

"You have done wrong. Let it alone," Giant said.

"What have I done wrong?" asked Rabbit. "When one kills game, he cuts it up and makes an equal distribution of the pieces."

"Let it alone, I say," said the Giant.

But Rabbit continued to insert the knife in the meat.

"I will blow that thing into the air," said the Giant.

"Blow me into the air! Blow me into the air!" said Rabbit.

So the Giant went closer to him, and when he blew at him the Rabbit went up into the air with his fur blown apart. Striding past, the Giant seized the deer, put it through his belt, and departed. That was his custom. He took all the deer that were killed, hung them on his belt, and took them to his lodge. He was a very tall person.

At night Rabbit wandered around, and at last went all around the Giant's lodge. He seized an insect and said to it, "Oh, insect! You shall go and bite the Giant right in the side."

PART 6: MYTHS ABOUT HEROES AND TRICKSTERS

At length when it was morning, it was said the Giant was ill. Then he died.

The people said, "Make a village for Rabbit!"

But Rabbit said, "I do not wish to be chief. I have left my old woman by herself, so I will return to her."

White Plume
(Sioux)

As told by Marie Mclaughlin

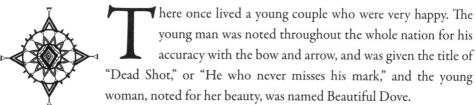

There once lived a young couple who were very happy. The young man was noted throughout the whole nation for his accuracy with the bow and arrow, and was given the title of "Dead Shot," or "He who never misses his mark," and the young woman, noted for her beauty, was named Beautiful Dove.

One day a stork paid this happy couple a visit and left them a fine big boy. The boy cried "Ina, ina" (mother, mother). "Listen to our son," said the mother, "he can speak, and hasn't he a sweet voice?" "Yes," said the father, "it will not be long before he will be able to walk." He set to work making some arrows, and a fine hickory bow for his son. One of the arrows he painted red, one blue, and another yellow. The rest he left the natural color of the wood. When he had completed them, the mother placed them in a fine quiver, all worked in porcupine quills, and hung them up over where the boy slept in his fine hammock of painted moose hide.

At times when the mother would be nursing her son, she would look up at the bow and arrows and talk to her baby, saying: "My son, hurry up and grow fast so you can use your bow and arrows. You will grow up to be as fine a marksman as your father." The baby would coo and stretch his little arms up towards the bright colored quiver as though he understood every word his mother had uttered. Time passed and the boy grew up to a good size, when one day his father said: "Wife, give our son the bow and arrows so that he may learn how to use them." The father taught his son how to string and unstring the bow, and also how to attach the arrow to the string. The red, blue and yellow arrows, he told the boy, were to be used only whenever there was any extra good shooting to be done, so the boy never used these three until he became a master of the art. Then he would practice on

PART 6: MYTHS ABOUT HEROES AND TRICKSTERS

eagles and hawks, and never an eagle or hawk continued his flight when the boy shot one of the arrows after him.

One day the boy came running into the tent, exclaiming: "Mother, mother, I have shot and killed the most beautiful bird I ever saw." "Bring it in, my son, and let me look at it." He brought the bird and upon examining it she pronounced it a different type of bird from any she had ever seen. Its feathers were of variegated colors and on its head was a topknot of pure white feathers. The father, returning, asked the boy with which arrow he had killed the bird. "With the red one," answered the boy. "I was so anxious to secure the pretty bird that, although I know I could have killed it with one of my common arrows, I wanted to be certain, so I used the red one." "That is right, my son," said the father. "When you have the least doubt of your aim, always use one of the painted arrows, and you will never miss your mark."

The parents decided to give a big feast in honor of their son killing the strange, beautiful bird. So a great many elderly women were called to the tent of Pretty Dove to assist her in making ready for the big feast. For ten days these women cooked and pounded beef and cherries, and got ready the choicest dishes known to the Indians. Of buffalo, beaver, deer, antelope, moose, bear, quail, grouse, duck of all kinds, geese and plover meats there was an abundance. Fish of all kinds, and every kind of wild fruit were cooked, and when all was in readiness, the heralds went through the different villages, crying out: "Ho-po, ho-po" (now all, now all), "Dead Shot and his wife, Beautiful Dove, invite all of you, young and old, to their tepee to partake of a great feast, given by them in honor of a great bird which their son has killed, and also to select for their son some good name which he will bear through life. So all bring your cups and wooden dishes along with your horn spoons, as there will be plenty to eat. Come, all you council men and chiefs, as they have also a great tent erected for you in which you hold your council."

Thus crying, the heralds made the circle of the village. The guests soon arrived. In front of the tent was a pole stuck in the ground and painted red, and at the top of the pole was fastened the bird of variegated colors; its wings stretched out to their full length and the beautiful white waving so beautifully from its topknot, it was the center of attraction. Half way up the pole was tied the bow and arrow of the young marksman. Long streamers of fine bead and porcupine work waved from the pole and presented a very striking appearance.

WHITE PLUME

The bird was faced towards the setting sun. The great chief and medicine men pronounced the bird "Wakan" (something holy).

When the people had finished eating they all fell in line and marched in single file beneath the bird, in order to get a close view of it. By the time this vast crowd had fully viewed the wonderful bird, the sun was just setting clear in the west, when directly over the rays of the sun appeared a cloud in the shape of a bird of variegated colors. The councilmen were called out to look at the cloud, and the head medicine man said that it was a sign that the boy would grow up to be a great chief and hunter, and would have a great many friends and followers.

This ended the feast, but before dispersing, the chief and councilmen bestowed upon the boy the title of White Plume.

One day a stranger came to the village, who was very thin and nearly starved. So weak was he that he could not speak, but made signs for something to eat. Luckily the stranger came to Dead Shot's tent, and as there was always a plentiful supply in his lodge, the stranger soon had a good meal served him. After he had eaten and rested he told his story.

"I came from a very great distance," said he. "The nations where I came from are in a starving condition. No place can they find any buffalo, deer nor antelope. A witch or evil spirit in the shape of a white buffalo has driven all the large game out of the country. Every day this white buffalo comes circling the village, and anyone caught outside of their tent is carried away on its horns. In vain have the best marksmen of the tribe tried to shoot it. Their arrows fly wide off the mark, and they have given up trying to kill it as it bears a charmed life. Another evil spirit in the form of a red eagle has driven all the birds of the air out of our country. Every day this eagle circles above the village, and so powerful is it that anyone being caught outside of his tent is descended upon and his skull split open to the brain by the sharp breastbone of the Eagle. Many a marksman has tried his skill on this bird, all to no purpose.

"Another evil spirit in the form of a white rabbit has driven out all the animals which inhabit the ground, and destroyed the fields of corn and turnips, so the nation is starving, as the arrows of the marksmen have also failed to touch the white rabbit. Anyone who can kill these three witches will receive as his reward, the choice of two of the most beautiful maidens of our nation. The younger one is the handsomer of the two and has also the

PART 6: MYTHS ABOUT HEROES AND TRICKSTERS

sweetest disposition. Many young, and even old men, hearing of this (our chief's) offer, have traveled many miles to try their arrows on the witches, but all to no purpose. Our chief, hearing of your great marksmanship, sent me to try and secure your services to have you come and rid us of these three witches."

Thus spoke the stranger to the hunter. The hunter gazed long and thoughtfully into the dying embers of the camp fire. Then slowly his eyes raised and looked lovingly on his wife who sat opposite to him. Gazing on her beautiful features for a full minute he slowly dropped his gaze back to the dying embers and thus answered his visitor:

"My friend, I feel very much honored by your chief having sent such a great distance for me, and also for the kind offer of his lovely daughter in marriage, if I should succeed, but I must reject the great offer, as I can spare none of my affections to any other woman than to my queen whom you see sitting there."

White Plume had been listening to the conversation and when his father had finished speaking, said: "Father, I am a child no more. I have arrived at manhood. I am not so good a marksman as you, but I will go to this suffering tribe and try to rid them of their three enemies. If this man will rest for a few days and return to his village and inform them of my coming, I will travel along slowly on his trail and arrive at the village a day or two after he reaches there."

"Very well, my son," said the father, "I am sure you will succeed, as you fear nothing, and as to your marksmanship, it is far superior to mine, as your sight is much clearer and aim quicker than mine."

The man rested a few days and one morning started off, after having instructed White Plume as to the trail. White Plume got together what he would need on the trip and was ready for an early start the next morning. That night Dead Shot and his wife sat up away into the night instructing their son how to travel and warning him as to the different kinds of people he must avoid in order to keep out of trouble. "Above all," said the father, "keep a good look out for Unktomi (spider); he is the most tricky of all, and will get you into trouble if you associate with him."

White Plume left early, his father accompanying him for several miles. On parting, the father's last words were: "Look out for Unktomi, my son, he is deceitful and treacherous." "I'll look out for him, father;" so saying he disappeared over a hill. On the way he tried his skill on several hawks and eagles and he did not need to use his painted arrows to kill them, but so skillful was he with the bow and arrows that he could bring down anything that flew with his common arrows. He was drawing near to the end of his destination when he had a large tract of timber to pass through. When he had nearly gotten through the timber he saw an old man sitting on a log, looking wistfully up into a big tree, where sat a number of prairie chickens.

"Hello, grandfather, why are you sitting there looking so downhearted?" asked White Plume. "I am nearly starved, and was just wishing someone would shoot one of those chickens for me, so I could make a good meal on it," said the old man. "I will shoot one for you," said the young man. He strung his bow, placed an arrow on the string, simply seemed to raise the arrow in the direction of the chicken (taking no aim). Twang went out the bow, zip went the arrow and a chicken fell off the limb, only to get caught on another in its descent. "There is your chicken, grandfather." "Oh, my grandson, I am too weak to climb up and get it. Can't you climb up and get it for me?" The young man, pitying the old fellow, proceeded to climb the tree, when the old man stopped him, saying: "Grandson, you have on such fine clothes, it is a pity to spoil them; you had better take them off so as not to spoil the fine porcupine work on them." The young man took off his fine clothes and climbed up into the tree, and securing the chicken, threw it down to the old man. As the young man was scaling down the tree, the old man said: "Iyashkapa, iyashkapa," (stick fast, stick fast). Hearing him say something, he asked, "What did you say, old man?" He answered, "I was only talking to myself." The young man proceeded to descend, but he could not move. His body was stuck fast to the bark of the tree. In vain did he beg the old man to release him. The old Unktomi, for he it was, only laughed and said: "I will go now and kill the evil spirits, I have your wonderful bow and arrows and I can not miss them. I will marry the chief's daughter, and you can stay up in that tree and die there."

So saying, he put on White Plume's fine clothes, took his bow and arrows and went to the village. As White Plume was expected at any minute, the whole village was watching for him, and when Unktomi came into sight the young men ran to him with a painted robe, sat him down on it and slowly raising him up they carried him to the tent of the chief. So certain were they that he would kill the evil spirits that the chief told him to choose one of the daughters at once for his wife. (Before the arrival of White Plume,

PART 6: MYTHS ABOUT HEROES AND TRICKSTERS

hearing of him being so handsome, the two girls had quarreled over which should marry him, but upon seeing him the younger was not anxious to become his wife.) So Unktomi chose the older one of the sisters, and was given a large tent in which to live. The younger sister went to her mother's tent to live, and the older was very proud, as she was married to the man who would save the nation from starvation. The next morning there was a great commotion in camp, and there came the cry that the white buffalo was coming. "Get ready, son-in-law, and kill the buffalo," said the chief.

Unktomi took the bow and arrows and shot as the buffalo passed, but the arrow went wide off its mark. Next came the eagle, and again he shot and missed. Then came the rabbit, and again he missed.

"Wait until tomorrow, I will kill them all. My blanket caught in my bow and spoiled my aim." The people were very much disappointed, and the chief, suspecting that all was not right, sent for the young man who had visited Dead Shot's tepee. When the young man arrived, the chief asked: "Did you see White Plume when you went to Dead Shot's camp?" "Yes, I did, and ate with him many times. I stayed at his father's tepee all the time I was there," said the young man. "Would you recognize him if you saw him again?" asked the chief. "Anyone who had but one glimpse of White Plume would surely recognize him when he saw him again, as he is the most handsome man I ever saw," said the young man.

"Come with me to the tent of my son-in-law and take a good look at him, but don't say what you think until we come away." The two went to the tent of Unktomi, and when the young man saw him he knew it was not White Plume, although it was White Plume's bow and arrows that hung at the head of the bed, and he also recognized the clothes as belonging to White Plume. When they had returned to the chief's tent, the young man told what he knew and what he thought. "I think this is some Unktomi who has played some trick on White Plume and has taken his bow and arrows and also his clothes, and hearing of your offer, is here impersonating White Plume. Had White Plume drawn the bow on the buffalo, eagle and rabbit today, we would have been rid of them, so I think we had better scare this Unktomi into telling us where White Plume is," said the young man.

"Wait until he tries to kill the witches again tomorrow," said the chief.

In the meantime the younger daughter had taken an axe and gone into the woods in search of dry wood. She went quite a little distance into the wood and was chopping a dry log. Stopping to rest a little she heard someone saying: "Whoever you are, come over here and chop this tree down so that I may get loose." Going to where the big tree stood, she saw a man stuck onto the side of the tree. "If I chop it down the fall will kill you," said the girl. "No, chop it on the opposite side from me, and the tree will fall that way. If the fall kills me, it will be better than hanging up here and starving to death," said White Plume, for it was he.

The girl chopped the tree down and when she saw that it had not killed the man, she said: "What shall I do now?" "Loosen the bark from the tree and then get some stones and heat them. Get some water and sage and put your blanket over me." She did as told and when the steam arose from the water being poured upon the heated rocks, the bark loosened from his body and he arose. When he stood up, she saw how handsome he was. "You have saved my life," said he. "Will you be my wife?" "I will," said she. He then told her how the old man had fooled him into this trap and took his bow and arrows, also his fine porcupine worked clothes, and had gone off, leaving him to die. She, in turn, told him all that had happened in camp since a man, calling himself White Plume, came there and married her sister before he shot at the witches, and when he came to shoot at them, missed every shot. "Let us make haste, as the bad Unktomi may ruin my arrows." They approached the camp and whilst White Plume waited outside, his promised wife entered Unktomi's tent and said: "Unktomi, White Plume is standing outside and he wants his clothes and bow and arrows." "Oh, yes, I borrowed them and forgot to return them; make haste and give them to him."

Upon receiving his clothes, he was very much provoked to find his fine clothes wrinkled and his bow twisted, while the arrows were twisted out of shape. He laid the clothes down, also the bows and arrows, and passing his hand over them, they assumed their right shapes again. The daughter took White Plume to her father's tent and upon hearing the story he at once sent for his warriors and had them form a circle around Unktomi's tent, and if he attempted to escape to catch him and tie him to a tree, as he (the chief) had determined to settle accounts with him for his treatment of White Plume, and the deception employed in winning the chief's eldest daughter. About midnight the guard noticed something crawling along close to the ground, and seizing him found it was Unktomi trying to make his escape before daylight, whereupon they tied him to a tree. "Why do

PART 6: MYTHS ABOUT HEROES AND TRICKSTERS

you treat me thus?" cried Unktomi, "I was just going out in search of medicine to rub on my arrows, so I can kill the witches." "You will need medicine to rub on yourself when the chief gets through with you," said the young man who had discovered that Unktomi was impersonating White Plume.

In the morning the herald announced that the real White Plume had arrived, and the chief desired the whole nation to witness his marksmanship. Then came the cry: "The White Buffalo comes." Taking his red arrow, White Plume stood ready. When the buffalo got about opposite him, he let his arrow fly. The buffalo bounded high in the air and came down with all four feet drawn together under its body, the red arrow having passed clear through the animal, piercing the buffalo's heart. A loud cheer went up from the village.

"You shall use the hide for your bed," said the chief to White Plume. Next came a cry, "the eagle, the eagle." From the north came an enormous red eagle. So strong was he, that as he soared through the air his wings made a humming sound as the rumble of distant thunder. On he came, and just as he circled the tent of the chief, White Plume bent his bow, with all his strength drew the arrow back to the flint point, and sent the blue arrow on its mission of death. So swiftly had the arrow passed through the eagle's body that, thinking White Plume had missed, a great wail went up from the crowd, but when they saw the eagle stop in his flight, give a few flaps of his wings, and then fall with a heavy thud into the center of the village, there was a greater cheer than before. "The red eagle shall be used to decorate the seat of honor in your tepee," said the chief to White Plume. Last came the white rabbit. "Aim good, aim good, son-in-law," said the chief. "If you kill him you will have his skin for a rug." Along came the white rabbit, and White Plume sent his arrow in search of rabbit's heart, which it found, and stopped Mr. Rabbit's tricks forever.

The chief then called all of the people together and before them all took a hundred willows and broke them one at a time over Unktomi's back. Then he turned him loose. Unktomi, being so ashamed, ran off into the woods and hid in the deepest and darkest corner he could find. This is why Unktomis (spiders) are always found in dark corners, and anyone who is deceitful or untruthful is called a descendant of the Unktomi tribe.

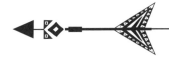

Coyote and Gray Fox
(Ponca)

As told by Katharine Berry Judson

Gray fox was very fat. Coyote said, "Younger brother, what has made you fat?" "Elder brother," said the Gray Fox, "I lie down on the trail in the way of those who carry crackers, and I pretend to be dead. When they throw me in the wagon, I lie there, kicking the crackers out. Then I leap out and start home eating. It is the crackers which make me fat. Elder brother, I wish you would do likewise. Elder brother, you have large feet, so I think will knock out a great many crackers."

Coyote went to the place and lay down in the trail. When the white man came along, he threw Coyote into the wagon. The white man thought, "It is not the first time he has acted in this way," so he tied the feet of Coyote. Having put the Coyote in the wagon, the white man went to his house. He threw Coyote out near an old outhouse. Then the white man brought a knife, and cut the cords which bound Coyote's feet. He acted as if Coyote was dead, so he threw him over his back and started off for the house.

But Coyote managed to get loose and ran homeward. He went back to get even with Gray Fox.

"Oh, younger brother," said Coyote, "you have made me suffer."

"You yourself are to blame," said Gray Fox. "Be silent and listen to me. You brought the trouble on yourself as you lay down in the place where the white man came with his load of goods."

"Oh, younger brother, you tell the truth," said Coyote. But Gray Fox had tempted him.

Coyote and the Dragon
(Nez Percé)

As told by Katharine Berry Judson

Long ago, in the Willamette Valley, there lived a monster who made all the people afraid. It lived in a cave. At night it would come from its cave, seize and eat people, and return to the cave in the morning. All night it would eat the people. Coyote heard of this monster and decided to help the people. Coyote was the cunningest and shrewdest of all the animals.

Now the monster could not endure daylight. It lived always in the dark. So one day when the sun was very bright and high up in the heavens, Coyote took his bow and arrows and went to a mountain top. He shot one of the arrows into the sun. Then he shot another into the lower end of the first one, and then another into the lower end of the second. At last Coyote had a chain of arrows that reached from the sun to the earth. Then he pulled the sun down. He pulled hard until it came down. Then he hid it in the Willamette River.

Now the monster thought night had come.

Everything was dark because the sun was hidden in the river. So the monster came out from his cave and attacked the people. Then Coyote broke the chain which held the sun down, and it sprang up in the sky again. The monster was blinded because the light was so bright. Then Coyote killed it.

When the pale-faces found the big bones of the monster and carried them away, Indians said evil would come of it.

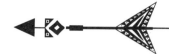 

How the Rabbit Lost His Tail
(Sioux)

As told by Marie L. Mclaughlin

Once upon a time there were two brothers, one a great Genie and the other a rabbit. Like all genies, the older could change himself into any kind of an animal, bird, fish, cloud, thunder and lightning, or in fact anything that he desired.

The younger brother (the rabbit) was very mischievous and was continually getting into all kinds of trouble. His older brother was kept busy getting Rabbit out of all kinds of scrapes.

When Rabbit had attained his full growth he wanted to travel around and see something of the world. When he told his brother what he intended to do, the brother said: "Now, Rabbit, you are Witkotko (mischievous), so be very careful, and keep out of trouble as much as possible. In case you get into any serious trouble, and can't get out by yourself, just call on me for assistance, and no matter where you are, I will come to you."

Rabbit started out and the first day he came to a very high house, outside of which stood a very high pine tree. So high was the tree that Rabbit could hardly see the top. Outside the door, on an enormous stool, sat a very large giant fast asleep. Rabbit (having his bow and arrows with him) strung up his bow, and, taking an arrow from his quiver, said:

"I want to see how big this man is, so I guess I will wake him up." So saying he moved over to one side and took good aim, and shot the giant upon the nose. This stung like fire and awoke the giant, who jumped up, crying: "Who had the audacity to shoot me on the nose?"

"I did," said Rabbit.

The giant, hearing a voice, looked all around, but saw nothing, until he looked down at the corner of the house, and there sat a rabbit. "I had hiccoughs this morning and thought that I was going to have a good big meal, and here is nothing but a toothful."

PART 6: MYTHS ABOUT HEROES AND TRICKSTERS

"I guess you won't make a toothful of me," said Rabbit, "I am as strong as you, though I am little."

"We will see," said the giant. He went into the house and came out, bringing a hammer that weighed many tons. "Now, Mr. Rabbit, we will see who can throw this hammer over the top of that tree."

"Get something harder to do," said Rabbit.

"Well, we will try this first," said the giant. With that he grasped the hammer in both hands, swung it three times around his head and sent it spinning through the air. Up, up, it went, skimming the top of the tree, and came down, shaking the ground and burying itself deep into the earth.

"Now," said the giant, "if you don't accomplish this same feat, I am going to swallow you at one mouthful." Rabbit said, "I always sing to my brother before I attempt things like this." So he commenced singing and calling his brother. "Cinye! Cinye!" (brother, brother) he sang. The giant grew nervous, and said: "Boy, why do you call your brother?"

Pointing to a small black cloud that was approaching very swiftly, Rabbit said: "That is my brother; he can destroy you, your house, and pine tree in one breath."

"Stop him and you can go free," said the giant. Rabbit waved his paws and the cloud disappeared.

From this place Rabbit continued on his trip towards the west. The next day, while passing through a deep forest, he thought he heard someone moaning, as though in pain. He stopped and listened; soon the wind blew and the moaning grew louder. Following the direction from whence came the sound, he soon discovered a man stripped of his clothing, and caught between two limbs of a tall elm tree. When the wind blew the limbs would rub together and squeeze the man, who would give forth the mournful groans.

"My, you have a fine place up there. Let us change. You can come down and I will take your place." (Now this man had been placed up there for punishment, by Rabbit's brother, and he could not get down unless someone came along and proposed to take his place on the tree).

"Very well," said the man. "Take off your clothes and come up. I will fasten you in the limbs and you can have all the fun you want."

Rabbit disrobed and climbed up. The man placed him between the limbs and slid down the tree. He hurriedly got into Rabbit's clothes, and just as he had completed his toilette, the wind blew very hard. Rabbit was nearly crazy with pain, and screamed and cried. Then he began to cry "Cinye, Cinye" (brother, brother). "Call your brother as much as you like, he can never find me." So saying the man disappeared in the forest.

Scarcely had he disappeared, when the brother arrived, and seeing Rabbit in the tree, said: "Which way did he go?" Rabbit pointed in the direction taken by the man. The brother flew over the top of the trees, soon found the man and brought him back, making him take his old place between the limbs, and causing a heavy wind to blow and continue all afternoon and night, for punishment to the man for having placed his brother up there.

After Rabbit got his clothes back on, his brother gave him a good scolding, and wound up by saying: "I want you to be more careful in the future. I have plenty of work to keep me as busy as I want to be, and I can't be stopping every little while to be making trips to get you out of some foolish scrape. It was only yesterday that I came five hundred miles to help you from the giant, and today I have had to come a thousand miles, so be more careful from this moment on."

Several days after this the Rabbit was traveling along the banks of a small river, when he came to a small clearing in the woods, and in the center of the clearing stood a nice little log hut. Rabbit was wondering who could be living here when the door slowly opened and an old man appeared in the doorway, bearing a tripe water pail in his right hand. In his left hand he held a string which was fastened to the inside of the house. He kept hold of the string and came slowly down to the river. When he got to the water he stooped down and dipped the pail into it and returned to the house, still holding the string for guidance.

Soon he reappeared holding on to another string, and, following this one, went to a large pile of wood and returned to the house with it. Rabbit wanted to see if the old man would come out again, but he came out no more. Seeing smoke ascending from the mud chimney, he thought he would go over and see what the old man was doing. He knocked at the door, and a weak voice bade him enter. He noticed that the old man was cooking dinner.

"Hello Tunkasina (grandfather), you must have a nice time, living here alone. I see that you have everything handy. You can get wood and water, and that is all you have to do. How do you get your provisions?"

PART 6: MYTHS ABOUT HEROES AND TRICKSTERS

"The wolves bring my meat, the mice my rice and ground beans, and the birds bring me the cherry leaves for my tea. Yet it is a hard life, as I am all alone most of the time and have no one to talk to, and besides, I am blind."

"Say, grandfather," said Rabbit, "let us change places. I think I would like to live here."

"If we exchange clothes," said the other, "you will become old and blind, while I will assume your youth and good looks." (Now, this old man was placed here for punishment by Rabbit's brother. He had killed his wife, so the genie made him old and blind, and he would remain so until someone came who would exchange places with him).

"I don't care for youth and good looks," said Rabbit, "let us make the change."

They changed clothes, and Rabbit became old and blind, whilst the old man became young and handsome.

"Well, I must go," said the man. He went out and cutting the strings close to the door, ran off laughing. "You will get enough of your living alone, you crazy boy," and saying this he ran into the woods.

Rabbit thought he would like to get some fresh water and try the string paths so that he would get accustomed to it. He bumped around the room and finally found the tripe water bucket. He took hold of the string and started out. When he had gotten a short distance from the door he came to the end of the string so suddenly, that he lost the end which he had in his hand, and he wandered about, bumping against the trees, and tangling himself up in plum bushes and thorns, scratching his face and hands so badly that the blood ran from them. Then it was that he commenced again to cry, "Cinye! Cinye!" (brother, brother). Soon his brother arrived, and asked which way the old man had gone.

"I don't know," said Rabbit, "I couldn't see which path he took, as I was blind."

The genie called the birds, and they came flying from every direction. As fast as they arrived the brother asked them if they had seen the man whom he had placed here for punishment, but none had seen him. The owl came last, and when asked if he had seen the man, he said "hoo-hoo."

"The man who lived here," said the brother.

"Last night I was hunting mice in the woods south of here and I saw a man sleeping beneath a plum tree. I thought it was your brother, Rabbit, so I didn't awaken him," said the owl.

"Good for you, owl," said the brother, "for this good news, you shall hereafter roam around only at night, and I will fix your eyes, so the darker the night the better you will be able to see. You will always have the fine cool nights to hunt your food. You other birds can hunt your food during the hot daylight." (Since then the owl has been the night bird).

The brother flew to the woods and brought the man back and cut the strings short, and said to him: "Now you can get a taste of what you gave my brother."

To Rabbit he said: "I ought not to have helped you this time. Anyone who is so crazy as to change places with a blind man should be left without help, so be careful, as I am getting tired of your foolishness, and will not help you again if you do anything as foolish as you did this time."

Rabbit started to return to his home. When he had nearly completed his journey he came to a little creek, and being thirsty took a good long drink. While he was drinking he heard a noise as though a wolf or cat was scratching the earth. Looking up to a hill which overhung the creek, he saw four wolves, with their tails intertwined, pulling with all their might. As Rabbit came up to them one pulled loose, and Rabbit saw that his tail was broken.

"Let me pull tails with you. My tail is long and strong," said Rabbit, and the wolves assenting, Rabbit interlocked his long tail with those of the three wolves and commenced pulling and the wolves pulled so hard that they pulled Rabbit's tail off at the second joint. The wolves disappeared.

"Cinye! Cinye! (Brother, brother.) I have lost my tail," cried Rabbit. The genie came and seeing his brother Rabbit's tail missing, said: "You look better without a tail anyway."

From that time on rabbits have had no tails.

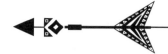 

Unktomi and the Arrowheads
(Sioux)

As told by Marie L. Mclaughlin

There were once upon a time two young men who were very great friends, and were constantly together. One was a very thoughtful young man, the other very impulsive, who never stopped to think before he committed an act.

One day these two friends were walking along, telling each other of their experiences in love making. They ascended a high hill, and on reaching the top, heard a ticking noise as if small stones or pebbles were being struck together.

Looking around they discovered a large spider sitting in the midst of a great many flint arrowheads. The spider was busily engaged making the flint rocks into arrow heads. They looked at the spider, but he never moved, but continued hammering away on a piece of flint which he had nearly completed into another arrowhead.

"Let's hit him," said the thoughtless one. "No," said the other, "he is not harming anyone; in fact, he is doing a great good, as he is making the flint arrowheads which we use to point our arrows."

"Oh, you are afraid," said the first young man. "He can't harm you, just watch me hit him." So saying, he picked up an arrowhead and throwing it at "Unktomi," hit him on the side. As Unktomi rolled over on his side, got up and stood looking at them, the young man laughed and said: "Well, let us be going, as your grandfather, "Unktomi," doesn't seem to like our company." They started down the hill, when suddenly the one who had hit Unktomi took a severe fit of coughing. He coughed and coughed, and finally small particles of blood came from his mouth. The blood kept coming thicker and in great gushes. Finally it came so thick and fast that the man could not get his breath and fell upon the ground dead.

UNKTOMI AND THE ARROWHEADS

The thoughtful young man, seeing that his friend was no more, hurried to the village and reported what had happened. The relatives and friends hurried to the hill, and sure enough, there lay the thoughtless young man still and cold in death. They held a council and sent for the chief of the Unktomi tribe. When he heard what had happened, he told the council that he could do nothing to his Unktomi, as it had only defended itself.

Said he: "My friends, seeing that your tribe was running short of arrowheads, I set a great many of my tribe to work making flint arrowheads for you. When my men are thus engaged they do not wish to be disturbed, and your young man not only disturbed my man, but grossly insulted him by striking him with one of the arrowheads which he had worked so hard to make. My man could not sit and take this insult, so as the young man walked away the Unktomi shot him with a very tiny arrowhead. This produced a haemorrhage, which caused his death. So now, my friends, if you will fill and pass the peace pipe, we will part good friends and my tribe shall always furnish you with plenty of flint arrowheads." So saying, Unktomi Tanka finished his peace smoke and returned to his tribe.

Ever after that, when the Indians heard a ticking in the grass, they would go out of their way to get around the sound, saying, Unktomi is making arrowheads; we must not disturb him.

Thus it was that Unktomi Tanka (Big Spider) had the respect of this tribe, and was never after disturbed in his work of making arrowheads.

How Master Lox Played a Trick on Mrs. Bear
(Micmac)

As told by Charles G. Leland

Don't live with mean people if you can help it. They will turn your greatest sorrow to their own account if they can. Bad habit gets to be devilish second nature. One dead herring is not much, but one by one you may make such a heap of them as to stink out a whole village.

As it happened to old Mrs. Bear, who was easy as regarded people, and thought well of everybody, and trusted all. So she took in for a house-mate another old woman. Their wigwam was all by itself, and the next neighbor was so far off that he was not their neighbor at all, but that of some other folks.

One night the old women made up a fire, and lay down and went to sleep Indian-fashion,—*witkusoodijik*,—heads and points, so that both could lie with their back to the fire.

Now while they were sound asleep, Lox, the Wolverine, or Indian Devil, came prowling round. Some people say it was Hespuns, the Raccoon; and it is a fact that Master Coon can play a very close game of deviltry on his own account. However, this time it must have been Lox, as you can see by the tracks.

While they were both sound asleep Lox looked in. He found the old women asleep, heads and points, and at once saw his way to a neat little bit of mischief. So, going into the woods, he cut a fine long sapling-pole of *ow-bo-goos*, and poked one end of it into the fire till it was a burning coal. Then he touched the soles of Mrs. Bear; and she, waking, cried out to the other, "Take care! you are burning me!" which the other denied like a thunder-clap.

Then Master Lox carefully applied the end of the hot pole to the feet of the other woman. First she dreamed that she was walking on hot sand and roasting rocks in summer-time, and then that the Mohawks were cooking her at the death-fire; and then she woke up, and, seeing where she was, began to blame Mrs. Bear for it all, just as if she were a Mohawk.

Ah, yes. Well, Master Lox, seeing them fighting in a great rage, burst out laughing, so that he actually burst himself, and fell down dead with delight. It was a regular side-splitter. When my grandfather said *that* we *always* laughed.

In the morning, when the women came out, there lay a dead devil at the door. He must indeed have looked like a Raccoon this time; but whatever he was, they took him, skinned him, and dressed him for breakfast. Then the kettle was hung and the water boiled, and they popped him in. But as soon as it began to scald he began to come to life. In a minute he was all together again, alive and well, and with one good leap went clear of the kettle. Rushing out of the lodge, he grabbed his skin, which hung on a bush outside, put it on, and in ten seconds was safe in the greenwood. He just saved himself with a whole skin.

Now Master Lox had precious little time, you will say, to do anymore mischief between his coming to life and running away; yet, short as the allowance was, he made a great deal of it. For even while jumping out his wits for wickedness came to him, and he just kicked the edge of the pot, so that it spilled all the scalding hot water into the fire, and threw up the ashes with a great splutter. They flew into the eyes of Dame Bear and blinded her.

Now this was hard on the old lady. She could not go out hunting, or set traps, or fish anymore; and her partner, being mean, kept all the nice morsels for herself. Mrs. Bear only got the leanest and poorest of the meat, though there was plenty of the best. As my grandfather used to say, Mrs. Bear might have fared better if she had used her eyes earlier.

One day, when she was sitting alone in the wigwam, Mrs. Bear began to remember all she had ever heard about eyes, and it came into her head that sometimes they were closed up in such a way that clever folk could cut them open again. So she got her knife and sharpened it, and, carefully cutting a little, saw the light of day. Then she was glad indeed, and with a little more cutting found that she could see as well as ever. And as good luck does not come single, the very first thing she beheld was an abundance of beautiful fat venison, fish, and maple-sugar hung up overhead.

PART 6: MYTHS ABOUT HEROES AND TRICKSTERS

Dame Bear said nothing about her having recovered her eyesight. She watched all the cooking going on, and saw the daintiest dinner, which all went into one platter, and a very poor lot of bones and scraps placed in another. Then, when she was called to eat, she simply said to the other woman, who kept the best, "Well, you have done well for yourself!"

The other saw that Mrs. Bear had recovered her sight. She was frightened, for Dame Bear was by far the better man of the two. So she cried out, "Bless me! what a mistake I've made! Why, I gave you the wrong dish. You know, my dear sister, that I always give you the best because you are blind."

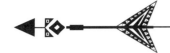

How the Ermine Got its Necklace
(Athabascan)

As told by Katharine Berry Judson

In the valley between Koyukuk and Yukon lived an old man, his wife, and two sons. The old man was too feeble to go out alone any longer, so he told the boys they must travel alone. Therefore they decided to go alone.

In the morning they found a porcupine trail. Following this downstream, they came to a large river running full of ice. At the edge of the water the track disappeared. The brothers leaped on a piece of ice and floated downstream. Again they landed and looked for food, when they found a fish had been left on the ice, and saw many sled tracks. They followed these. They then heard a faint crying. Going on cautiously, they saw a porcupine carrying a load. They asked it why it cried. When it did not answer, they clubbed it dead, cooked it, and ate it.

Going on, they saw a village. An old woman came out, saw them, and called to the people of the village to prepare food for them. The brothers entered a large house, where an old man was seated on a caribou skin. They sat down on either side of him on caribou skins and began to eat. Seeing only young women, besides the old man and woman, the brothers asked where the young men were. The young women said there were none, but that they could do many difficult things which even men could hardly do. The elder brother boasted that he could do more than they. But the young women laughed. They said they were simply answering his question.

In the morning the young women went hunting. The brothers went with them. Then the women outran the elder brother and teased him. He became angry and said:

"You can not do one thing. Stand at a distance and shoot at me. If I am not hit, I will shoot at you."

PART 6: MYTHS ABOUT HEROES AND TRICKSTERS

The younger man warned his brother; but the elder one was still angry and insisted. Finally the women consented to shoot at him. As they shot he leaped, but four arrows struck him together and he fell dead. The younger brother mourned for him.

When he wished to return and asked the way, he was told it was dangerous and they described to him the monsters he would meet. Nevertheless he started.

After traveling for some time, he saw a cliff with a nest of enormous birds. The old ones were away, but he found a young eaglet.

"What do your parents do when they come?" he asked.

"When they come," the eaglet answered, "it becomes dark, it blows, and there is thunder. When it is my mother coming, it rains. When it is my father who comes, it hails."

The young man killed the bird. Then he waited. Soon it became dark, and thundered, and rained, while the air was blown against him by the beating of the wings of the Thunder bird. The young man shot it, and springing forward, killed it with his moose-horn club. When the other bird came, he killed it too.

He went on until he came to a porcupine as high as a hill, which lived in a cave. Through this cave the young man had to pass for he could find no way around it. Hiding outside the cave, he made a noise to attract the porcupine's attention. It at once started to back out, lashing its tail against the mountain side until the enormous quills were stuck all over the mountain and the tail itself was quite bare.

Then as it left the cave, the young man shot it and clubbed it to death.

Traveling on farther, he found the tracks of an enormous lynx. This the women had told him was the strongest of the monsters. Here, too, he tried to go around it but could not. Then he tried to shoot it, but the lynx caught the arrows in his claws. Seeing no way of escape, the young man gave up hope. Then the lynx ordered him to clear away the snow so that he could eat him more at ease, and to heap up the wood for the fire by which the young man was to be cooked. The young man did this, but the lynx told him to get still more firewood. The young man did this, going farther each time to get the wood. Soon he heard someone say:

"Brother, stand quickly on my back and I will carry you away."

"Where are you?" he asked.

"Here."

Looking down, he saw an ermine at his feet. He said, "I am afraid I will kill you if I step on your back."

"No, jump on me. I will carry you."

Then he jumped hard, but the ermine did not even move.

"Your back is too small. I can not sit on it."

"Lay a stick across my back, and put another across my neck for your feet."

He laid the sticks across the ermine and sat down. Immediately it carried him to his house. The young man's parents were glad for his safe return. They gave the ermine a shell necklace.

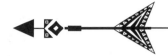 

The Legend of O-na-wut-a-qut-o
(Ojibwa)

Anonymous

A long time ago there lived an aged Odjibwa and his wife on the shores of Lake Huron. They had an only son, a very beautiful boy, named O-na-wut-a-qut-o, or He that catches the clouds. The family were of the totem of the beaver. The parents were very proud of their son, and wished to make him a celebrated man; but when he reached the proper age he would not submit to the We-koon-de-win, or fast. When this time arrived they gave him charcoal instead of his breakfast, but he would not blacken his face. If they denied him food he sought bird's eggs along the shore, or picked up the heads of fish that had been cast away, and broiled them. One day they took away violently the food he had prepared, and cast him some coals in place of it. This act decided him. He took the coals and blackened his face and went out of the lodge. He did not return, but lay down without to sleep. As he lay, a very beautiful girl came down from the clouds and stood by his side.

"O-na-wut-a-qut-o," she said, "I am come for you. Follow in my footsteps."

The young man rose and did as he was bid. Presently he found himself ascending above the tops of the trees, and gradually he mounted up step by step into the air, and through the clouds. At length his guide led him through an opening, and he found himself standing with her on a beautiful plain.

A path led to a splendid lodge, into which O-na-wut-a-qut-o followed his guide. It was large, and divided into two parts. At one end he saw bows and arrows, clubs and spears, and various warlike instruments tipped with silver. At the other end were things exclusively belonging to women. This was the house of his fair guide, and he saw that she had on a frame a broad rich belt of many colors that she was weaving.

"My brother is coming," she said, "and I must hide you."

Putting him in one corner she spread the belt over him, and presently the brother came in very richly dressed, and shining as if he had points of silver all over him. He took down from the wall a splendid pipe, and a bag in which was a-pa-ko-ze-gun, or smoking mixture. When he had finished smoking, he laid his pipe aside, and said to his sister—

"Nemissa," (elder sister) "when will you quit these practices? Do you forget that the greatest of the spirits has commanded that you shall not take away the children from below? Perhaps you think you have concealed O-na-wut-a-qut-o, but do I not know of his coming? If you would not offend me, send him back at once."

These words did not, however, alter his sister's purpose. She would not send him back, and her brother, finding that she was determined, called O-na-wut-a-qut-o from his hiding-place.

"Come out of your concealment," said he, "and walk about and amuse yourself. You will grow hungry if you remain there."

At these words O-na-wut-a-qut-o came forth from under the belt, and the brother presented a bow and arrows, with a pipe of red stone, richly ornamented, to him. In this way he gave his consent to O-na-wut-a-qut-o's marriage with his sister, and from that time the youth and the girl became husband and wife.

O-na-wut-a-qut-o found everything exceedingly fair and beautiful around him, but he found no other people besides his wife and her brother. There were flowers on the plains, there were bright and sparkling streams, there were green valleys and pleasant trees, there were gay birds and beautiful animals, very different from those he had been accustomed to. There was also day and night as on the earth, but he observed that every morning the brother regularly left the lodge and remained absent all day, and every evening his sister departed, but generally for only a part of the night.

O-na-wut-a-qut-o was curious to solve this mystery, and obtained the brother's consent to accompany him in one of his daily journeys. They traveled over a smooth plain which seemed to stretch to illimitable distances all around. At length O-na-wut-a-qut-o felt the gnawing of hunger and asked his companion if there was no game about.

"Patience, my brother," replied he; "we shall soon reach the spot where I eat my dinner, and you will then see how I am provided."

PART 6: MYTHS ABOUT HEROES AND TRICKSTERS

After walking on a long time they came to a place where several fine mats were spread, and there they sat down to refresh themselves. At this place there was a hole in the sky and O-na-wut-a-qut-o, at his companion's request, looked through it down upon the earth. He saw below the great lakes and the villages of the Indians. In one place he saw a war-party stealing on the camp of their enemies. In another he saw feasting and dancing. On a green plain some young men were playing at ball, and along the banks of a stream were women employed in gathering the a-puk-wa for mats.

"Do you see," asked the brother, "that group of children playing beside a lodge? Observe that beautiful and active lad," said he, at the same time darting something from his hand. The child immediately fell on the ground, and was carried by his companions into the lodge.

O-na-wut-a-qut-o and his companion watched and saw the people below gathering about the lodge. They listened to the she-she-gwau of the meeta, to the song he sang asking that the child's life might be spared. To this request O-na-wut-a-qut-o's companion made answer—

"Send me up the sacrifice of a white dog."

A feast was immediately ordered by the parents of the child. The white dog was killed, his carcass was roasted, all the wise men and medicine-men of the village assembling to witness the ceremony.

"There are many below," said O-na-wut-a-qut-o's companion, "whom you call great in medical skill. They are so, because their ears are open; and they are able to succeed, because when I call they hear my voice. When I have struck one with sickness they direct the people to look to me, and when they make me the offering I ask, I remove my hand from off the sick person and he becomes well."

While he was saying this, the feast below had been served. Then the master of the feast said—

"We send this to thee, Great Manito," and immediately the roasted animal came up. Thus O-na-wut-a-qut-o and his companion got their dinner, and after they had eaten they returned to the lodge by a different path.

In this manner they lived for some time, but at last the youth got weary of the life. He thought of his friends, and wished to go back to them. He could not forget his native village and his father's lodge, and he asked his wife's permission to return. After some persuasion she consented.

"Since you are better pleased," she said, "with the cares and ills and poverty of the world, than with the peaceful delights of the sky and its boundless prairies, go. I give you my permission, and since I have brought you hither I will conduct you back. Remember, however, that you are still my husband. I hold a chain in my hand by which I can, whenever I will, draw you back to me. My power over you will be in no way diminished. Beware, therefore, how you venture to take a wife among the people below. Should you ever do so, you will feel what a grievous thing it is to arouse my anger."

As she uttered these words her eyes sparkled, and she drew herself up with a majestic air. In the same moment O-na-wut-a-qut-o awoke. He found himself on the ground near his father's lodge, on the very spot where he had thrown himself down to sleep. Instead of the brighter beings of a higher world, he found around him his parents and their friends. His mother told him that he had been absent a year. For some time O-na-wut-a-qut-o remained gloomy and silent, but by degrees he recovered his spirits, and he began to doubt the reality of all he had seen and heard above. At last he even ventured to marry a beautiful girl of his own tribe. But within four days she died. Still he was forgetful of his first wife's command, and he married again. Then one night he left his lodge, to which he never returned. His wife, it is believed, recalled him to the sky, where he still dwells, walking the vast plains.

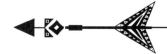 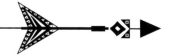

The Adventures of the Great Hero Pulowech, or the Partridge
(Micmac)

As told by Charles G. Leland

Wee-yig-yik-keseyook. A tale of old times. Two men once lived together in one wigwam in the woods, on the border of a beautiful lake. Many hard-wood trees made their pictures in it. One of these Indians was Pulowech, the Partridge in the Micmac tongue, but who is called by the Passamaquoddy Mitchihess; but the other was Wejek (M.), the Tree Partridge.

Now it befell that one day Pulowech was walking along the shore, when it was winter, and he beheld three girls, fair and fine, with flowing hair, sitting on the ice braiding their locks. Then he knew that they were of the fairy kind, who dwell in the water; and, verily, these were plentier of old than they are now,—to our sorrow be it said, for they were good company for the one who could get them. And Pulowech, knowing this, said, "I will essay this thing, and perchance I may catch one or two of them; which will be a great comfort, for a pretty girl is a nice thing to have about the wigwam." So he sought to secure them by stealing softly along; but one cried, "*Ne miha skedap!*" "I see a man!" P., and they all went head over heels, first best time, into the water; and verily that was a cold duck for December in the Bay of Fundy.

But though Pulowech had never hunted for sea-girls, yet he had fished for seals, who are greatly akin unto them, being almost as slippery; and wotting well that no man hath the mitten till he is refused thirty times and many more, he went about it in another wise. For this time he got many fir boughs, strewing them about as if blown by the wind, and hiding himself behind them, again came up and made a sudden dart. Then the maids, crying as before, "*Ne miha skedap!*" "I see a, man!" went with a dive into the deep. But this time he caught, if not the hair, at least the hair-string, of the fairest, which remained in his hand. And, gazing on this, it came into his mind that he had got that which was her charm, or life, and that she could not live without it, or her cherished *sakultobee* (M.). And taking it home, he tied it to the place in the wigwam above that wherein he slept. Nor had he waited long before she came, and, with little ado, remained with him as his wife.

Now Pulowech, being himself addicted to sorcery, knew that there were divers knaves of the same stamp prowling about the woods, who would make short work of a wife if they could find a plump young one in the way,—they being robbers, ravishers, and cannibals withal. Therefore he warned his bride to keep well within doors when he was away, and to open to none, which she, poor soul, meant to obey with all her might. But being alone at midnight, and hearing a call outside, even "*Pantahdooe*!" M., "Open the door to me!" she wondered greatly who it might be. And it was a very wicked wizard, a *boo-oin*, or pow-wow; and he, being subtle and crafty, and knowing of her family, so imitated the voices of her brothers and sisters; beseeching her to let them in, that her very heart ached. "O sister, we have come from afar!" they cried. "We missed you, and have followed you. Let us in!" And yet again she heard a sad and very earnest voice, and it was that of her old mother, crying, "*N'toos, n'toos, pantahdooe*!" M., "My daughter! my daughter! open unto me!" and she verily wist that it must be so. But when she heard the voice of her dear old father, shaking and saying, "*Pantahdooe loke cyowchee*!" "Open the door, for I am very cold!" she could resist no more, and, springing up, opened it to those who were without. And then the evil sorcerers, springing on her like mad wolves, dragged her away and devoured her. They did not leave two of her little bones one with another.

Now when *Wejek*, the Tree Partridge, came in and found his friend's wife gone, he was so angry that, without waiting, he set forth to seek her. And this was not wisely done, since, falling among them, he was himself slain. Then Pulowech, returning last of all, and finding no one, sought by means of magic to know where friend and wife might be. For taking a *woltes*, or a wooden dish, he filled it with water, and charmed it with a spell, and placed it in the back part of his wigwam, just opposite the door. So he laid him down to sleep, and in the morning when he arose he looked upon the dish,—even the dish of divination,— and lo! it was half full of blood. Then he knew that the twain had been murdered.

PART 6: MYTHS ABOUT HEROES AND TRICKSTERS

Then gathering all his arms, he went forth for revenge, and passed many days on the path, tracking the *boo-oin*; and having the eyesight of sorcery, he one day beheld very far away, upon an exceeding high cliff, the knee of a man sticking out of the stone, and knew that a sorcerer had hidden himself in the solid rock, even as a child might hide itself in a pile of feathers. Then throwing his tomahawk he cut away the knee, and the *boo-oin*, his spell broken, remained hard and fast forever in the ledge. And yet, anon, a little further on, he saw a foot projecting from a wall, and this he likewise cut off, and with that he had slain two.

And as he went further he found by the way a poor little squirrel, even *Meeko*, who was crawling along, half dead, in sorry plight. And taking her up he made her well, and placing her in his bosom, said, "Rest there yet a while, *Meeko*, for thou must fight to-day, and that fiercely. Yet fear not, for I will stand by thee, and when I tap thy back, then shalt thou bring forth thy young!"

Then going ever on, he saw from the mountains far in a lake below a flock of wild geese sporting merrily, even the *Senum-kwak'*. But he wist right well that these also were of the *boo-oin*, whom he sought, and placing a spell on his bow, and singing a charm over his arrows that they should not miss, he slew the wild fowl one by one, and tying their heads together, he carried them in a bunch upon his back. And truly he deemed it a good bag of game for one day.

And yet further on he came to a wigwam, and entering it saw a man there seated, whom he knew at once was of the enemy. For he who sat there glared at him grimly; he did not say to him, "*'Kutakumoogwal!*" "Come higher up!" as they do who are hospitable. But having cooked some meat, and given it in a dish to Pulowech's hand, he snatched it back again, and said he would sooner give it to his dog. And this he did more than once, saying the same thing. But Pulowech kept quiet. Then the rude man said, "Hast thou met with aught to-day, thou knave?" And the guest replied, "Truly I saw a fellow's knee sticking out of a stone, and I cut it off. And yet, anon, I saw a foot coming from a rock, and this I also chopped. And further on there was a flock of wild geese, and them I slew; there was not one left,—no, not one. And if you will look without there you may see them all dead, and much good may it do you!"

Then the savage sorcerer burst forth in all his rage: "Come on, then, our dogs must fight this out!" "Thou sayest well," replied Pulowech; "truly I am fond of a good dog-fight, so bring out thy pup!" And that which the man brought forth was terrible; for it was no dog, but a hideous savage beast, known to Micmacs as the *Weisum*.

But that which Pulowech produced was quite as different from a dog as was the *Weisum*; for it was only *Meeko*, a poor little squirrel, and half dead at that, which he laid carefully before the fire that it might revive. But anon it began to revive, and grew until it was well-nigh as great as the *Weisum*. And then there was indeed a battle as of devils and witches; he who had been a hundred miles away might have heard it.

But anon it seemed that the *Weisum* was getting the better of *Meeko*. Then Pulowech did but tap the squirrel on the back, when lo! she brought forth two other squirrels, and these grew in an instant to be as large as their mother, and the three were soon too many for the beast. "Ho! call off your dogs!" cried the *boo-oin*; "you have beaten. But spare mine, since, indeed, he does not belong to me, but to my grandmother, who is very fond of him."

Pulowech, who held to his own in all things like a wolverine, was the last man alive to think of, and he encouraged the squirrels until they had torn the *Weisum* to rags.

Then he who had staked it, bitterly lamented, saying, "Alack, my poor grandmother! Alas, how she will wail when she hears that her *Weisum* is dead! Woe the day that ever I did put him up! Alas, my grandmother!" For all which the cruel Pulowech, the hard-hearted, impenitent Partridge, did not care the hair of a dead musk-rat.

Now the host, who had thus suddenly grown so tender-hearted, said, "Let us sail forth upon the river in a canoe." Then they were soon on the stream, and rushing down a rapid like a dart. And anon they came to a terribly high cliff, in which there was a narrow cavern into which the river ran. And on it, thundering through this door of death, borne on a boiling surge, the bark was forced furiously into darkness. And Pulowech sat firmly in his seat, and steered the boat with steady, certain hand; but just as he entered the horrible hole, glancing around, he saw the sorcerer leap ashore. For the evil man, believing that no one had ever come alive out of the cavern, had betrayed him into it.

Yet ever cool and calm the mighty man went on, for danger now was bringing out all the force of his magic; and soon the stream grew smoother, the rocks disappeared from its bed, and then from afar there was a brightness, and he was soon in the daylight and sunshine on a beautiful stream, and by the banks thereof there grew the *wabeyu-beskwan*, or water-lilies, and very pleasant it was to him to feel the wind again. So using his paddle

PART 6: MYTHS ABOUT HEROES AND TRICKSTERS

he saw a smoke rising from a cave in the rocks, And landing and softly stepping up heard talking within.

Nor had he listened long ere he knew the voice of the man who had lured him into the canoe, and he was telling his grandmother how, one after the other, all the best *boo-oin* of their band had been slain by a mighty sorcerer. But when she heard from him how her beloved, or the one who had inspired the *Weisum*, had been beaten, her wrath burst forth in a storm, like the raving of devils, like a mad wind on the waves. And she said, "If Pulowech were but before me, were he but alive, I would roast him." The man, hearing this, cried, "Aye; but he is *not* alive, for I sent him afloat down into the dark cavern!"

And then Pulowech, stepping in before them, said, "And yet I am alive. And do thou, woman, *bak sok bok sooc*!" (roast me to death). Then she scowled horribly at him, but said naught; and he, sitting down, looked at them.

This woman was of the Porcupines, who are never long without raising their quills, and they are fond of heat. Now there was in the cave much hemlock bark, and this she began to heap on the fire. Then it blazed, it crackled and roared; but Pulowech sat still, and said naught, neither did his eyes change. And he called unto himself all his might, the might of his magic did he awaken, and the spirit came unto him very terribly, so that all the *boo-oin*, with their vile black witchcraft, were but as worms before him, the Great and Terrible One. And when the fire had burned low he brought in by his will great store of bark, so that the whole cave was filled, and closing the door he lighted the fuel. Then the Porcupines, who were those who had slain his wife and friend, howled for mercy, but he was deaf as a stone to their cries. Then the roof and sides of the cavern cracked with the heat, the red-hot stones fell in heavy blocks, the red flames rose in the thickest smoke, but Pulowech sat and sang his song until the witch and wizard were burned to cinders; yea, till their white bones crumbled to ashes beneath his feet. And then he arose and went unto his home.

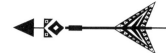

The Peace with the Snakes
(Blackfoot)

As told by George Bird Grinnell

In those days there was a Piegan chief named Owl Bear. He was a great chief, very brave and generous. One night he had a dream: he saw many dead bodies of the enemy lying about, scalped, and he knew that he must go to war. So he called out for a feast, and after the people had eaten, he said:—

"I had a strong dream last night. I went to war against the Snakes, and killed many of their warriors. So the signs are good, and I feel that I must go. Let us have a big party now, and I will be the leader. We will start to-morrow night."

Then he told two old men to go out in the camp and shout the news, so that all might know. A big party was made up. Two hundred men, they say, went with this chief to war. The first night they traveled only a little way, for they were not used to walking, and soon got tired.

In the morning the chief got up early and went and made a sacrifice, and when he came back to the others, some said, "Come now, tell us your dream of this night."

"I dreamed good," said Owl Bear. "I had a good dream. We will have good luck."

But many others said they had bad dreams. They saw blood running from their bodies.

Night came, and the party started on, traveling south, and keeping near the foot-hills; and when daylight came, they stopped in thick pine woods and built war lodges. They put up poles as for a lodge, and covered them very thick with pine boughs, so they could build fires and cook, and no one would see the light and smoke; and they all ate some of the food they carried, and then went to sleep.

Again the chief had a good dream, but the others all had bad dreams, and some talked about turning back; but Owl Bear laughed at them, and when night came, all started on. So they traveled for some nights, and all kept dreaming bad except the chief. He always

PART 6: MYTHS ABOUT HEROES AND TRICKSTERS

had good dreams. One day after a sleep, a person again asked Owl Bear if he dreamed good. "Yes," he replied. "I have again dreamed of good luck."

"We still dream bad," the person said, "and now some of us are going to turn back. We will go no further, for bad luck is surely ahead."

"Go back! go back!" said Owl Bear. "I think you are cowards; I want no cowards with me." They did not speak again. Many of them turned around, and started north, toward home.

Two more days' travel. Owl Bear and his warriors went on, and then another party turned back, for they still had bad dreams. All the men now left with him were his relations. All the others had turned back. They traveled on, and traveled on, always having bad dreams, until they came close to the Elk River. Then the oldest relation said, "Come, my chief, let us all turn back. We still have bad dreams. We can not have good luck."

"No," replied Owl Bear, "I will not turn back."

Then they were going to seize him and tie his hands, for they had talked of this before. They thought to tie him and make him go back with them. Then the chief got very angry. He put an arrow on his bow, and said: "Do not touch me. You are my relations; but if any of you try to tie me, I will kill you. Now I am ashamed. My relations are cowards and will turn back. I have told you I have always dreamed good, and that we would have good luck. Now I don't care; I am covered with shame. I am going now to the Snake camp and will give them my body. I am ashamed. Go! go! and when you get home put on women's dresses. You are no longer men."

They said no more. They turned back homeward, and the chief was all alone. His heart was very sad as he traveled on, and he was much ashamed, for his relations had left him.

Night was coming on. The sun had set and rain was beginning to fall. Owl Bear looked around for some place where he could sleep dry. Close by he saw a hole in the rocks. He got down on his hands and knees and crept in. Here it was very dark. He could see nothing, so he crept very slowly, feeling as he went. All at once his hand touched something strange. He felt of it. It was a person's foot, and there was a moccasin on it. He stopped, and sat still. Then he felt a little further. Yes, it was a person's leg. He could feel the cowskin legging.

THE PEACE WITH THE SNAKES

Now he did not know what to do. He thought perhaps it was a dead person; and again, he thought it might be one of his relations, who had become ashamed and turned back after him.

Pretty soon he put his hand on the leg again and felt along up. He touched the person's belly. It was warm. He felt of the breast, and could feel it rise and fall as the breath came and went; and the heart was beating fast. Still the person did not move. Maybe he was afraid. Perhaps he thought that was a ghost feeling of him.

Owl Bear now knew this person was not dead. He thought he would try if he could learn who the man was, for he was not afraid. His heart was sad. His people and his relations had left him, and he had made up his mind to give his body to the Snakes. So he began and felt all over the man,—of his face, hair, robe, leggings, belt, weapons; and by and by he stopped feeling of him. He could not tell whether it was one of his people or not.

Pretty soon the strange person sat up and felt all over Owl Bear; and when he had finished, he took the Piegan's hand and opened it and held it up, waving it from side to side, saying by signs, "Who are you?"

Owl Bear put his closed hand against the person's cheek and rubbed it; he said in signs, "Piegan!" and then he asked the person who he was. A finger was placed against his breast and moved across it *zigzag*. It was the sign for "Snake."

"*Hai yah!*" thought Owl Bear, "a Snake, my enemy." For a long time he sat still, thinking. By and by he drew his knife from his belt and placed it in the Snake's hand, and signed, "Kill me!" He waited. He thought soon his heart would be cut. He wanted to die. Why live? His people had left him.

Then the Snake took Owl Bear's hand and put a knife in it and motioned that Owl Bear should cut his heart, but the Piegan would not do it. He lay down, and the Snake lay down beside him. Maybe they slept. Likely not.

So the night went and morning came. It was light, and they crawled out of the cave, and talked a long time together by signs. Owl Bear told the Snake where he had come from, how his party had dreamed bad and left him, and that he was going alone to give his body to the Snakes.

Then the Snake said: "*I* was going to war, too. I was going against the Piegans. Now I am done. Are you a chief?"

PART 6: MYTHS ABOUT HEROES AND TRICKSTERS

"I am the head chief," replied Owl Bear. "I lead. All the others follow."

"I am the same as you," said the Snake. "I am the chief. I like you. You are brave. You gave me your knife to kill you with. How is your heart? Shall the Snakes and the Piegans make peace?"

"Your words are good," replied Owl Bear. "I am glad."

"How many nights will it take you to go home and come back here with your people?" asked the Snake.

Owl Bear thought and counted. "In twenty-five nights," he replied, "the Piegans will camp down by that creek."

"My trail," said the Snake, "goes across the mountains. I will try to be here in twenty-five nights, but I will camp with my people just behind that first mountain. When you get here with the Piegans, come with one of your wives and stay all night with me. In the morning the Snakes will move and put up their lodges beside the Piegans."

"As you say," replied the chief, "so it shall be done." Then they built a fire and cooked some meat and ate together.

"I am ashamed to go home," said Owl Bear. "I have taken no horses, no scalps. Let me cut off your side locks?"

"Take them," said the Snake.

Owl Bear cut off the chiefs braids close to his head, and then the Snake cut off the Piegan's braids. Then they exchanged clothes and weapons and started out, the Piegan north, the Snake south.

"Owl Bear has come! Owl Bear has come!" the people were shouting.

The warriors rushed to his lodge. *Whish*! how quickly it was filled! Hundreds stood outside, waiting to hear the news.

For a long time the chief did not speak. He was still angry with his people. An old man was talking, telling the news of the camp. Owl Bear did not look at him. He ate some food and rested. Many were in the lodge who had started to war with him. They were now ashamed. They did not speak, either, but kept looking at the fire. After a long time the chief said: "I traveled on alone. I met a Snake. I took his scalp and clothes, and his weapons. See, here is his scalp!" And he held up the two braids of hair.

No one spoke, but the chief saw them nudge each other and smile a little; and soon they went out and said to one another: "What a lie! That is not an enemy's scalp; there is no flesh on it. He has robbed some dead person."

Someone told the chief what they said, but he only laughed and replied:—

"*I* do not care. They were too much afraid even to go on and rob a dead person. They should wear women's dresses."

Near sunset, Owl Bear called for a horse, and rode all through camp so every one could hear, shouting out: "Listen! listen! To-morrow we move camp. We travel south. The Piegans and Snakes are going to make peace. If anyone refuses to go, I will kill him. All must go."

Then an old medicine man came up to him and said: "*Kyi*, Owl Bear! listen to me. Why talk like this? You know we are not afraid of the Snakes. Have we not fought them and driven them out of this country? Do you think we are afraid to go and meet them? No. We will go and make peace with them as you say, and if they want to fight, we will fight. Now you are angry with those who started to war with you. Don't be angry. Dreams belong to the Sun. He gave them to us, so that we can see ahead and know what will happen. The Piegans are not cowards. Their dreams told them to turn back. So do not be angry with them anymore."

"There is truth in what you say, old man," replied Owl Bear; "I will take your words."

In those days the Piegans were a great tribe. When they traveled, if you were with the head ones, you could not see the last ones, they were so far back. They had more horses than they could count, so they used fresh horses every day and traveled very fast. On the twenty-fourth day they reached the place where Owl Bear had told the Snake they would camp, and put up their lodges along the creek. Soon some young men came in, and said they had seen some fresh horse trails up toward the mountain.

"It must be the Snakes," said the chief; "they have already arrived, although there is yet one night." So he called one of his wives, and getting on their horses they set out to find the Snake camp. They took the trail up over the mountain, and soon came in sight of the lodges. It was a big camp. Every open place in the valley was covered with lodges, and the hills were dotted with horses; for the Snakes had a great many more horses than the Piegans.

PART 6: MYTHS ABOUT HEROES AND TRICKSTERS

Some of the Snakes saw the Piegans coming, and they ran to the chief, saying: "Two strangers are in sight, coming this way. What shall be done?"

"Do not harm them," replied the chief. "They are friends of mine. I have been expecting them." Then the Snakes wondered, for the chief had told them nothing about his war trip.

Now when Owl Bear had come to the camp, he asked in signs for the chiefs lodge, and they pointed him to one in the middle. It was small and old. The Piegan got off his horse, and the Snake chief came out and hugged him and kissed him, and said: "I am glad you have come to-day to my lodge. So are my people. You are tired. Enter my lodge and we will eat." So they went inside and many of the Snakes came in, and they had a great feast.

Then the Snake chief told his people how he had met the Piegan, and how brave he was, and that now they were going to make a great peace; and he sent some men to tell the people, so that they would be ready to move camp in the morning. Evening came. Everywhere people were shouting out for feasts, and the chief took Owl Bear to them. It was very late when they returned. Then the Snake had one of his wives make a bed at the back of the lodge; and when it was ready he said: "Now, my friend, there is your bed. This is now your lodge; also the woman who made the bed, she is now your wife; also everything in this lodge is yours. The parfleches, saddles, food, robes, bowls, everything is yours. I give them to you because you are my friend and a brave man."

"You give me too much," replied Owl Bear. "I am ashamed, but I take your words. I have nothing with me but one wife. She is yours."

Next morning camp was broken early. The horses were driven in, and the Snake chief gave Owl Bear his whole band,—two hundred head, all large, powerful horses.

All were now ready, and the chiefs started ahead. Close behind them were all the warriors, hundreds and hundreds, and last came the women and children, and the young men driving the loose horses. As they came in sight of the Piegan camp, all the warriors started out to meet them, dressed in their war costumes and singing the great war song. There was no wind, and the sound came across the valley and up the hill like the noise of thunder. Then the Snakes began to sing, and thus the two parties advanced. At last they met. The Piegans turned and rode beside them, and so they came to the camp. Then they got off their horses and kissed each other. Every Piegan asked a Snake into his lodge to eat

THE PEACE WITH THE SNAKES

and rest, and the Snake women put up their lodges beside the Piegan lodges. So the great peace was made.

In Owl Bear's lodge there was a great feast, and when they had finished he said to his people: "Here is the man whose scalp I took. Did I say I killed him? No. I gave him my knife and told him to kill me. He would not do it; and he gave me his knife, but I would not kill him. So we talked together about what we should do, and now we have made peace. And now (turning to the Snake) this is your lodge, also all the things in it. My horses, too, I give you. All are yours."

So it was. The Piegan took the Snake's wife, lodge, and horses, and the Snake took the Piegan's, and they camped side by side. All the people camped together, and feasted with each other and made presents. So the peace was made.

For many days they camped side by side. The young men kept hunting, and the women were always busy drying meat and tanning robes and cowskins. Buffalo were always close, and after a while the people had all the meat and robes they could carry. Then, one day, the Snake chief said to Owl Bear: "Now, my friend, we have camped a long time together, and I am glad we have made peace. We have dug a hole in the ground, and in it we have put our anger and covered it up, so there is no more war between us. And now I think it time to go. To-morrow morning the Snakes break camp and go back south."

"Your words are good," replied Owl Bear. "I too am glad we have made this peace. You say you must go south, and I feel lonesome. I would like you to go with us so we could camp together a long time, but as you say, so it shall be done. To-morrow you will start south. I too shall break camp, for I would be lonesome here without you; and the Piegans will start in the home direction."

The lodges were being taken down and packed. The men sat about the fireplaces, taking a last smoke together.

They were now great friends. Many Snakes had married Piegan women, and many Piegans had married Snake women. At last all was ready. The great chiefs mounted their horses and started out, and soon both parties were strung out on the trail.

Some young men, however, stayed behind to gamble a while. It was yet early in the morning, and by riding fast it would not take them long to catch up with their camps. All

PART 6: MYTHS ABOUT HEROES AND TRICKSTERS

day they kept playing; and sometimes the Piegans would win, and sometimes the Snakes.

It was now almost sunset. "Let us have one horse race," they said, "and we will stop." Each side had a good horse, and they ran their best; but they came in so close together it could not be told who won. The Snakes claimed that their horse won, and the Piegans would not allow it. So they got angry and began to quarrel, and pretty soon they began to fight and to shoot at each other, and some were killed.

Since that time the Snakes and Piegans have never been at peace.

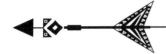 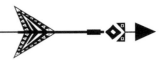

The Adventures of Kivioq
(Inuit)

As told by Evelyn Wolfson

Kivioq's father had been killed by an angry hunter several months before he was born. His mother vowed to avenge her husband's death and plotted to get even. Soon after the little boy was born, his mother wrapped his tiny body in the skin of a newborn seal and sewed it together so tightly that it fit just like his own. Kivioq's mother taught her young son how to hold his breath under water. They practiced each day until Kivioq grew so comfortable under water that his mother had to wait long periods of time for her young son to come up for air. One day Kivioq's mother said, "You are ready for the sea, my son." And she took him down to the shore. Kivioq's mother rubbed his sleek sealskin suit and smiled at her young son. "Swim out to sea," she said. "And when you see kayaks, show yourself above the water. The men will quickly paddle toward you. Let them come close, then duck under the water and hold your breath until you have led them far out to sea. After they are far enough away, I will raise a great storm, turn over their kayaks, and they will all drown."

Kivioq did as he was told and swam out to sea.

"Look," cried one hunter from his kayak. "There is a seal. Let's follow it."

Kivioq let the kayaks come close, then he dove down under the water and disappeared. When he resurfaced, he was far out at sea, and the men's kayaks were right behind him. Kivioq quickly dove under the water again, and the men paddled rapidly after him.

Suddenly, an angry wind sent huge waves over the tops of the kayaks, and one by one, the little boats disappeared beneath the water. Only one kayak and hunter remained and continued to follow Kivioq. But soon this single hunter grew tired and stopped to rest. No sooner had he laid the paddle across his kayak than a great wave washed over him. Kivioq never saw the young hunter again.

PART 6: MYTHS ABOUT HEROES AND TRICKSTERS

Kivioq bobbed up and down in the water looking for more hunters until he was certain his mother had sought her complete revenge. Then he swam to the nearest island and went ashore. He found one small house, which had no windows or roof. Kivioq climbed up the wall of the house and looked down inside. An old witch sat on the sleeping platform tanning a human skin. From the top of the wall Kivioq blew down on the witch's head, then drew back so she could not see him. The witch looked up, but her thick wrinkled eyelids were so big and heavy that they fell down over her eyes and shrouded her sight. "Strange, my house has never leaked before," muttered the old witch.

Kivioq blew down on the witch again. This time she cut off her heavy eyelids with her tanning knife and looked up toward the top of the wall. Kivioq gasped at the sight of her hideous red-black eyes and let go his grip of the side of the house. He landed on the ground just in time for the old witch to greet him at the door. "Please come in," she said in a kind voice. "Let me hang up your clothes to dry."

Kivioq went inside and took off his wet clothing. The old witch hung the clothing on a long line that stretched across the room, and Kivioq jumped up onto the sleeping platform to stay warm.

"Wait here," said the old witch. "I must go out and get some more fuel for the fire."

Suddenly Kivioq began to fear that the old witch meant to cook him. He got down off the sleeping platform and began to poke around the room. "Oh," he gasped out loud as his hand brushed against a pile of human skulls. "What are these?" One of the skulls spoke up, "You had better get out of here in a hurry if you do not wish to join us!"

Kivioq reached for his clothing on the line above him. But each time he grabbed at his anorak, the line flew up into the air and out of reach. Desperate, Kivioq rubbed the small white feather that hung around his neck and called out to the bird who was his helping spirit, "Snow Bunting, Snow Bunting, where are you? Please help me."

Snow Bunting flew into the house and brushed her wings against the line that held Kivioq's clothing. The clothing fell to the floor, and Kivioq put it on as quickly as possible. Then he rushed out of the house, down to the shore, and jumped into the water.

Soon the old witch came running after him waving her long pointed knife. Frustrated that she could not reach him, but eager to show Kivioq her great powers, the old witch gashed open a granite boulder on shore, just as easily as if she were cutting a piece of fresh meat.

232

Kivioq quickly responded by throwing his harpoon at an even larger boulder that jutted up out of the sea. The great stone split in two and fell into the water. "That is the way I would have harpooned you," cried Kivioq.

The old witch smiled gleefully. She was so impressed with Kivioq's great strength that she called out, "Please come back, I want you to be my husband."

Kivioq swam away as fast as he could go. The angry old witch hurled her knife after him. It skidded over the water and eventually turned into a great ice floe. Thereafter, the sea began to freeze over every winter.

After Kivioq had escaped far from the angry witch, he stole a kayak and began to paddle from shore to shore in search of a place to settle. At first he stopped on a small island where two giant caterpillars, helping spirits of the old witch, tried to steal his kayak. He escaped just in time, back to the sea. Snow Bunting came to warn him that the witch had sent a giant clam after him, and Kivioq looked up just in time to dodge two huge shells that threatened to swallow him whole.

At last Kivioq returned home, but his mother was gone and the village was empty. He mourned for many months before he decided to seek a wife. Kivioq walked until he came upon a small stone house nestled against low-growing shrubs by the side of a lake. He called out, "Is anyone at home?" A sweet-looking old lady with graying hair came out to greet him. The old lady, who was really a wolf in human form, invited Kivioq in to meet her daughter. Kivioq entered the small stone house and was surprised to see that the daughter had the same graying hair as the mother, even though she was very young. After Kivioq had been with the women for two winters and had taught them how to hunt caribou, he asked the young girl to be his wife. Kiviok's young bride had become an excellent hunter, but her mother was too old to run fast and seldom brought down an animal.

In the evening Kivioq brought caribou home in his kayak, and his young wife waded out into the lake to retrieve the dead animals. Kivioq admired his wife's strength and beauty. Her knees never wobbled under a heavy load, and her shoulders stayed straight back when she walked.

But the old lady sneered at her robust daughter, "You are so young and strong you can show off for your new husband. But I am just as strong." The young girl ignored the old lady and continued to sew her husband's caribou-skin anorak.

PART 6: MYTHS ABOUT HEROES AND TRICKSTERS

One day while the daughter waited for Kivioq to come home, the old lady sneaked up behind her and hit her on the head with a rock. Then, the jealous old woman stripped her daughter of her beautiful young skin and stepped into it herself. The new young skin covered the old woman's wrinkled face, bony arms and hands, and torso, but it would not stretch all the way down to her feet. Still, she was pleased with her new appearance, and she covered up the old skin of her legs with high boots.

Before long, Kivioq called from his kayak, and the old lady, disguised as his wife, slipped out the door to greet him. "You forgot to take off your boots," scolded Kivioq. But the old lady pretended she did not hear him and kept walking out toward the kayak. "Take off your boots," he protested again. "Boots do not belong in the water."

Finally the old lady took off the boots and threw them on the shore. After she reached Kivioq's kayak she grabbed hold of the caribou, just as her daughter had always done, and hoisted it onto her shoulder. But the animal's weight made her shoulders bend forward and her knees buckle. Kivioq thought his wife must be very tired.

He watched closely as his wife struggled to walk toward shore. Then he looked down in the water and saw two thin wrinkled legs below the fine young skin of his wife. Immediately, Kivioq understood his jealous mother-in-law's terrible deed.

"You cruel old woman. You have taken my wife from me," he shouted. And he turned his kayak around and paddled off in the opposite direction.

Kivioq never looked behind him. And he never again saw the old she-wolf who was his mother-in-law.

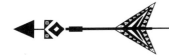 

Nanebojo and the Geese
(Ojibwa)

As told by Katharine Berry Judson

Nanebojo lived with his grandmother. His parents had been killed by a war party. Now Nanebojo resolved to leave that place with his grandmother. He told the Indians that a stranger was coming who would harm all of them.

Then Nanebojo climbed to the top of a maple tree. He poured water into it; therefore the sap in the maple is now watery and thin. It has to be boiled before it becomes sugar. Nanebojo also went through the cornfields and pulled off all the ears of corn except one or two. Therefore now cornstalks have but one or two ears. They used to have ten or twelve.

Then Nanebojo went away.

Nanebojo and his grandmother traveled until they reached Lake Erie. Then they journeyed to Lake St. Clair. Grandmother went on ahead.

Nanebojo saw ducks in Lake St. Clair, but he could not think how to capture them. At last he remembered. He went to his grandmother and told her to make him a sack.

"What for?" asked grandmother.

"Never mind what for," answered her grandson. So Grandmother made the sack.

Nanebojo took the sack and went along the lake shore to where there was a hill, with a short stretch of flat land between the hill and the water. He climbed to the top of the hill, got into the sack, closed the neck, and rolled down the hill. Then he got out and walked up again, laughing heartily all the time. Again he rolled down the hill, shouting loudly.

Now the ducks heard him. They came out of the water and waddled around him. They came closer and closer. After a while, one duck grew bold. He said, "Let us roll downhill just once."

Nanebojo said, "Oh, no indeed, you go away! Every time I do anything you come around and bother me!" Then he went up the hill again with his sack on his back, and rolled himself downhill, laughing loudly.

Again the ducks said, "Let us roll downhill just once."

Nanebojo said, "Very well. You may roll downhill just once," and he told them to get into the bag. Just then some geese flew by overhead. They stopped to watch. Nanebojo also saw them.

Nanebojo carried the ducks to the top of the hill, laid down the bag, filled it with ducks, tied the neck, and started rolling it down the hill. He ran beside it, laughing very loudly, while the ducks quacked. They all made much noise. When the bag of ducks reached the bottom of the hill, Nanebojo emptied out the bag, and told them to go away. Then he went up the hill with the sack on his shoulder, and again he rolled downhill, laughing loudly, but always keeping one eye on the ducks and one on the geese. "If I lose one, I may get the other," he said. Every time he rolled down, the geese came nearer. Nanebojo pretended not to see them. At last they came very near indeed and asked him if they might roll down. "Let us roll down just once," they said.

Nanebojo said, "No!" and kept right on rolling downhill. The geese were about to fly away when Nanebojo said, "Oh, well. If you want to, you may roll down once."

The geese were very glad to get into the sack. Nanebojo squeezed them in together very tightly, saying, "If you are close together, you will have more fun." Then he shouldered the sack and started up the hill.

Nanebojo walked a long, long time. He walked up to the top of the hill and then he walked down on the other side. The geese after a while thought he had walked too long a time. They called out, "Where are you going?" but he made no answer and walked straight on.

When Nanebojo reached his grandmother, he said, as he laid down the sack, "You heat some water while I go and get more from the spring." Then he went out after he had said, "Do not untie the sack." When he had left the lodge, Grandmother untied the sack, wondering what was in it. At once the geese flew out and got away. Not one was left.

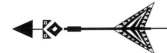 

Ûñtsaiyĭ, the Gambler
(Cherokee)

As told by James Mooney

Thunder lives in the west, or a little to the south of west, near the place where the sun goes down behind the water. In the old times he sometimes made a journey to the east, and once after he had come back from one of these journeys a child was born in the east who, the people said, was his son. As the boy grew up it was found that he had scrofula sores all over his body, so one day his mother said to him, "Your father, Thunder, is a great doctor. He lives far in the west, but if you can find him he can cure you."

So the boy set out to find his father and be cured. He traveled long toward the west, asking of every one he met where Thunder lived, until at last they began to tell him that it was only a little way ahead. He went on and came to Ûñtiguhĭ, on Tennessee, where lived Ûñtsaiyĭ, "Brass." Now Ûñtsaiyĭ was a great gambler, and made his living that way. It was he who invented the *gatayûstĭ* game that we play with a stone wheel and a stick. He lived on the south side of the river, and everybody who came that way he challenged to play against him. The large flat rock, with the lines and grooves where they used to roll the wheel, is still there, with the wheels themselves and the stick turned to stone. He won almost every time, because he was so tricky, so that he had his house filled with all kinds of fine things. Sometimes he would lose, and then he would bet all that he had, even to his own life, but the winner got nothing for his trouble, for Ûñtsaiyĭ knew how to take on different shapes, so that he always got away.

As soon as Ûñtsaiyĭ saw him he asked him to stop and play a while, but the boy said he was looking for his father, Thunder, and had no time to wait. "Well," said Ûñtsaiyĭ, "he lives in the next house; you can hear him grumbling over there all the time"—he meant the Thunder—"so we may as well have a game or two before you go on." The boy said he

PART 6: MYTHS ABOUT HEROES AND TRICKSTERS

had nothing to bet. "That's all right," said the gambler, "we'll play for your pretty spots." He said this to make the boy angry so that he would play, but still the boy said he must go first and find his father, and would come back afterwards.

He went on, and soon the news came to Thunder that a boy was looking for him who claimed to be his son. Said Thunder, "I have traveled in many lands and have many children. Bring him here and we shall soon know." So they brought in the boy, and Thunder showed him a seat and told him to sit down. Under the blanket on the seat were long, sharp thorns of the honey locust, with the points all sticking up, but when the boy sat down they did not hurt him, and then Thunder knew that it was his son. He asked the boy why he had come. "I have sores all over my body, and my mother told me you were my father and a great doctor, and if I came here you would cure me."

"Yes," said his father, "I am a great doctor, and I'll soon fix you."

There was a large pot in the corner and he told his wife to fill it with water and put it over the fire. When it was boiling, he put in some roots, then took the boy and put him in with them. He let it boil a long time until one would have thought that the flesh was boiled from the poor boy's bones, and then told his wife to take the pot and throw it into the river, boy and all. She did as she was told, and threw it into the water, and ever since there is an eddy there that we call Ûñ'tiguhĭ', "Pot-in-the-water." A service tree and a calico bush grew on the bank above. A great cloud of steam came up and made streaks and blotches on their bark, and it has been so to this day. When the steam cleared away she looked over and saw the boy clinging to the roots of the service tree where they hung down into the water, but now his skin was all clean. She helped him up the bank, and they went back to the house. On the way she told him, "When we go in, your father will put a new dress on you, but when he opens his box and tells you to pick out your ornaments be sure to take them from the bottom. Then he will send for his other sons to play ball against you. There is a honey-locust tree in front of the house, and as soon as you begin to get tired strike at that and your father will stop the play, because he does not want to lose the tree."

When they went into the house, the old man was pleased to see the boy looking so clean, and said, "I knew I could soon cure those spots. Now we must dress you." He brought out a fine suit of buckskin, with belt and headdress, and had the boy put them on. Then he opened a box and said, "Now pick out your necklace and bracelets." The boy looked, and the box was full of all kinds of snakes gliding over each other with their heads up. He was not afraid, but remembered what the woman had told him, and plunged his hand to the bottom and drew out a great rattlesnake and put it around his neck for a necklace. He put down his hand again four times and drew up four copperheads and twisted them around his wrists and ankles. Then his father gave him a war club and said, "Now you must play a ball game with your two elder brothers. They live beyond here in the Darkening land, and I have sent for them." He said a ball game, but he meant that the boy must fight for his life. The young men came, and they were both older and stronger than the boy, but he was not afraid and fought against them. The thunder rolled and the lightning flashed at every stroke, for they were the young Thunders, and the boy himself was Lightning. At last he was tired from defending himself alone against two, and pretended to aim a blow at the honey-locust tree. Then his father stopped the fight, because he was afraid the lightning would split the tree, and he saw that the boy was brave and strong.

The boy told his father how Ûñtsaiyĭ' had dared him to play, and had even offered to play for the spots on his skin. "Yes," said Thunder, "he is a great gambler and makes his living that way, but I will see that you win." He brought a small cymling gourd with a hole bored through the neck, and tied it on the boy's wrist. Inside the gourd there was a string of beads, and one end hung out from a hole in the top, but there was no end to the string inside. "Now," said his father, "go back the way you came, and as soon as he sees you he will want to play for the beads. He is very hard to beat, but this time he will lose every game. When he cries out for a drink, you will know he is getting discouraged, and then strike the rock with your war club and water will come, so that you can play on without stopping. At last he will bet his life, and lose. Then send at once for your brothers to kill him, or he will get away, he is so tricky."

The boy took the gourd and his war club and started east along the road by which he had come. As soon as Ûñtsaiyĭ' saw him he called to him, and when he saw the gourd with the bead string hanging out he wanted to play for it. The boy drew out the string, but there seemed to be no end to it, and he kept on pulling until enough had come out to make a circle all around the playground. "I will play one game for this much against your stake," said the boy, "and when that is over we can have another game."

They began the game with the wheel and stick and the boy won. Ûñtsaiyĭ' did not

PART 6: MYTHS ABOUT HEROES AND TRICKSTERS

know what to think of it, but he put up another stake and called for a second game. The boy won again, and so they played on until noon, when Ûñtsaiyĭ' had lost nearly everything he had and was about discouraged. It was very hot, and he said, "I am thirsty," and wanted to stop long enough to get a drink. "No," said the boy, and struck the rock with his club so that water came out, and they had a drink. They played on until Ûñtsaiyĭ' had lost all his buckskins and beaded work, his eagle feathers and ornaments, and at last offered to bet his wife. They played and the boy won. Then Ûñtsaiyĭ' was desperate and offered to stake his life. "If I win I kill you, but if you win you may kill me." They played and the boy won.

"Let me go and tell my wife," said Ûñtsaiyĭ', "so that she will receive her new husband, and then you may kill me." He went into the house, but it had two doors, and although the boy waited long Ûñtsaiyĭ' did not come back. When at last he went to look for him he found that the gambler had gone out the back way and was nearly out of sight going east.

The boy ran to his father's house and got his brothers to help him. They brought their dog—the Horned Green Beetle—and hurried after the gambler. He ran fast and was soon out of sight, and they followed as fast as they could. After a while they met an old woman making pottery and asked her if she had seen Ûñtsaiyĭ' and she said she had not. "He came this way," said the brothers. "Then he must have passed in the night," said the old woman, "for I have been here all day." They were about to take another road when the Beetle, which had been circling about in the air above the old woman, made a dart at her and struck her on the forehead, and it rang like brass—*ûñtsaiyĭ*'! Then they knew it was Brass and sprang at him, but he jumped up in his right shape and was off, running so fast that he was soon out of sight again. The Beetle had struck so hard that some of the brass rubbed off, and we can see it on the beetle's forehead yet.

They followed and came to an old man sitting by the trail, carving a stone pipe. They asked him if he had seen Brass pass that way and he said no, but again the Beetle—which could know Brass under any shape—struck him on the forehead so that it rang like metal, and the gambler jumped up in his right form and was off again before they could hold him. He ran east until he came to the great water; then he ran north until he came to the edge of the world, and had to turn again to the west. He took every shape to throw them off the track, but the Green Beetle always knew him, and the brothers pressed him so hard

UÑTSAIYĬ', THE GAMBLER

that at last he could go no more and they caught him just as he reached the edge of the great water where the sun goes down.

They tied his hands and feet with a grapevine and drove a long stake through his breast, and planted it far out in the deep water. They set two crows on the end of the pole to guard it and called the place *Kâgûñ'yĭ*, "Crow place." But Brass never died, and can not die until the end of the world, but lies there always with his face up. Sometimes he struggles under the water to get free, and sometimes the beavers, who are his friends, come and gnaw at the grapevine to release him. Then the pole shakes and the crows at the top cry *Ka! Ka! Ka!* and scare the beavers away.

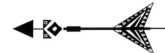 

The Fallen Star
(Dakota)

As told by Katharine Berry Judson

A people had this camp. And there were two women sleeping out of doors and looking up at the stars.

One of them said, "I wish that that large and bright shining star were my husband."

The other said, "I wish the star that shines less brightly were my husband."

And immediately both were carried upward, they say. They found themselves in a beautiful country which was full of beautiful twin flowers. And they found that the star which had shone most brightly was a large man; the other star was only a young man. So the two stars married the two women and they lived in that beautiful Star Country.

Now in that country was a plant, the Teepsinna, with large, attractive stalks. The wife of the large star wanted to dig them. Her husband said, "No; no one does so here."

Then the camp moved. When the woman had pitched her tepee, and came inside to lay the mats, she saw there a beautiful teepsinna. She said to herself, "I will dig this; no one will see me."

So she took her digging stick and dug the teepsinna; but when she pulled it out of the earth, the foundation of the Star Country broke and she fell through with her baby. So the woman died; but the baby was not injured. It lay there stretched out.

An old man came that way. When he saw that the baby was alive, he took it in his blanket and took it to his own lodge. He said to his wife, "Old woman, I saw something today that made my heart feel badly."

"What was it?" she asked.

"A woman lay dead; and a little baby boy lay beside her kicking."

"Why did you not bring it home, old man?" she asked.

"Here it is," he said. Then he took it out of his blanket.

The wife said, "Old man, let us adopt this child."

The old man said, "We will swing it around the tepee." He whirled it up through the smoke hole. It went whirling around and around and fell down, and came creeping into the tent.

Again he took up the baby and threw it up through the smoke hole. It got up and came into the tent walking. Again the old man whirled him out. In came a boy with some green sticks. He said, "Grandfather, I wish you would make me arrows."

Again the old man whirled him out. No one knows where he went. This time he came back into the tepee a long man, with many green sticks. He said, "Grandfather, make me arrows of these."

So the old man made him arrows, and he killed a great many buffaloes, and they made a large tepee, and built up a high sleeping place in the back part of the tepee, and were very rich in dried meat.

The old man said, "Old woman, I am glad we are well off; I will proclaim it abroad." So when morning came, he went to the top of the tent, and sat, and said, "I, I have abundance laid up. I eat the fat of the animals."

That is how the meadow lark came to be made, they say. It has a yellow breast and black in the middle, which is the yellow of that morning, and they say the black stripe is made by a smooth buffalo horn worn for a necklace.

The young man said, "Grandfather, I want to go visiting."

"Yes," said the old man. "When one is young is the time to go visiting."

The young man went and came to a people, and lo! they were engaged in shooting arrows through a hoop. And there was a young man who was simply looking on. By and by he said, "My friend, let us go to your house."

So they came to his lodge. Now this young man also had been raised by his grandmother, and lived with her, they say.

"Grandmother, I have brought my friend home with me; get him something to eat," said the grandson.

Grandmother said, "What shall I do?"

Then the visiting young man said, "How is it, grandmother?"

PART 6: MYTHS ABOUT HEROES AND TRICKSTERS

She said, "The people are about to die of thirst. All who go for water will not come back again."

Fallen Star said, "My friend, take a kettle; we will go for water."

"With difficulty have I raised my grandchild," objected the old woman.

"You are afraid of trifles," said the grandson. So he went with Star-born.

They reached the side of the lake. By the water of the lake stood troughs half full of water.

Star-born called out, "You who they say have killed every one who has come for water, where have you gone? I have come for water."

Then immediately whither they went is not manifest. Behold, there was a long house which was extended, and it was full of young men and women. Some of them were dead and some were dying.

"How did you come here?" asked Star-born.

They replied, "What do you mean? We came for water and something swallowed us."

Something kept striking on the head of Star-born.

"What is this?" he said.

"Get away," they replied, "that is the heart."

Then he drew out his knife and cut it to pieces. Suddenly something made a great noise. In the great body, these people were swallowed up. When the heart died, death came to the body. Then Star-born cut a great hole in the side, and came out, bringing the young men and the young women. All came to life again.

So the people were thankful and offered him two wives.

But he said, "I am journeying. My friend here will marry them."

Then Star-born went on, they say. Again he found a young man standing where they were shooting through a hoop. He said, "I will look on with my friend," and went and stood beside him.

Then the other said, "My friend, let us go home," so he went with him to his tepee.

"Grandmother, I have brought my friend home with me," he said. "Get him something to eat."

Grandmother replied, "How shall I do as you say?"

"How is it?" said Star-born.

"This people are perishing for wood," she said; "when anyone goes for wood, he never comes home again."

Star-born said, "My friend, take the packing strap; we will go for wood."

The old woman protested. "This one, my grandchild, I have raised with difficulty," she said. He answered, "Old woman, what you are afraid of are trifles," and went with the young man. "I am going to bring wood," he said. "If any wish to go, come along."

"The young man who came from somewhere says this," they said, so they followed him.

They had now reached the wood. They found it tied up in bundles. He ordered them to carry it home, but he stood still and said, "You who killed everyone who came to this wood, where have you gone?"

Then, suddenly, where he went was not made manifest. And lo! a tepee, and in it some young men and young women; some were eating, and some were waiting.

He said to them, "How came you here?"

They answered, "What do you mean? We came for wood and something brought us here. Now you also are lost."

He looked behind him, and lo! there was a hole.

"What is this?" he asked.

"Stop!" they said. "That is the thing itself."

He drew out an arrow and shot it. Then suddenly it opened out and behold! it was the ear of an owl in which they had been shut up. When it was killed, it opened out. Then he said, "Young men and women, come out," so they went home.

Again they offered him two wives. But he said, "My friend will marry them. I am traveling."

Again he passed on. And he came to a dwelling place of people and found them shooting the hoop. There stood a young man looking on. He joined him as his friend. While they stood there together, he said:

"Friend, let us go to your home." So he went with him to his tepee.

The young man said, "Grandmother, I have brought my friend home with me; get him something to eat."

She said, "Where shall I get it from, that you say that?"

"Grandmother, how is it that you say so?" asked the stranger.

PART 6: MYTHS ABOUT HEROES AND TRICKSTERS

She replied, "Waziya treats this people very badly. When they go out to kill buffalo, he takes it all, and now they are starving to death."

Now Waziya was a giant who caused very cold weather and blizzards.

Then he said, "Grandmother, go to him and say, 'My grandchild has come on a journey and has nothing to eat; so he has sent me to you.'"

So the old woman went and standing at a distance, cried, "Waziya, my grandchild has come on a journey and has nothing to eat; so he has sent me to you."

He replied, "Bad old woman, get you home; what do you mean by coming here?"

The old woman came home crying, and saying that Waziya had threatened to kill some of her relations.

Star-born said, "My friend, take your strap; we will go there."

The old woman interfered: "I have with difficulty raised my grandchild."

Grandchild replied to this by saying, "Grandmother is very much afraid." So the two went together.

When they came to the house of Waziya, they found a great deal of dried meat outside. He put as much on his friend as he could carry, and sent him home with it; then Star-born entered the tepee of Waziya, and said to him, "Waziya, why did you answer my grandmother as you did when I sent her to you?"

Waziya only looked angry.

Hanging there was a bow of ice. "Waziya, why do you keep this?" he said.

The giant replied, "Hands off; whoever touches that gets a broken arm."

Star-born said, "I will see if my arm breaks." He took the ice bow and snapped it into many pieces, and then started home.

The next morning all the people went on the chase and killed many buffaloes. But, as he had done before, the Waziya went all over the field, gathered up all the meat, and put it in his blanket.

Star-born was cutting up a fat cow. Waziya came and stood there. He said, "Who cuts this up?"

"I am," answered Star-born.

Waziya said, "From where have you come that you act so haughtily?"

"Whence have you come, Waziya, that you act so proudly?" he retorted.

THE FALLEN STAR

Waziya said, "Fallen Star, whoever points his finger at me dies." The young man thought, "I will point my finger at him and see if I die." He pointed his finger, but it made no difference.

Then Fallen Star said, "Waziya, whoever points his finger at me, his hand loses all use." So Waziya thought, "I will point my finger and see." He pointed his finger. His forearm lost all use. Then he pointed his finger with the other hand. It was destroyed even to the elbow.

Then Fallen Star drew out his knife and cut up Waziya's blanket, and all the buffalo meat he had gathered there fell out. Fallen Star called to the people, "Henceforth kill and carry home."

So the people took the meat and carried it to their tepees.

The next morning, they say, it was rumored that the blanket of Waziya, which had been cut to pieces, had been sewed up by his wife. He was about to shake it.

The giant stood with his face toward the north and shook his blanket. Then the wind blew from the north. Snow fell all about the camp so that the people were all snowed in. They were much troubled. They said, "We did live in some fashion before; but now this young man has acted so we are in great trouble."

But he said, "Grandmother, find me a fan."

Then she made a road under the snow, and went to people and said, "My grandchild says he wants a fan."

"What does he mean by saying that?" they asked and gave him one.

Now the snow reached to the top of the lodges, and so Fallen Star pushed up through the snow, and sat on the ridge of the lodge. While the wind was blowing to the south, he sat and fanned himself and made the wind come from the south. Then the heat became great. The snow went as if boiling water had been poured over it. All over the ground there was a mist. Waziya and his wife and children all died with the great heat. But the youngest child, the littlest child of Waziya, took refuge in the hole made by the tent pole, where there was a frost, and so he lived. So they say that is all that is left of Waziya now, just the littlest child.

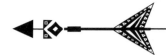

The Destruction of Monsters
(Shuswap)

As told by Katharine Berry Judson

There were many monsters in the Fraser River and the North Thompson River. Tlecsa was the eldest of four brothers who lived near Kamloops, and there were many evil beings in that country who killed all the Indians, so the four brothers decided to destroy them. There were the four Grizzly Bear sisters, and the huge elk which stood in the Thompson River just where it flows out of Kamloops Lake and swallowed all who came down the river, even a canoe with people. There was the great ram of the mountain sheep who lived on a cliff in Bonaparte Valley and killed people by blowing his breath upon them. Every one of these was killed by Tlecsa and his magic.

Then the brothers followed up the Bonaparte River until they came to a chasm which is now near the old fifty-nine-mile post, on the old Caribou road. Here lived Great Beaver and his friends. They were not cannibals, but the Indians feared their magic. The Indians did not know how to catch or kill them, but Tlecsa said, "I will eat beaver flesh," so he started after him. But first he made a beaver spear, and tied a piece of white bark around each wrist so his brothers could see him, if he were dragged under water.

Tlecsa went up to Great Beaver and harpooned him. Beaver at once dragged him into the creek. His brothers watched him for a while and then lost sight of him, and at once began to search for him in all the nearby creeks. They even dug ditches in many places. At last they dug a deep ditch along the largest creek, and then they found him. When they dug near him, he said, "Be careful not to hurt me. I am here." Great Beaver had dragged him into his own house in the bank, but there Tlecsa had killed Great Beaver. At once the brothers killed many beavers and took their skins. They also ate Big Beaver. Tlecsa said, "Hereafter beaver shall be speared by mankind. The Indians shall use their flesh and skins.

THE DESTRUCTION OF MONSTERS

Beavers shall no longer have magic power;" and it was so.

Now Tlecsa and his brothers wandered around through the mountains and through Bonaparte Valley, and after a while they went up the Marble Cañon. On a high cliff lived Great Eagle, who swooped down on the Indians in the valley. He would catch an Indian and dash him against the rocks and bring him to the young eaglets in his nest. Tlecsa said, "I shall ornament myself with eagle feathers."

Now when his brothers were not looking, Tlecsa put some white paint in one side of his mouth, and some red paint in the other side. Soon Great Eagle saw him. Swooping down, he clutched him, and then, flying high on the cliffs, dashed him against the rocks. Tlecsa warded off the blow with his flaker, and let the red paint flow out of his mouth upon the rocks. His brothers below, watching, said, "He is dead. See his blood."

Again Great Eagle dashed Tlecsa against the rocks, and the white paint flowed from his mouth over the rocks. His brothers below, watching, said, "He is dead. See his brains."

Now Great Eagle also thought he was dead, so he laid him on a ledge of rocks near the nest. At once Tlecsa killed Great Eagle and pulled out his tail feathers. Then he tied an eaglet to each wrist and commanded them to fly down with him. When they reached the valley far below, Tlecsa pulled the large feathers out of the eaglets' wings and tails, and gave them to his brothers. He said to the eaglets, "Hereafter you shall be ordinary eagles. You shall have no power to kill people, and Indians shall ornament their heads and weapons with your feathers;" and it was so.

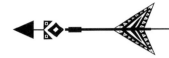
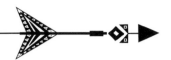

The Boy Who Became a God
(Navajo)

As told by Katharine Berry Judson

The Tolchini, a clan of the Navajos, lived at Wind Mountains. One of them used to take long visits into the country. His brothers thought he was crazy. The first time on his return, he brought with him a pine bough; the second time, corn.

Each time he returned he brought something new and had a strange story to tell. His brothers said: "He is crazy. He does not know what he is talking about."

Now the Tolchini left Wind Mountains and went to a rocky foothill east of the San Mateo Mountain. They had nothing to eat but seed grass. The eldest brother said, "Let us go hunting," but they told the youngest brother not to leave camp. But five days and five nights passed, and there was no word. So he followed them.

After a day's travel he camped near a canon, in a cave-like place. There was much snow but no water so he made a fire and heated a rock, and made a hole in the ground. The hot rock heated the snow and gave him water to drink. Just then he heard a tumult over his head, like people passing. He went out to see what made the noise and saw many crows crossing back and forth over the canon. This was the home of the crow, but there were other feathered people there, and the chaparral cock. He saw many fires made by the crows on each side of the cavern. Two crows flew down near him and the youth listened to hear what was the matter.

The two crows cried out, "Somebody says. Somebody says."

The youth did not know what to make of this.

A crow on the opposite side called out, "What is the matter? Tell us! Tell us! What is wrong?"

The first two cried out, "Two of us got killed. We met two of our men who told us."

Then they told the crows how two men who were out hunting killed twelve deer, and a party of the Crow People went to the deer after they were shot. They said, "Two of us who went after the blood of the deer were shot."

The crows on the other side of the cavern called, "Which men got killed?"

"The chaparral cock, who sat on the horn of the deer, and the crow who sat on its backbone."

The others called out, "We are not surprised they were killed. That is what we tell you all the time. If you go after dead deer you must expect to be killed."

"We will not think of them longer," so the two crows replied. "They are dead and gone. We are talking of things of long ago."

But the youth sat quietly below and listened to everything that was said.

After a while the crows on the other side of the canon made a great noise and began to dance. They had many songs at that time. The youth listened all the time. After the dance a great fire was made and he could see black objects moving, but he could not distinguish any people. He recognized the voice of Hasjelti. He remembered everything in his heart. He even remembered the words of the songs that continued all night. He remembered every word of every song. He said to himself, "I will listen until daylight."

The Crow People did not remain on the side of the canon where the fires were first built. They crossed and recrossed the canon in their dance. They danced back and forth until daylight. Then all the crows and the other birds flew away to the west. All that was left was the fires and the smoke.

Then the youth started for his brothers' camp. They saw him coming. They said, "He will have lots of stories to tell. He will say he saw something no one ever saw."

But the brother-in-law who was with them said, "Let him alone. When he comes into camp he will tell us all. I believe these things do happen for he could not make up these things all the time."

Now the camp was surrounded by pinon brush and a large fire was burning in the center. There was much meat roasting over the fire. When the youth reached the camp, he raked over the coals and said. "I feel cold."

Brother-in-law replied, "It is cold. When people camp together, they tell stories to one another in the morning. We have told ours, now you tell yours."

PART 6: MYTHS ABOUT HEROES AND TRICKSTERS

The youth said, "Where I stopped last night was the worst camp I ever had." The brothers paid no attention but the brother-in-law listened.

The youth said, "I never heard such a noise." Then he told his story. Brother-in-law asked what kind of people made the noise.

The youth said, "I do not know. They were strange people to me, but they danced all night back and forth across the canon and I heard them say my brothers killed twelve deer and afterwards killed two of their people who went for the blood of the deer. I heard them say, 'That is what must be expected. If you go to such places, you must expect to be killed.'"

The elder brother began thinking. He said, "How many deer did you say were killed?"

"Twelve."

Elder brother said, "I never believed you before, but this story I do believe. How do you find out all these things? What is the matter with you that you know them?"

The boy said, "I do not know. They come into my mind and to my eyes."

Then they started homeward, carrying the meat. The youth helped them.

As they were descending a mesa, they sat down on the edge to rest. Far down the mesa were four mountain sheep. The brothers told the youth to kill one.

The youth hid in the sage brush and when the sheep came directly toward him, he aimed his arrow at them. But his arm stiffened and became dead. The sheep passed by.

He headed them off again by hiding in the stalks of a large yucca. The sheep passed within five steps of him, but again his arm stiffened as he drew the bow.

He followed the sheep and got ahead of them and hid behind a birch tree in bloom. He had his bow ready, but as they neared him they became gods. The first was Hasjelti, the second was Hostjoghon, the third Naaskiddi, and the fourth Hadatchishi. Then the youth fell senseless to the ground.

The four gods stood one on each side of him, each with a rattle. They traced with their rattles in the sand the figure of a man, drawing lines at his head and feet. Then the youth recovered and the gods again became sheep. They said, "Why did you try to shoot us? You see you are one of us." For the youth had become a sheep.

The gods said, "There is to be a dance, far off to the north beyond the Ute Mountain. We want you to go with us. We will dress you like ourselves and teach you to dance. Then we will wander over the world."

Now the brothers watched from the top of the mesa but they could not see what the trouble was. They saw the youth lying on the ground, but when they reached the place, all the sheep were gone. They began crying, saying, "For a long time we would not believe him, and now he has gone off with the sheep."

They tried to head off the sheep, but failed. They said, "If we had believed him, he would not have gone off with the sheep. But perhaps some day we will see him again."

At the dance, the five sheep found seven others. This made their number twelve. They journeyed all around the world. All people let them see their dances and learn their songs. Then the eleven talked together and said, "There is no use keeping this youth with us longer. He has learned everything. He may as well go back to his people and teach them to do as we do."

So the youth was taught to have twelve in the dance, six gods and six goddesses, with Hasjelti to lead them. He was told to have his people make masks to represent the gods.

So the youth returned to his brothers, carrying with him all songs, all medicines, and clothing.

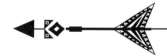 

The Adventures of Tcikápis
(Cree)

As told by Alanson Skinner

Once there was a young boy named Tcikápis who lived alone with his sister. Their mother and father had been slain by an animal called "Katcī'tos" before the boy could remember. One day, when he grew old enough to go out hunting he asked his sister what color the hair of his parents had been. She replied, "Our father was dark, and our mother was light." He took his bow and arrows and went out singing a song, the gist of which was that he would like to meet the animal that killed his father and mother. The bear appeared, "Are you looking for me?" he asked. "Do you eat people," asked Tcikápis, "when you meet them?" "Oh no," said the bear, "I run away." "Then I don't want you," said Tcikápis. Other animals came and answered his questions in the same manner. At last came the "Katcī'tos." "Are you looking for me?" he asked. "Do you eat people?" asked Tcikápis. "Yes," answered the animal. "How strong are you?" asked Tcikápis. "As strong as that Jackpine," said the animal pointing to a tree.

Tcikápis turned around and fired his arrow at the tree to try his strength. He shivered it to splinters. This frightened the animal who started to run away. Tcikápis hastened and picked up his arrow. The animal was out of sight, but Tcikápis fired where it had disappeared. He ran to the spot and found it dead, split from head to tail by his arrow. In its belly he found the hair of his father and mother which he recognized by its color. He took it home to his sister.

One day Tcikápis told his sister to set some hooks for fish. She did so. Then Tcikápis took his bow, turned up, and got into it like a canoe, for he had the power to make himself very small or as large as a normal man. He went sailing along when up came a great fish. The fish was about to swallow Tcikápis, canoe and all, when he said, "Swallow me whole, don't bite me." The fish did so and went away. Tcikápis looked from the fish's stomach out of his mouth and saw the hook his sister had set. "What is that over there? " he said to the fish. The fish went to see and took the bait. Later Tcikápis' sister pulled in the line and caught the fish. When she gutted it, out stepped Tcikápis. His sister scolded him for this but he only laughed.

One time during the winter, Tcikápis heard someone out on the ice, chiseling beaver. He said to his sister, "I am going out to help those people catch beaver." "Do not go," said his sister, "they are 'Big Fellows' (giants) and they are catching big beaver and they will get you to take hold of a beaver's tail and you will only be pulled in so they will laugh at you." "Never fear," said Tcikápis, "I am going."

Tcikápis made himself very small and went out to the river. The "Big Fellows" laughed at him and asked him to take hold of a beaver's tail and pull it out, because they expected to see him pulled in so that they could laugh at him. Tcikápis took hold of a beaver's tail and pulled it out without difficulty. He threw it over his shoulder and walked away to his lodge. When the "Big Fellows" saw this, they shouted, "Here, bring back our beaver," Tcikápis replied, "It is my beaver, I caught it."

When he reached home, his sister was frightened and said, "Tonight the 'Big Fellows' will come and kill us." Tcikápis only laughed and said, "I am not afraid of them." That night he changed his wigwam into stone. The "Big Fellows" came and tried to break it in, but it was solid rock and Tcikápis only laughed at them.

One day Tcikápis heard some girls scraping skin. He said to his sister, "I am going to see those girls." His sister said, "Do not do so, their mother eats people." But Tcikápis was not afraid and went over where the girls were. There were two of them.

He began to make love to them, and very soon the old woman heard them talking and laughing. She came up, and Tcikápis said to the girls, "Do you mind if I kill your mother?" The girls said, "No," for she killed all their lovers. Tcikápis replied, "When she goes to cook me, tell her to sit close to the pot if she likes to see the grease come up."

Tcikápis had a bladder full of grease under his coat, and when the old woman threw him in the pot he let it bubble up. It began to boil soon. After a time, the girls said, "Mother, if you like to see the grease come up, sit closer to the pot." She did so, and Tcikápis leaped out and scalded her to death. Then Tcikápis went home and brought the girls with him. "Here are two girls, sister," he said, "to keep you company so that you will not be lonely anymore."

PART 6: MYTHS ABOUT HEROES AND TRICKSTERS

"What mischief have you been up to now?" said his sister. "Nothing," said Tcikápis, "I have only killed the old woman and the girls said that they were willing I should do it."

Tcikápis climbed up a tree one day. When he got on the top of the tree he began to blow on it, and it began to grow. It grew until it reached the sky. Tcikápis got off, and there he found a beautiful path. (It was the road the sun traveled across the heavens every day.) Tcikápis wondered what made this fine path, so he lay down to wait. Presently, the sun came along. "Get out of my way," said the sun to Tcikápis. "Come on, and step over me," said Tcikápis rudely.

The sun refused, but after some argument, finding Tcikápis would not move, he came and stepped over him. It was so hot that it burned Tcikápis' caribou-skin coat. This made Tcikápis very angry and determined to be revenged so he set a snare for the sun. Next day, when the sun came along its path it was caught in the snare, and struggled to get loose. When it struggled there were great flashes of light and dark or day and night. This, of course, would not do, so Tcikápis tried to let the sun loose, but it was so hot that it burned him when he went near it. At length, Tcikápis persuaded the shrew who has a very long nose, to gnaw it loose.

After this, Tcikápis decided to go up above to live. He descended and got his two wives and his sister. They all climbed into the tree, and Tcikápis, began to blow on it. The tree grew higher and higher, so high that his sister and his two wives grew dizzy and they would fall off, but every time they fell off Tcikápis would catch them and put them back again.

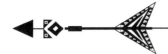 

The Story of Ashish
(Klamath)

As told by Katharine Berry Judson

Ashish, they say, having many people with him, gambled. While on their way gambling, they built fires. Purple-blue was the fire of Ashish; the fire of Silver-Fox was yellow only; the fire of Kemush was smoke only.

Then they shot at the target. Ashish hit it straight; Silver-Fox slightly missed the mark; Kemush hit this side of the mark. All the others struck far this side of the mark. After doing so they began gambling again. They bet on many things. Then Ashish won over them. About noon all the men had lost all they had. Then they went to their lodges.

Now Ashish had five wives. Mud Hen was one wife of Ashish; Long-tail Squirrel was one wife; Sandhill Crane was one wife; Mallard was one wife; Chaffinch was one wife.

Then Kemush plotted secretly. After daybreak he plotted against Ashish. Then Kemush began to weep, pretending to remember the inherited place where his father had killed eagles. Now declared Kemush to Ashish, "Far away is the killing place of the young eagles. I kill them not, being afraid." Then they set out together, Kemush and Ashish. Now Kemush coveted Little Squirrel, the wife of Ashish.

Then they saw eagles. Kemush pointed out the pine for Ashish to climb up. Then the eagles flew on the pine. Ashish climbed up, but as he climbed the tree grew. Far up, the pine now touched the sky. Ashish having climbed to the top, saw only the young ones of a lark, although it was the eyrie of an eagle. Thus Ashish wept, sitting in the eyrie.

Then Kemush went away. He dressed himself to appear like Ashish. He came back to the lodge from the pine tree.

Now the wives of Ashish became suspicious. "This one is Kemush," — thus said the wives of Ashish. Next morning they all went with those who were in the habit of gambling

PART 6: MYTHS ABOUT HEROES AND TRICKSTERS

with Ashish. They built a fire while gambling. And from the fire of Kemush smoke only curled up. Then they suspected, and said, "This is not Ashish. This is Kemush," —thus said those afar off, "Ashish did not come. The fire of Ashish is not burning there."

Thus said the followers in the distance. Those in the distance also said, "Ye will find out this man after he has shot at the mark. Ashish always hits straight."

Then they shot. Kemush struck far this side of the mark. Silver-Fox missed a little. Then they commenced gambling and they won over Kemush. All day long they won many stakes. Then they went back to the lodges. Then they quit gambling for they missed Ashish.

Now Ashish's wives wept constantly and left their lodges to dig roots. Four wives put pitch on their heads. Only Mallard mourned not for Ashish.

Then Ashish heard the weeping cries of Sandhill Crane, and Ashish wept hearing them. Now Ashish was far away close to the sky. He was nothing but bones. Then two butterflies flew up close to the sky and saw Ashish. Then they flew back, having seen him. They returned home and said to their father, "A good man will soon perish. Far off, close to the sky, we saw that man, nothing but bones. He will soon die." Thus they said to their father.

The father ordered them early next morning to fly up with a basket strung around them. So the butterflies carried food up there, carrying water also. They raised up Ashish in that eyrie. Then inquired those butterflies, "What are you doing up here?"

Then Ashish said, "Kemush sent me after the eagles. And I climbed the small pine and it grew up under me. The pine grew up during my climbing. Then I saw eagles. Of the lark saw I only the young." So Ashish said, giving explanations to them.

Then the butterflies spread a wildcat's skin in the willow basket. They placed Ashish in it, after giving him food, giving him water also. Then they took him in the basket down to the ground. Thus he returned. Then he lay sick a long time, then he recovered.

Part 7:
Myths about Birds

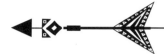 

Origin of Birds
(Ojibwa)

As told by George E. Laidlaw

One time a man shot another with his bow and arrow for stealing his wife. He watched the actions of his wife and this man and saw them sleeping together in a bush, when he shot them with his arrows and killed them both. He went to work and cut up about half the man into little bits and threw these up in the air. The pieces of meat did not fall back again, but became different birds, such as the blue jay, robins and others. He cut some more pieces a little bigger and threw these up in the air too, when they became gulls, cranes and such-like birds.

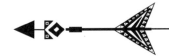 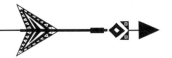

The Origin of the Raven and the Macaw, Totems of Winter and Summer
(Zuni)

As told by Frank Hamilton Cushing

He who was named Yanáuluha carried ever in his hand a staff which now in the daylight appeared plumed and covered with feathers of beautiful colors—yellow, blue-green, and red, white, black, and varied. Attached to it were shells and other potent contents of the under-world. When the people saw all these things and the beautiful baton, and heard the song-like tinkle of the sacred shells, they stretched forth their hands like little children and cried out, asking many questions.

Yanáuluha, and other priests (shiwanáteuna) having been made wise by teaching of the masters of life (god-beings) with self-magic-knowing (yam tsépan *ánikwanan*), replied: "It is a staff of extension, wherewith to test the hearts and understandings of children." Then he balanced it in his hand and struck with it a hard place and blew upon it. Amid the plumes appeared four round things, seeds of moving beings, mere eggs were they, two blue like the sky or turkis; two dun-red like the flesh of the Earth-mother.

Again the people cried out with wonder and ecstasy, and again asked they questions, many.

"These be," said he who was named Yanáuluha, "the seed of living things; both the cherishers and annoyancers, of summer time; choose ye without greed which ye will have for to follow! For from one twain shall issue beings of beautiful plumage, colored like the verdure and fruitage of summer; and whither they fly and ye follow, shall be everlastingly manifest summer, and without toil, the pain whereof ye ken not, fields full fertile of food shall flourish there. And from the other twain shall issue beings evil, uncolored, black, piebald with white; and whither these two shall fly and ye follow, shall strive winter with summer; fields furnished only by labour such as ye wot not of shall ye find there, and contended for between their offspring and yours shall be the food-fruits thereof."

"The blue! the blue!" cried the people, and those who were most hasty and strongest strove for the blue eggs, leaving the other eggs for those who had waited. "See," said they as they carried them with much gentleness and laid them, as one would the new-born, in soft sand on the sunny side of a cliff, watching them day by day, "precious of color are these; surely then, of precious things they must be the seed!" And "Yea verily!" said they when the eggs cracked and worms issued, presently becoming birds with open eyes and with pin-feathers under their skins, "Verily we chose with understanding, for see! yellow and blue, red and green are their dresses, even seen through their skins!" So they fed the pair freely of the food that men favor—thus alas! cherishing their appetites for food of all kinds! But when their feathers appeared they were *black* with white bandings; for ravens were they! And they flew away mocking our fathers and croaking coarse laughs!

And the other eggs held by those who had waited and by their father Yanáuluha, became gorgeous macaws and were wafted by him with a toss of his wand to the far southward summer-land. As father, yet child of the macaw, he chose as the symbol and name of himself and as father of these his more deliberate children—those who had waited—the macaw and the kindred of the macaw, the Múla-kwe; whilst those who had chosen the ravens became the Raven-people, or the Kâ′kâ-kwe.

Thus first was our nation divided into the People of Winter and the People of Summer. Of the Winter those who chose the raven, who were many and strong; and of the Summer those who cherished the macaw, who were fewer and less lusty, yet of prudent understanding because more deliberate. Hence, Yanáuluha their father, being wise, saw readily the light and ways of the Sun-father, and being made partaker of his breath, thus became among men as the Sun-father is among the little moons of the sky; and speaker to and of the Sun-father himself, keeper and dispenser of precious things and commandments, Pékwi Shíwani Éhkona (and Earliest Priest of the Sun). He and his sisters became also the

PART 7: MYTHS ABOUT BIRDS

seed of all priests who pertain to the Midmost clan-line of the priest-fathers of the people themselves "masters of the house of houses." By him also, and his seed, were established and made good the priests-keepers of things.

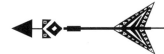 

The Thunder Bird
(Comanche)

As told by Katharine Berry Judson

In the olden times, a hunter once shot at a large bird which was flying above him. It fell to the ground. It was so large he was afraid to go to it alone, so he went back to the camp for others.

When they came back to the place where the bird had been shot, thunder was rolling through the ravine. Flashes of lightning showed the place where the bird lay. They came nearer. Then the lightning flashed so that they could not see the bird. One flash killed a hunter.

The other Indians fled back to the camp. They knew it was the Thunder Bird.

Once the Thunder Bird, in the days of the grandfathers, came down to the ground and alighted there. You may know that is so, because the grass remains burned off a large space, and the outlines are those of a large bird with outspread wings.

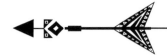 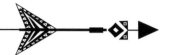

When Chickadee Climbed a Tree
(Shuswap)

As told by Katharine Berry Judson

Once Grizzly Bear told her grandson that if ever any of his arrows should catch in a tree, and beyond his reach, not to climb the tree. At first the boy did just as Grandmother said; but he lost many arrows. Now one day he shot his best arrow at a bird that was sitting in a tree. The bird flew away and the arrow stuck in a branch just beyond his reach. It was his very best arrow.

Then the boy forgot and climbed that tree to get the arrow. Just as he came near it, the tree suddenly grew and the arrow was far out of his reach. The boy climbed again, but just as he reached out his hand to take it, the tree shot up and again it was far out of his reach. This happened many times. So the boy kept on climbing.

Now as the boy looked down, he saw that the earth was far below him, and there were no branches at all on the tree trunk. He could not climb down, so he began to climb from branch to branch after his arrow, and the tree grew higher and higher until it broke through the floor of the Sky Land. Its lower branches were just level with the floor. And only then was the boy able to reach his arrow. Then he pulled it out, and climbed off the branch into the Sky Country.

Now the Sky Country was a great plain, covered lightly with snow. There were no signs of people. He said to himself, "There is no use in wandering aimlessly around in this way. I will set my arrow on end, and follow whichever way it falls."

Then he did so. He traveled the way the arrow fell and came to some chips which showed him that some people had been there felling a tree. Then he came to some fresher chips. Then he traveled on until he came to a lodge, with a mat door.

Then someone opened the door and he went in. Afterward he became the chickadee.

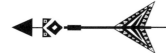 

Story of the Hummingbird
(Shoshone)

As told by Julia Darrow Cowles

"See!" said the Indian grandfather, as he sat in the opening of his tepee. "See the little Fire Bird! How swiftly it darts! Now it drinks honey from the flowers. How fast its wings move!"

A little Indian boy stood quietly at his grandfather's side. "I see the fire on its throat," he said softly, and then, as the bird darted away, he begged, "Tell me the story of the little Fire Bird, grandfather. I like the story." Then the grandfather told this tale, which his grandfather had told to him:

Long, long ago the Indian people lived in a country where it was cold, and the snow fell for many, many days.

The falling snow covered the tracks of the forest children, so the hunters could find little meat. Many times the Indian children cried to the Great Spirit for warmth, and for better hunting.

Far to the west of the Indian village there was a high mountain; and often the people watched the red sun as he sank from sight beyond the mountain, and all the sky was filled with brightness.

One night a little child went running about the tepees calling, "Come, come; see the sun! See the sun!"

The people looked toward the west. All the sky was bright; and they said, "The sun is touching the mountain top."

But the brightness did not fade away as they watched. Instead, while darkness fell all about the village, the red fire burned brighter and brighter at the top of the mountain. The people cried, "The sun is resting. He does not move. He does not sink behind the mountain!" Then they were frightened, for they knew not what to think.

PART 7: MYTHS ABOUT BIRDS

All night they watched, and still the bright light shone above the mountain top. It flashed, and threw fiery darts far into the heavens; and the Indians said, "The sun is angry. Perhaps he will destroy the earth's children."

Then their wonder grew as far away in the east a light began to glow. It grew brighter and brighter,—and then the sun arose on the eastern horizon! The people knew then that the light upon the mountain was not the light of the sun.

"There is *fire* in the mountain," they cried, "and fire is warm. It is beckoning to us with its hands. Let us move nearer to the fire mountain. It will not be so cold there."

So the people of the village marched westward toward the mountain. The bright light had gone, but a cloud of smoke hung above it. For several days they journeyed, and at last they reached the foot of the mountain, and there they camped.

Then two of their bravest warriors climbed up the mountain, until they came to its very top, and there they looked down into a great opening, shaped like a mammoth bowl, and it was full of fire! Then they hastened down and told the people.

The people rejoiced, and said, "The fire in the mountain will keep us warm. It will be good to live here." And they made them a new village at the foot of the mountain.

For many moons the people dwelt there, hunting and fishing, making their beads and moccasins. Then one day a strange noise was heard. It was as though the mountain coughed—a great, hoarse, rumbling cough, like that of some huge giant.

The people stood still and listened! There was another sound like the first, but heavier, more convulsive.

Then a great flash of fire shot up from the mountain top, and fell again. Then another, and another, and each time the fire leaped higher.

"Let us run!" cried the people. "Let us run!" Even as they spoke there was a great burst of fire and smoke, and huge stones were thrown high in the air, and a stream came pouring down the side of the mountain—a stream that looked like liquid fire.

Then the Indians ran, indeed, and there was no time to save anything but their own lives!

Many streams followed the first one, coming like fiery serpents down the mountain side, and above were heavy smoke clouds, shot with bursting rocks.

Far away the Indian people ran, crying, "The Fire Spirit is angry! What have we done that he should destroy our homes?"

STORY OF THE HUMMINGBIRD

At last they stopped, and turned to look back at the fire mountain. The flames were gone: only a cloud of smoke hung about. But the fiery streams had burned all that was in their way; and rocks and ashes had buried what the fire streams had not destroyed.

Then the people prayed to the Great Spirit, and as the Great Spirit looked down upon the mountain and saw what destruction had been wrought, he said, "Your flames shall be put out; your fires shall be quenched." And even as the Great Spirit spoke, the fires grew ashen in color, and the flames trembled and sank away.

But in the center of the great bowl of the mountain, where the fires had been, one little flame hung quivering. The Great Spirit saw it, and he said, "Little flame, you alone shall stay. But I will give to you a new form. You shall have wings, and live among the earth's people, and drink the honey of its flowers. Little flame, you shall carry the color of the fire upon your throat. You shall be known as the Humming Bird, and every child will love you."

Owl and Raven
(Inuit)

As told by Katharine Berry Judson

Owl and Raven were close friends. One day Raven made a new dress, dappled black and white, for Owl. Owl, in return, made for Raven a pair of whalebone boots and then began to make for her a white dress. When Owl wanted to fit the dress, Raven hopped about and would not sit still. Owl became very angry and said, "If I fly over you with a blubber lamp, don't jump," Raven continued to hop about. At last Owl became very angry and emptied the blubber lamp over the new white dress. Raven cried, "Qaq! Qaq!" Ever since that day Raven has been black all over.

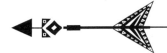 

Ball Game of the Birds and Animals
(Cherokee)

As told by Katharine Berry Judson

Once the Animals challenged the Birds to a great ball play, and the Birds accepted. The Animals met near the river, in a smooth grassy field. The Birds met in the tree top over by the ridge.

Now the leader of the Animals was Bear. He was very strong and heavy. All the way to the river he tossed up big logs to show his strength and boasted of how he would win against the Birds. Terrapin was with the Animals. He was not the little terrapin we have now, but the first Terrapin. His shell was so hard the heaviest blows could not hurt him, and he was very large. On the way to the river he rose on his hind feet and dropped heavily again. He did this many times, bragging that thus he would crush any bird that tried to take the ball from him. Then there was Deer, who could outrun all the others. And there were many other animals.

Now the leader of the Birds was Eagle; and also Hawk, and the great Tlanuwa. They were all swift and strong of flight.

Now first they had a ball dance. Then after the dance, as the birds sat in the trees, two tiny little animals no larger than field mice climbed up the tree where Eagle sat. They crept out to the branch tips to Eagle.

They said, "We wish to play ball."

Eagle looked at them. They were four-footed. He said, "Why don't you join the Animals? You belong there."

"The Animals make fun of us," they said. "They drive us away because we are small."

Eagle pitied them. He said, "But you have no wings."

Then at once Eagle and Hawk and all the Birds held a council in the trees. At last they said to the little fellows, "We will make wings for you."

PART 7: MYTHS ABOUT BIRDS

But they could not think just how to do it. Then a Bird said, "The head of our drum is made of groundhog skin. Let us make wings from that." So they took two pieces of leather from the drum and shaped them for wings. They stretched them with cane splints and fastened them on the forelegs of one of the little animals. So they made Tlameha, the Bat. They began to teach him.

First they threw the ball to him. Bat dropped and circled about in the air on his new wings. He did not let the ball drop. The Birds saw at once he would be one of their best men.

Now they wished to give wings also to the second little animal, but there was no more leather. And there was no more time. Then somebody said they might make wings for the other man by stretching his skin. Therefore two large birds took hold from opposite sides with their strong bills. Thus they stretched his skin. Thus they made Tewa, the Flying Squirrel.

Then Eagle threw to him the ball. At once Flying Squirrel sprang after it, caught it in his teeth, and carried it through the air to another tree nearby.

Then the game began. Almost at the first toss, Flying Squirrel caught the ball and carried it up a tree. Then he threw it to the Birds, who kept it in the air for some time. When it dropped to the earth, Bear rushed to get it, but Martin darted after it and threw it to Bat, who was flying near the ground. Bat doubled and dodged with the ball, and kept it out of the way of Deer. At last Bat threw it between the posts. So the Birds won the game.

Bear and Terrapin, who had boasted of what they would do, never had a chance to touch the ball.

Because Martin saved the ball when it dropped to the ground, the Birds afterwards gave him a gourd in which to build his nest. He still has it.

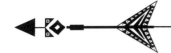 

The Race Between Humming Bird and Crane
(Cherokee)

As told by Katharine Berry Judson

Humming Bird and Crane were both in love with a pretty woman. She liked Humming Bird, who was handsome. Crane was ugly, but he would not give up the pretty woman. So at last to get rid of him, she told them they must have a race, and that she would marry the winner. Now Humming Bird flew like a flash of light; but Crane was heavy and slow.

The birds started from the woman's house to fly around the world to the beginning. Humming Bird flew off like an arrow. He flew all day and when he stopped to roost he was far ahead.

Crane flew heavily, but he flew all night long. He stopped at daylight at a creek to rest. Humming Bird waked up, and flew on again, and soon he reached a creek, and behold! there was Crane, spearing tadpoles with his long bill. Humming Bird flew on.

Soon Crane started on and flew all night as before. Humming Bird slept on his roost.

Next morning Humming Bird flew on and Crane was far, far ahead. The fourth day, Crane was spearing tadpoles for dinner when Humming Bird caught up with him. By the seventh day Crane was a whole night's travel ahead. At last he reached the beginning again. He stopped at the creek and preened his feathers, and then in the early morning went to the woman's house. Humming Bird was far, far behind.

But the woman declared she would not marry so ugly a man as Crane. Therefore she remained single.

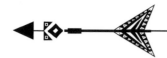 

Prairie Falcon's Marriage
(Miwok)

As told by Edward Winslow Gifford

"Going, going to marry Prairie Falcon," Green Heron said. "Give me a large basket. Give me a basket, so that I may give it to Meadowlark." The two left that night after they had married the chief. "Where is my daughter going?" said Green Heron. When tiny returned, Coyote followed them. Coyote said, "You, Green Heron, what will you do when the chief becomes hungry?" Thus spoke Coyote, when he told them to prepare food for the chief.

Eagle told California Jay to obtain food. Then Coyote said to Eagle, "We go now to hunt rabbits." Coyote continued to California Jay, "Yes, that is all right. Let's go." "Whatever you people say is good," said Eagle to Jay. Then they departed.

Jay and Coyote went hunting. Coyote ran away and hid behind a rock.

Green Heron told his daughters to pound acorns. They said. "Yes." They went over to the mortar, where they pounded acorns. The chief arose from his bed to marry one of the girls. He had never known any girl intimately. Then he went to the assembly house and told his wife to pound acorns on the following day. Prairie Falcon told his sister to take the acorns to the girls. One of the girls, Meadowlark, gave birth to a boy baby. After she had given birth to the child, she pounded acorns. The Eagle visited her while she pounded acorns. He took her, Prairie Falcon's wife. "Why is that chief deceiving me by taking my wife away from me?" said Prairie Falcon, and he became very angry.

Prairie Falcon decided to go away. He said to his sister, "Give me a bow and arrow. I am going into the world." He killed one quail with an arrow. He took the quail with him. He said, "I do not think my sister eats anything." Then he traveled over the world, along the water towards the north. After that he returned home. He told his sister to tell no one where he had been.

"I will kill my wife, if she follows me. She deceived me, when she married me," said Prairie Falcon. Then he went around the world, returning again to his sister.

After returning to his sister, he visited his sister's husband, Lizard. Lizard threw the fire to him. Lizard said to his wife, "What will your brother do over there?" Then Prairie Falcon said to his sister, "I think he does not wish me to remain."

"Hold back your dogs," said Prairie Falcon's sister to Lizard, for Lizard had rattle snakes and bears for dogs. "I do not want them to bite me," said Prairie Falcon to his sister.

"I go now to the place where my father died," said Prairie Falcon to his sister. His sister objected, saying, "Do not go; remain here," for she feared for him. Their father had died at the place to which he was going. "No, I go. My father went there and I go, too," said Prairie Falcon. His sister then said, "Well, you may go, then. Remember, if anything happens to you, that you did not mind me, when I told you not to go."

"You watch my wife, for she might follow me," said Prairie Falcon to his sister. "If she comes, I will kill her. She is a pretty woman, but I will kill her, nevertheless." His sister said, "Do not kill her, for she will save your life when you arrive at your destination."

His wife followed him all the way. He looked back to find that she followed him. She was coming. Prairie Falcon said to his brother-in-law, Lizard, "Watch her closely, for I shall take her. I do not think that I shall kill her." Lizard watched her and Prairie Falcon took her. "Yes, I am going," said Prairie Falcon. "Do not give me that girl," he said to Lizard.

He went north. He told his sister not to tell his wife where he had gone. "I go to the north," he said. "I go to the north. I feel lonesome." Thus he spoke to his sister, as he was leaving. "It is all right if they kill me. I go around the water. I do not think I shall come back. I go around the water. I think that will be the last of me. I do not think that you will see me anymore."

He changed his mind, after he talked with his sister, and went to the south instead. He finally arrived at his destination.

Lizard said to his wife, "Your brother will be back, so the fire tells me." Prairie Falcon's sister said, "Our brother has returned."

Upon his return, Prairie Falcon found that his wife had started for the place to which he had been. He set out again to overtake her. He overtook her before she arrived at her

PART 7: MYTHS ABOUT BIRDS

destination. Then they proceeded on their journey together. Prairie Falcon said, "I go to the place where my father died. I shall take my wife with me."

He arrived there and found that his father, Owl, still lived. Prairie Falcon remained with his father. His father said to him, after he had stayed with him a while, "If they want your wife, give her to them, because she will save your life."

Prairie Falcon's brother-in-law, Lizard, told his wife that her brother had gone.

Prairie Falcon told his wife not to come near him after they had arrived at their destination. "Keep away from me," he said. Lizard threw the tire on the ground. Prairie Falcon told his father, "Fire comes." His wife saw the fire coming. Prairie Falcon told his father to return.

All of the ground was burned after Lizard threw the fire. Prairie Falcon told his wife that a large fire was coming. "We had better hurry or it will catch us." His wife replied that she did not believe him. She pulled two hairs from herself and threw them on the ground. They became a lake. She did this after Prairie Falcon left. She entered the lake and stayed in the water, while the fire burned around it. She swam around the lake. Finally she came out of it and went to her father. Upon meeting her father (Meadowlark man), she said, "We are safe now, the fire has gone out." Meadowlark's wife said to him, "We go to the place to which Prairie Falcon has gone." Then they went. They obtained a large rock, which rolled upon the wife's leg.

Prairie Falcon told his wife that they had arrived at their destination. "They are going to have a game with me," he said. "If they win, they will kill me."

Prairie Falcon's father, Owl, helped him. He helped Prairie Falcon in the game, which they played. Prairie Falcon called strong winds from every direction to help him in the race. The big wind came as they started the jumping contest. Prairie Falcon jumped about before he jumped through the hole. He jumped through the hole. It snapped at him, but just missed him. He said to his wife, "We have gone through one place safely. Now we are going to my father."

Prairie Falcon's father said that he dreamed that his son was coming. "I am going to meet him. He is on his way, coming to see me. He is coming. I think they will kill him when he arrives here."

The people told him that his son had arrived. "We can have a game with him," they said. "He has arrived. He has brought his wife with him." Thus spoke Chief Mountain Sheep to his people. Mountain Sheep gave a festival in which games were played.

Mountain Sheep said, "We are going to have a big festival. We are going to have a football game. Get Prairie Falcon's wife. Bring his wife. I like his wife. He can have my wife." They took Prairie Falcon's wife and brought another woman to him. They held a festival. They told Prairie Falcon that he could have his wife back after the games were over. Prairie Falcon replied, "All right." Then, upon second thought, he said, "No. I would rather have my wife with me. I will send the string of beads." Eagle said, "All right. I will take the beads over there."

The other girl went to Prairie Falcon, but Prairie Falcon told her not to come near him, told her to stay away. She slept in a different place. Then she went to Mountain Sheep and told him that Prairie Falcon did not sleep with her. Prairie Falcon's wife went to Mountain Sheep's house and stayed there overnight. Everyone liked her.

Prairie Falcon told Gopher to dig tunnels in the ground on Mountain Sheep's side of the field, so that he would stumble when he ran. Then Gopher made tunnels in the ground. Next day they played football. Roadrunner helped Prairie Falcon and Dove; so did Kingbird. They ran. Owl kicked the ball: then Prairie Falcon's side won.

Next day they played more games. Prairie Falcon won the first game played. Owl kicked the ball; from where it landed Coyote kicked it; then Dove. After that they played another game.

Then Prairie Falcon said to his father, "Give me my arrows. Mountain Sheep is tired. They will kill me, father, if they win the game. I shall forestall them." Then he killed Mountain Sheep with arrows. After he had killed him, he returned home.

He returned home to his sister. Then he told his wife that she should bathe. "After that we will go home," he said. Owl bathed her. After she had been bathed, they started for home.

Prairie Falcon told his sister not to worry. "I have been over to Mountain Sheep's place," he said. "That is all for Mountain Sheep. I killed him, just as he killed my father."

Prairie Falcon came again to the hole through which he had passed. He called upon the winds from every direction to help him pass safely through it. He told his wife to cling

PART 7: MYTHS ABOUT BIRDS

to him tightly, when he jumped. His wife clasped him tightly about the waist. The hole opened just as he prepared to jump. Then he jumped through it.

When he had passed to the other side of the hole, he said to his wife, "We are going home." Then he went to his sister's house again. He told her that he had killed all of the people on the other side.

His sister told him not to talk thus while his brother-in-law (Lizard) was listening. Then Prairie Falcon became angry and went home. Then he went beyond his home. He said that he would never return to that place again. He took his son with him. He did not sleep in his home, but went beyond it.

He left his wife at the assembly house. He told her that he did not know whether he would return or not. He arrived at a large rock, which was his father-in-law's place. His father-in-law (Green Heron) asked him if he wanted anything to eat. He also asked him if he had won in the game. Prairie Falcon replied. "Yes, I went there and killed the chief."

He stayed at his father-in-law's place for two nights. Then his father came to take him home. He told Prairie Falcon that his wife was worrying about him. Prairie Falcon came down from the large rock and talked with his father. He told his father that he did not desire to return. Then Dove and Coyote came behind him. They told him that they had left one and that they had not found the other one. Dove and Coyote were given bear hides to sit upon. Then they told him to marry the girl with whom he had been going. He did not reply.

His father asked him what he ate, while he was traveling. He told his father that he had nothing to eat. His father told him that he would get him a quail, if he would marry.

"Quail is the only thing I ever eat," said Prairie Falcon to his father. His father went hunting.

[Prairie Falcon's assembly house was at Goodwin's ranch near Montezuma in Tuolumne County. Mountain Sheep's village was at the south end of the world.]

Redbird and Blackbird
(Ojibwa)

As told by Katharine Berry Judson

Once there were two men named Redbird and Blackbird. They had a house on the shore of the lake, and they lived on wild potatoes. They spent all their time digging for wild potatoes, and that was all the food they ever had.

One day Blackbird said to Redbird, "There are great fields of wild rice across the lake. We ought to go and gather it." So the very next day they crossed the lake and found themselves among large fields of wild rice. They began gathering the rice, then they saw people nearby. They went to the people and said, "How do you do?"

The people said, "We have never seen you before." Blackbird said, "No. We live on the other side of the lake. We live on the wild potatoes we find there." The people said, "Well, you did right in coming over here. You ought to have good food."

Then Blackbird and Redbird shook hands all around and went home.

Now these people talked about the wild potatoes. Just about that time, Redbird said to Blackbird, "Those people are planning to attack us, for our wild potatoes. What shall you do?" Blackbird said at once what he would do. Then Redbird said what he would do. The very next day those people came. Redbird heard their voices. At once he began to grow smaller and smaller until he was only a single feather lying on the ground. When Blackbird heard their voices, he hit himself against the house, and soon there was only an awl standing there.

The people came and searched everywhere. They said, "No, we can't find those men," so they went home.

Blackbird and Redbird were a little afraid they would come back. So they changed themselves into birds. Redbird flew to the woods, but Blackbird went over the lake to live.

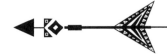

War with the Sky People
(Thompson River)

As told by Katharine Berry Judson

The people of Sky Land stole Swan's wife. Swan at once called all the Earth People to a great council. They agreed to make war on the Sky People.

Now they gathered their bows and arrows. Swan was their chief. Each man began to fire his arrows at the sky. Every one came down. Every man tried to shoot an arrow into the Sky Land, until at last only Wren was left. Then Wren shot an arrow. The people watched, but it did not come back to earth. They watched a long time. It had stuck in the sky. Wren fired another arrow. That did not come down. It had stuck in the notch of the first one. Wren fired many arrows. Not one came back, though all the birds and animals were watching carefully. They at last could see the chain of arrows, and Wren shot more arrows until the chain reached the earth.

Now all the Bird People and the Animal People climbed over the arrow chain and went up into Sky Land and fought the Sky People. Grizzlies lived there, and Black Bear and Elk. And the Sky People won the fight. The Earth People began to retreat in great haste. They came down over the arrow chain, but when about half the people had reached the ground, the chain broke. Those who could not get down had to go back to Sky Land. Some of them were made prisoners and some were killed.

There used to be many more birds and animals than there are now; so the Indians say. There are fewer now because of this war.

The Eagle and the Hunter
(Wyandot)

As told by Marius Barbeau

I will now tell the story of events that have really happened long ago. A man was in the habit of hunting game. He was fond above all, of killing deer; and, after he had skinned them, he used to shout, "O you eagles, come and have something to eat!" The eagles, it is said, would gather there, only to be slain by the hunter. And it was always happening in the same manner; time and time again the man went out hunting, killing, and skinning deer, and calling the eagles to eat the venison, with the fixed purpose of killing them.

Some people found out what he was in the habit of doing. So they warned him. "You had better give up killing the eagles, for they might destroy you!" He did not mind their advice, however, and kept on slaying eagles, skinning and cutting up the deer, and again calling out, "O you eagles! Come here and have some meat to swallow!" And, as usual, it was only with the intent of killing them.

One day, the chief of the eagles herself came there. Then the man was so frightened that he ran away. As she was just about to catch him, he ran towards a hollow log lying close by and crawled into it. The Eagle came down and, seizing the log in her talons, she carried it to her nest, in which two young ones were sitting. She had thus taken the log to her nest, for her little ones to eat the man inside it.

After quite a long while, the Eagle started off in search of food for her young birds; and, while she was away, the hunter crawled out of the log, now his usual dwelling, and ate some of the meat to be found there. That is really how he managed to keep alive. Then he tied the young eagles' bills.

After three days, the eagle-mother began to worry, because her children could no

PART 7: MYTHS ABOUT BIRDS

longer eat. She spoke to the hunter, saying, "Pray tell me what to do, for they are quite sick now and unable to swallow anything. How could they ever recover?" The man replied, "It is a very simple matter: take me back home!" She was now willing to do so; so they agreed upon a pact whereby the Eagle, for one, gave the man a charm to bring about the realization of whatever he wished for, and the hunter, on his side, promised never again to kill anymore eagles.

That is why the Eagle then took him back to the place where he belonged. His folks were quite surprised upon seeing him again and quite glad indeed, for they were now sure that the eagles had destroyed him.

Soon the hunter started again for the hunt; and, as was his habit, he killed and skinned the deer, again to call them, "Come to eat, O you eagles! because I won't kill eagles any longer."

And so it truly happened; the eagles came down and had plenty to eat, for the man had thus complied with the pact made with the chief of all the eagles.

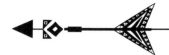 

Sedna, Goddess of the Sea
(Inuit)

As told by Evelyn Wolfson

A very long time ago, a young girl named Sedna lived with her widowed father in a small sealskin tent along the coast of Baffin Island. Sedna, who was beautiful, smart, independent, and willful, wanted a husband who was her equal. In fact, she was so particular that she turned down every suitor who came to visit. Sedna's father, Kinuk, did not mind that his daughter was so fussy because he loved her dearly and did not want to lose her.

One day, a long, sleek kayak carrying a handsome young man pulled up along the shore. Sedna asked her father if he recognized the style of the young man's clothing. "I have never seen an anorak with such beautiful black-and-white stripes," she said to her father.

"It is most unusual," he agreed. "And look at the stranger's spear. It is made of ivory." Although Sedna and her father were very curious about the young man, they remained hidden from view inside their little tent.

But the stranger cried out to Sedna: "Come to me. You will never be hungry, and you will live in a tent made of the most beautiful skins. You will rest on soft bearskins. Your lamp will always be filled with oil, your pot with meat."

Sedna pushed aside the thick caribou hide that covered the front entrance of her tent and peeked out. "Oh," she gasped. "He is indeed handsome." But Sedna had a reputation to protect, and she could not run to the shore and join the handsome young man while the people of her village looked on. So she closed the tent flap and stood quietly.

The young man stepped out of his kayak, and, using the tip of his ivory spear, drew a picture in the sand. "This is the land to which I will take you," he said as he scratched a scene of rolling hills, fat animals, and large comfortable houses. "I have many furs to give you," he shouted. "And I will place necklaces of ivory around your neck."

PART 7: MYTHS ABOUT BIRDS

Sedna stepped out from the door of the tent and in a shy voice asked, "Am I the only girl in the territory without a husband? Are there no other women to pursue than one who does not wish to marry?"

The young man's smiled broadened. "There are many women for such a rich man as myself. But I want only you."

Sedna was charmed. She had known handsome men before, but she had never been enchanted by their words. She went back indoors, filled a small sealskin pouch with her sewing needles, and walked slowly down to the shore. Sedna's father did not protest.

He believed he could not have made a better choice himself. The old man smiled and waved goodbye to his beautiful daughter.

The handsome young man lifted Sedna gently into his kayak and turned quickly out to sea. That evening, their kayak stopped alongside a rocky coast backed by low rolling hills. There were no houses and no fat animals— just hundreds of loons.

Sedna stepped hesitantly out of the kayak and turned to ask her new husband the whereabouts of the beautiful home he had described, but when she turned around, she was being followed not by her husband, but by an elegant loon with black on his back and white on his breast and belly. "Oh," she cried. "I have run away with the spirit-bird!"

"I used my power to transform myself into a human after I fell in love with you," said the young loon. "Otherwise, you would not have come away with me."

Sedna cried inconsolably. She could not imagine living among a flock of loud birds, who waddled around on webbed feet, let alone marrying one. She begged and begged to be returned to her home. "Please," she said. "I will give you my bag of sewing needles, if you will let me go home. I will give you anything I own."

Her loon husband fluffed up the nest of loose plants he had made for her and ignored her pleas. He brought her dozens of fresh fish and fed her well. But still she begged to go home.

When Sedna had failed to return home, even to visit, her father set out to find her. The old man wandered for many days from one island to another in search of his daughter. At last he spotted the long sleek kayak that belonged to the handsome suitor, and he went ashore. The father was puzzled: there were no houses on the island, just hundreds of black and white loons. He called out his daughter's name, "Sedna. Sedna. Where are you?"

But he was answered only by the cry of the loons. Then he looked up and saw his once-beautiful daughter sitting on a nest sobbing. "Oh, my child. I will take you home." He took her in his arms, carried her to his kayak, and they paddled away as quickly as possible.

When Sedna's husband came home, he asked the other birds, "Where is my wife?"

"Her father came and took her away," they cried.

Quickly, Loon-Husband turned back into a human, jumped into his sleek kayak, and gave chase.

Sedna's father saw the young husband approaching in his kayak, and he hid Sedna underneath a pile of furs. "Where is my wife? I want to see her," demanded her husband. The old man ignored him and paddled on.

Sedna's husband suddenly grew very angry and whirled his paddle madly in the air. Then he struck the water with his paddle, first on one side of the boat and then the other. His head and body gyrated back and forth in the tight little kayak, and water splashed all around him. Suddenly, the young man's handsome anorak turned back into shiny black and white feathers, and the spirit-bird rose up out of his kayak. As the great bird flapped its wings, the strange, wild cry of the loon filled the air.

Within moments, a furious storm rose up out of the sea, and giant waves smacked against the little kayak where Sedna still hid under a cover of heavy furs. Although Sedna's father wanted to save his beautiful daughter, he was consumed with fear. The spirit-bird was seeking revenge, and the old man knew he must appease the angry spirit. There was only one way to satisfy the spirit-bird, and that was to throw his daughter overboard. Once her father had made this horrible sacrifice, Sedna struggled to keep her head above the water as giant waves washed over her. When at last she was able to grip the gunwales of her father's kayak, he was seized with fear, and cut away her half-frozen fingers. "I must," he cried, steeling himself against his own agony. "The spirit-bird makes the sea angry and demands your life."

Sedna's body slowly disappeared beneath the icy waters, and her grieving father returned home. The old man lay down on a thick pile of caribou hides inside the little tent he and Sedna had shared for so many years, and wept.

During the night, another storm filled the sea with giant waves. This time, the waves washed far up on shore and lashed against the little tent where Sedna's father lay sleeping.

PART 7: MYTHS ABOUT BIRDS

When the last wave returned to the sea that night, it took the old man with it, down to Sedna's home at the bottom of the sea.

Sedna glared at her father with a single large, hollow eye that shone like a winter moon on her defiant face—the other eye had been lost in the storm at sea. Her father recognized the thick black braids that hung down his daughter's back, but the youthful beauty he had known had been replaced by the proud face of a great spirit-goddess.

Sea animals had been created from the joints of Sedna's severed hands: the first joint of her fingers became the seals of the sea; the second joint the whales of the sea; and the third joint the walruses of the sea. When Sedna was in a good mood, she made the animals plentiful, and no one went hungry.

Sedna protected the animals she had created from her dismembered fingers and reigned over a vast region where human souls, including her father's, were imprisoned as punishment after death.

Part 8:
Myths about Fire and Light

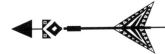 

The Origin of Daylight
(Nanaimo modification of the Tlingit legend)

As told by Katharine Berry Judson

When the earth was very new and young, it was dark and cold and gray. Even the stars were black. There was no light anywhere for Gull kept it in a small box which he guarded carefully. His cousin, Raven, was tired of the dark. He wished for the daylight. One day when Gull and Raven were out walking, Raven thought, "I wish Gull would run a thorn into his foot." Hardly had he thought so, when, in the darkness, Gull stepped on a thorn. "Sqenán! My foot!" cried Gull. "A thorn?" asked Raven. "Let me see it. I will take it out."

But it was so dark Raven could not see the thorn. He asked Gull to open the box and make it light. Gull opened it just a little way and the light was very faint.

Raven said, "You must give me more light."

Gull answered, "Sqenán!"

So Raven pretended not to see the thorn. Instead of pulling it out, he pushed it in deeper and deeper, saying, "You must give me more light."

"Sqenán! Sqenán! My foot! my foot!" cried Gull. Raven pushed the thorn in deeper and deeper until Gull at last opened the box. That is the way the daylight came.

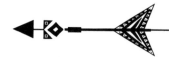 

Old Man Steals the Sun's Leggings
(Blackfoot)

As told by Frank D. Linderman

Firelight—what a charm it adds to storytelling. How its moods seem to keep pace with situations pictured by the oracle, offering shadows when dread is abroad, and light when a pleasing climax is reached; for interest undoubtedly tends the blaze, while sympathy contributes or withholds fuel, according to its dictates.

The lodge was alight when I approached and I could hear the children singing in a happy mood, but upon entering, the singing ceased and embarrassed smiles on the young faces greeted me; nor could I coax a continuation of the song.

Seated beside War Eagle was a very old Indian whose name was Red Robe, and as soon as I was seated, the host explained that he was an honored guest; that he was a Sioux and a friend of long standing. Then War Eagle lighted the pipe, passing it to the distinguished friend, who in turn passed it to me, after first offering it to the Sun, the father, and the Earth, the mother of all that is.

In a lodge of the Blackfeet the pipe must never be passed across the doorway. To do so would insult the host and bring bad luck to all who assembled. Therefore if there be a large number of guests ranged about the lodge, the pipe is passed first to the left from guest to guest until it reaches the door, when it goes back, unsmoked, to the host, to be refilled ere it is passed to those on his right hand.

Briefly War Eagle explained my presence to Red Robe and said:

"Once the Moon made the Sun a pair of leggings. Such beautiful work had never been seen before. They were worked with the colored quills of the Porcupine and were covered with strange signs, which none but the Sun and the Moon could read. No man ever saw such leggings as they were, and it took the Moon many snows to make them. Yes, they were wonderful leggings and the Sun always wore them on fine days, for they were bright to look upon.

"Every night when the Sun went to sleep in his lodge away in the west, he used the leggings for a pillow, because there was a thief in the world, even then. That thief and rascal was Old Man, and of course the Sun knew all about him. That is why he always put his fine leggings under his head when he slept. When he worked he almost always wore them, as I have told you, so that there was no danger of losing them in the daytime; but the Sun was careful of his leggings when night came and he slept.

"You wouldn't think that a person would be so foolish as to steal from the Sun, but one night Old Man—who is the only person who ever knew just where the Sun's lodge was—crept near enough to look in, and saw the leggings under the Sun's head.

"We have all traveled a great deal but no man ever found the Sun's lodge. No man knows in what country it is. Of course we know it is located somewhere west of here, for we see him going that way every afternoon, but Old Man knew everything—except that he could not fool the Sun.

"Yes—Old Man looked into the lodge of the Sun and saw the leggings there—saw the Sun, too, and the Sun was asleep. He made up his mind that he would steal the leggings so he crept through the door of the lodge. There was no one at home but the Sun, for the Moon has work to do at night just as the children, the Stars, do, so he thought he could slip the leggings from under the sleeper's head and get away.

"He got down on his hands and knees to walk like the Bear-people and crept into the lodge, but in the black darkness he put his knee upon a dry stick near the Sun's bed. The stick snapped under his weight with so great a noise that the Sun turned over and snorted, scaring Old Man so badly that he couldn't move for a minute. His heart was not strong—wickedness makes every heart weaker—and after making sure that the Sun had not seen him, he crept silently out of the lodge and ran away.

"On the top of a hill Old Man stopped to look and listen, but all was still; so he sat down and thought.

"'I'll get them to-morrow night when he sleeps again'; he said to himself. 'I need those leggings myself, and I'm going to get them, because they will make me handsome as the Sun.'

PART 8: MYTHS ABOUT FIRE AND LIGHT

"He watched the Moon come home to camp and saw the Sun go to work, but he did not go very far away because he wanted to be near the lodge when night came again.

"It was not long to wait, for all the Old Man had to do was to make mischief, and only those who have work to do measure time. He was close to the lodge when the Moon came out, and there he waited until the Sun went inside. From the bushes Old Man saw the Sun take off his leggings and his eyes glittered with greed as he saw their owner fold them and put them under his head as he had always done. Then he waited a while before creeping closer. Little by little the old rascal crawled toward the lodge, till finally his head was inside the door. Then he waited a long, long time, even after the Sun was snoring.

"The strange noises of the night bothered him, for he knew he was doing wrong, and when a Loon cried on a lake nearby, he shivered as with cold, but finally crept to the sleeper's side. Cautiously his fingers felt about the precious leggings until he knew just how they could best be removed without waking the Sun. His breath was short and his heart was beating as a war-drum beats, in the black dark of the lodge. Sweat—cold sweat, that great fear always brings to the weak-hearted—was dripping from his body, and once he thought that he would wait for another night, but greed whispered again, and listening to its voice, he stole the leggings from under the Sun's head.

"Carefully he crept out of the lodge, looking over his shoulder as he went through the door. Then he ran away as fast as he could go. Over hills and valleys, across rivers and creeks, toward the east. He wasted much breath laughing at his smartness as he ran, and soon he grew tired.

"'Ho!' he said to himself, 'I am far enough now and I shall sleep. It's easy to steal from the Sun—just as easy as stealing from the Bear or the Beaver.'

"He folded the leggings and put them under his head as the Sun had done, and went to sleep. He had a dream and it waked him with a start. Bad deeds bring bad dreams to us all. Old Man sat up and there was the Sun looking right in his face and laughing. He was frightened and ran away, leaving the leggings behind him.

"Laughingly the Sun put on the leggings and went on toward the west, for he is always busy. He thought he would see Old Man no more, but it takes more than one lesson to teach a fool to be wise, and Old Man hid in the timber until the Sun had traveled out of sight. Then he ran westward and hid himself near the Sun's lodge again, intending to wait for the night and steal the leggings a second time.

"He was much afraid this time, but as soon as the Sun was asleep he crept to the lodge and peeked inside. Here he stopped and looked about, for he was afraid the Sun would hear his heart beating. Finally he started toward the Sun's bed and just then a great white Owl flew from off the lodge poles, and this scared him more, for that is very bad luck and he knew it; but he kept on creeping until he could almost touch the Sun.

"All about the lodge were beautiful linings, tanned and painted by the Moon, and the queer signs on them made the old coward tremble. He heard a night-bird call outside and he thought it would surely wake the Sun; so he hastened to the bed and with cunning fingers stole the leggings, as he had done the night before, without waking the great sleeper. Then he crept out of the lodge, talking bravely to himself as cowards do when they are afraid.

"'Now,' he said to himself, 'I shall run faster and farther than before. I shall not stop running while the night lasts, and I shall stay in the mountains all the time when the Sun is at work in the daytime!'

"Away he went—running as the Buffalo runs—straight ahead, looking at nothing, hearing nothing, stopping at nothing. When day began to break Old Man was far from the Sun's lodge and he hid himself in a deep gulch among some bushes that grew there. He listened a long time before he dared to go to sleep, but finally he did. He was tired from his great run and slept soundly and for a long time, but when he opened his eyes—there was the Sun looking straight at him, and this time he was scowling. Old Man started to run away but the Sun grabbed him and threw him down upon his back. My! but the Sun was angry, and he said:

"'Old Man, you are a clever thief but a mighty fool as well, for you steal from me and expect to hide away. Twice you have stolen the leggings my wife made for me, and twice I have found you easily. Don't you know that the whole world is my lodge and that you can never get outside of it, if you run your foolish legs off? Don't you know that I light all of my lodge every day and search it carefully? Don't you know that nothing can hide from me and live? I shall not harm you this time, but I warn you now, that if you ever steal from me again, I will hurt you badly. Now go, and don't let me catch you stealing again!'

PART 8: MYTHS ABOUT FIRE AND LIGHT

"Away went Old Man, and on toward the west went the busy Sun. That is all.

"Now go to bed; for I would talk of other things with my friend, who knows of war as I do. Ho!"

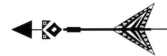

The Northern Lights
(Wabanski)

As told by Katharine Berry Judson

Old Chief M'Sartto, Morning Star, had one son only, so different from other boys of the tribe as to be a worry to Old Chief. He would not stay and play with the others, but would take his bow and arrows and leave home for days at a time, always going toward the North. When he come home, they say, 'Where you been? What you see?' But he say nothing.

"At last Old Chief say his wife, 'That boy must be watched. I will follow him.'

"So next time Chief M'Sartto kept in his trail and travel for long time. Suddenly his eyes close an' he could not hear. He had a curious feeling, then know nothing. By'm-by his eyes open in a queer light country, no sun, no moon, no stars, but country all lighted by strange light. He saw many beings, but all different from his people. They gather 'round and try to talk, but he not understand their language. M'Sartto did not know where to go or what to do. He well treated by this strange tribe. He watch their games and was 'tracted to wonderful game of ball he never saw before. It seemed to turn the light to many colors and players all had lights on their heads and all wore very curious belts called Menquan, or Rainbow belts.

"In few days an old man came and speak to M'Sartto in his own language and ask him if he know where he was.

"Old Chief say, 'No.'

"Then old man say, 'You are in country of Wa-ba-ban, Northern Lights. I came here many years ago. I was the only one here from the "Lower Country" as we call it; but now there is a boy comes to visit us every few days.'

"Then M'Sartto asked how old man got there, what way he come.

"Old man say, 'I follow path called Spirits' Path, Ket-a-gus-wowt,—Milky Way.'

PART 8: MYTHS ABOUT FIRE AND LIGHT

"'This must be path I come,' said Old Chief. 'Did you have queer feeling as if you lost all knowledge when you traveled?'"

"'Yes,' say old man, 'I could not hear or see.'"

"Then say M'Sartto, 'We did come by same path. Can you tell me how I get home again?'"

"'Yes, Chief of Wa-ba-ban will send you home safe.'"

"'Well, can you tell me where I can see my boy?—the boy that comes here to visit you is mine.'"

"Then old man tell M'Sartto, 'You will see him playing ball if you watch.'"

"Chief M'Sartto very glad to hear this, and when man went round to tepees telling all to go have ball game, M'Sartto went too. When game began he saw many beautiful colors.

"Old man ask him, 'Do you see your boy there?'"

"Old Chief said he did. 'The one with the brightest light is my son.'"

"Then they went to Chief of Northern Lights, and old man said, 'Chief of Lower Country wants to go home and also wants his boy.'"

"So Chief of Northern Lights calls his people together to bid good-bye to M'Sartto and his son; then ordered two K'che Sippe, Great Birds, to carry them home. When they went traveling Milky Way he felt the same strange way he did when going and when he came to his sense he found himself near home. His wife very glad he come, for when boy told her his father was safe she pay no notice, as she afraid M'Sartto was lost."

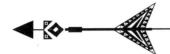

The Theft of Fire
(Miwok)

As told by Edward Winslow Gifford

Lizard saw the smoke. He said: "Smoking below, smoking below, smoking below, smoking below. My grandmother starts a fire to cook acorns. It is very lonely."

Flute-player (Mouse) was sent down the mountains into the valley to secure the fire. Flute-player departed, taking with him two flutes. He finally arrived at the assembly house from which the smoke was issuing. He found it crowded, but he was welcomed and the people persuaded him to play. He played and he played.

Then they put a feather mat over the smoke hole at the top of the house and shut the feathers in the door. They closed the door with the feather dress. They told the doorkeeper to close the door tight.

Flute-man played continuously. The people fell asleep and snored. Flute-player remained awake and played. Finally, he concluded that all were fast asleep. He arose and took two coals from the fire, placing them in his flute. Then he put two coals in the second flute. He proceeded to the door, cut loose the feathers, passed out, and started homeward.

The people awoke to find him gone and with him the fire. Hail and Rain were sent in pursuit, for they were the two swiftest travelers among the valley people. Hail went, but Flute-man heard Hail and Rain coming, so he threw one of his flutes under a buckeye tree. Rain asked him what he had done with the fire. "You stole our fire," Rain said. Flute-player denied it. Then Rain returned home. The placing of the flute, with the coals in it, under the buckeye tree resulted in the fire always being in the buckeye.

When Rain started back, Flute-man took his fire from under the buckeye and again proceeded homeward. He arrived at home safely and brought the fire into the assembly

PART 8: MYTHS ABOUT FIRE AND LIGHT

house. He told the people that Rain had taken one flute with coals in it. He said, "Rain took one flute from me. I have only one left."

The chief told Flute-player to build a fire, and the latter produced the coals from his remaining flute. A large fire was made. It was then that people lost their language. Those close to the fire talked correctly. The people at the north side of the assembly house talked brokenly. Those at the south side talked altogether different; so did those at the west side and at the east side. This was because of the cold.

Coyote brought entrails and threw them on the tire, extinguishing it. The people became angry and expelled Coyote, telling him to remain outside and to eat his food raw. That is why Coyote always eats his meat uncooked.

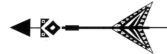 

How Beaver Stole Fire from the Pines
(Nez Percé)

As told by R. L. Packard

Once, before there were any people in the world, the different animals and trees lived and moved about and talked together just like human beings. At this time the pine-trees had the secret of fire, and guarded it jealously from the rest of the world, so that, no matter how cold it was, nobody could get any fire to warm himself by, unless he was a pine. At length an unusually cold season came, and all the animals were in danger of freezing to death because they could get no fire; but all plans to find out their secret from the pines were in vain, until Beaver hit upon one which proved successful.

At a certain place on Grande Ronde River, in Idaho, the pines were about to hold a great council. They had built a large fire at which to warm themselves, after coming out of the icy water from bathing, and had posted sentinels round about to keep off all the animals and other intruders, who might steal their fire secret. But Beaver had hidden under the bank near the fire before the sentinels had been posted, and so escaped their notice. After a while, a live coal rolled down the bank close by Beaver, which he seized and hid in his breast, and then ran away as fast as he could. The pines immediately raised the hue and cry, and started after him. Whenever he was hard pressed, Beaver darted from side to side, and dodged his pursuers, and when he had a good start he kept a straight course. Hence the Grande Ronde River is very tortuous in some parts of its course and then straight for some distance, because it preserves the direction Beaver took in his flight.

After running a long time, the pines grew tired and decided to abandon the chase. So most of them halted in a body on the river banks, where they remain in great numbers

PART 8: MYTHS ABOUT FIRE AND LIGHT

to this day, and form a growth so dense that hunters can hardly get through it. A few, however, kept on after Beaver, but they finally gave out one after another, and they also remain scattered at intervals along the banks of the river in the places where they stopped.

There was one cedar running with the foremost pines, and although he despaired of capturing Beaver, he said to the few pines still in the chase, "Although we can not catch Beaver, I will keep on to the top of the hill yonder, and see how far he is ahead." So he ran to the top of the hill, and saw Beaver far ahead, just diving into Big Snake River where the Grande Ronde enters it, so that further pursuit was out of the question. He saw Beaver dart across Big Snake River and give fire to some willows on the opposite bank, and recross farther on and give fire to the birches, and so on to certain other kinds of wood. Since then, all who have wanted fire have got it from these particular woods, because they have fire in them and give it up more readily than other kinds when rubbed together in the ancient way.

Cedar still stands all alone on the very top of the hill where he stopped in the chase after Beaver, near the junction of the Grande Ronde and Big Snake rivers. He is very old; so old that his top is dead, but he still stands as a proof of the truth of the story. That the chase was a very long one is shown by there being no cedars within a hundred miles upstream from where he stands. The old people point him out to the children as they pass by, and say, "See, there is old Cedar standing in the very spot where he stopped chasing Beaver." Reubens gave an instance of so useful a practical application of this little fable that it seems to show intention to that effect on the part of the first tellers. He said that in his boyhood, he and some companions were once on a fishing expedition, and had wandered too far from home to return at night. They had caught some salmon, but could not cook them because they had no matches with which to start a fire, and were therefore in danger of passing a hungry night. Fortunately, this story occurred to one of the party, and among them they recalled the different kinds of wood to which Beaver had given fire in his flight and which they understood to be, on that account, preferable as kindling woods. Accordingly, they took pieces of two of the kinds mentioned (the top of a small tree of one kind and a piece of root of the other), made a small cavity in one of them, and rapidly turned the pointed end of the other therein until they were able to kindle a fire by friction after the manner of the "old timers."

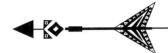 

The Flying Heads
(Wyandot)

As told by Marius Barbeau

Ages and ages ago the Wyandots were migrating from a distant country. They were moving all their villages. In the course of their migration they came to a large river with exceedingly steep and rocky shores. This river belonged to some Giants, and these opposed the crossing of the Wyandots.

These Giants were all medicine men. They were of immense size, being as tall as the highest tree. They lived in the stone caverns under the bed of the river. They were cruel and wicked cannibals.

The Wyandots made canoes and attempted to cross over. When a canoe loaded with Wyandots pushed out into the stream, the Giants thrust up from the hidden depths of the water their huge hands, and dragged down both canoe and passengers. The Wyandots were carried to the stone caverns of the Giants, where they were tortured at the fiery stake, and afterwards devoured.

The Wyandots were terrified. They could neither advance nor retreat. A solemn Council was called to deliberate upon their fearful dilemma. At the Council a powerful "medicine" was made, by the aid of which it was learned that the Giants could be captured and destroyed if a ring of fire could be built about them when they came out of their caves under the river.

Upon the same night of the Council, the Wyandots saw, on a high cliff on the opposite side of the river, the Giants dancing about the fires in which they were torturing some Wyandots captured a few days before.

The Little Turtle said:

"I can make a great fire from the Lightning. It will go all about the Giants. How can our warriors cross over the river?"

PART 8: MYTHS ABOUT FIRE AND LIGHT

The Big Turtle said:

"Let the Little Turtle and his warriors get upon my back. I will carry them on the bottom of the river, under the water, and the Giants will not see us."

It was so done. The warriors of the Little Turtle crept about the camp of the Giants. Then the Little Turtle brought the Thunder and the Lightning. The Lightning leaped into a great wall, all about the Giants, while the Thunder bore them to the earth. The warriors of the Little Turtle rushed upon the Giants and seized them.

The Little Turtle carried the Giants to a high rock that overhung the river. Here the head of each Giant was cut off and thrown down into the raging water. But the surprise of the Wyandots, and their dismay also, was great when at the dawning of the day they saw all these Giant Heads rise from the waters, with streaming hair covered with blood which shone like lightning. They rose from the troubled waters uttering horrible screams, screeches, and yells, flew along the river, and disappeared.

The Wyandots destroyed the caves of the Giants. They then crossed over the river and continued their journey. They came to the point where Montreal now stands. The Flying Heads plagued the Wyandots. They were more dangerous and troublesome during rainy, foggy, or misty weather. They could enter a cloud of fog, or mist, or rime, and in it approach a Wyandot village unseen. They were cruel and wicked hooh'-kehs and cannibals. They caused sickness; they were vampires, and lay in wait for people, whom they caught and devoured. They carried away children; they blighted the tobacco and other crops; they stole and devoured the game after the hunter had killed it.

Fire was the most potent agency with which to resist them. The Lightning sometimes killed one. The Little People often helped the Wyandots drive them away from their villages. I could never learn that it was supposed that the Flying Heads were ever either entirely expelled or that they voluntarily departed from the Wyandot country.

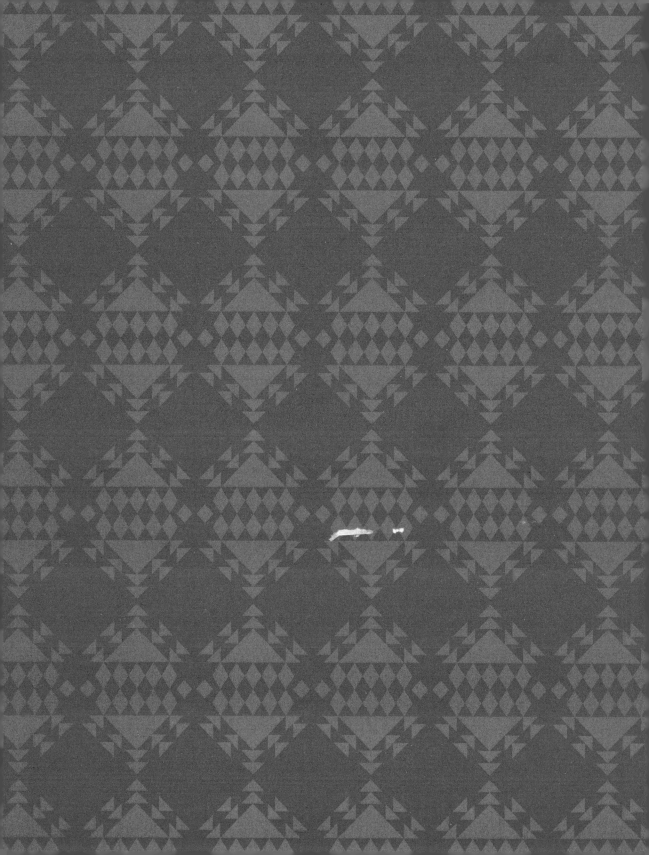